The flo
face.

There wa̲s

"A crypt," Annja said, without realizing she'd spoken the thought aloud.

"Most perceptive." It was a woman's voice.

The light began to move. The woman placed an oil-filled lantern on top of a great stone sarcophagus close to where Annja lay bound.

"How long was I out?" Annja asked.

"Four hours, nearly five. You must have the constitution of a horse. That dose should have put you out for much longer, unless he managed to screw that up, too." The woman's eyes flicked to a dark heap in the corner.

"Is he dead?"

She nodded. "I should hope so." She made the shape of a gun with her fingers and thumb and mimed putting a bullet through his brain.

Did she really value life so cheaply? "And me? Am I just another loose end to be put out of my misery?"

"Oh, no, not at all. You're far more important than that. I am sure my brother will tell you all about it."

"Brother?"

"Enough with the questions. You're almost as bad as your friend. The pretty one. Garin."

"I suppose you killed him, too."

"Of course not. He's been most helpful."

Annja thought of everything Roux had told her about the midnight visit and the theft from the vault and muttered, "I'll kill him."

"Not until we're finished with him."

Titles in this series:

ROGUE Angel

Alex Archer

DAY OF ATONEMENT

A GOLD EAGLE BOOK FROM

WORLDWIDE ®

TORONTO • NEW YORK • LONDON
AMSTERDAM • PARIS • SYDNEY • HAMBURG
STOCKHOLM • ATHENS • TOKYO • MILAN
MADRID • WARSAW • BUDAPEST • AUCKLAND

Recycling programs
for this product may
not exist in your area.

First edition May 2015

ISBN-13: 978-0-373-62174-3

Day of Atonement

Special thanks and acknowledgment to
Steven Savile for his contribution to this work.

Printed in U.S.A.

The
LEGEND

...THE ENGLISH COMMANDER TOOK
JOAN'S SWORD AND RAISED IT HIGH.
The broadsword, plain and unadorned,
gleamed in the firelight. He put the tip against
the ground and his foot at the center of the blade.
The broadsword shattered, fragments falling
into the mud. The crowd surged forward,
peasant and soldier, and snatched the shards
from the trampled mud. The commander tossed
the hilt deep into the crowd.
Smoke almost obscured Joan, but she continued
praying till the end, until finally the flames climbed
her body and she sagged against the restraints.

Joan of Arc died that fateful day in France,
but her legend and sword are reborn...

1

On a winter's night
Twenty years ago

"You have my attention," Roux said.

The young man who sat across from him had been insistent, refusing to be put off no matter how many times Roux ducked the meeting. His excuses had become more and more elaborate, but that only made the young man try harder. That dogged persistence paid off. Eventually. The old man had been tempted to arrange the sit-down in a very public space, given the personality type that kind of persistence hinted at. There were some people he didn't invite into his home, but Roux was tired. The search for the fragments of the blade wasn't going well, with what he thought might be the final shard eluding him still, so just this once Muhammad could come to the mountain, or, in this case, chateau.

He regretted that decision now. Something about the intense young man's scrutiny was decidedly uncomfortable. It wasn't so much the stare as it was the slight twitch of his lower lip, like it was fighting back the urge to smile. It made his skin crawl. One thing the years had done for Roux was to offer an education in human nature. He liked to think himself a reasonable judge of character. This boy—because that's what he was, really, a boy in man's clothing—was somehow off.

So he waited, knowing the young man had something to get off his chest, and equally sure he didn't want to hear it.

"I thought I might, eventually."

"So how can I help you?"

"I suspect it's more a case of how I can help you." He settled a briefcase on the Louis XIV coffee table that acted as a barrier between them.

Roux winced as the young man pushed the case back an inch and thumbed the locks. It was all he could do not to reach out and slap the stupid boy. The table was a priceless work of art; the briefcase was not. "I wasn't aware that I needed any help," Roux said.

"Then allow me to enlighten you, Mr. Roux." He drew a manila folder out of the briefcase. Roux had seen a million of these over the years. In his experience, they never contained good news when they were hand delivered like this. He sank back into his chair and feigned disinterest. The young man didn't need to know his curiosity had been piqued.

Roux picked up the business card the young man had given him when he first turned up at his door. The name was the same as the one in Roux's appointment diary. Patrice Moerlen, freelance journalist. After the seventh call he had done his due diligence and had some of his people run background checks on the man that would have made the CIA envious, and by the time he had finally agreed to the sit-down Roux knew everything there was to know about Patrice Moerlen, and had his own dossier almost twice as thick as the folder the journalist pulled from his briefcase.

"I saw this picture of you in a magazine," he said, handing over the first clipping.

Roux had seen it before.

He had been disappointed that the photograph had been published, but it couldn't be helped. The photograph had been taken at a charity event organized by an old friend, and obligations to the social compact necessitated he attend, because that's what friends did. He'd been promised it was going to be a low-key gathering, but the late addition of one of those Hollywood darlings with too-blond hair and an impossibly plastic smile and her politico beau had transformed it into an irresistible honeypot for the paparazzi.

"Not the most flattering, I'll grant you, but hardly a crime against humanity," Roux said. "I rarely accept invitations to events like that, but you know how it is. Sometimes it's hard to say no."

"I understand," the young man said, smiling. "The thing is, seeing it, I couldn't help but think your face looked familiar."

"I have one of those faces," Roux said, not liking where this was going. "Isn't that what they say? It's embarrassing sometimes because everyone thinks they've seen me before, or that I remind them of someone else."

"Which is what I thought at first. In my line of work I see a lot of faces. So I decided to check, just to be sure."

"So." Roux offered a slight smile. "Who did you think I reminded you of?"

"No one in particular, not some celebrity at least. But I had this nagging feeling that I'd seen you in another picture."

He picked the next piece of paper from the folder and handed it over.

Roux remembered the picture being taken, even if he had forgotten the joke that had put a smile on everyone's lips a long time ago.

The young man picked out the faces one by one.

"Bobby Kennedy, JFK and someone beside them, a third man, who you must admit bears a striking resemblance to you."

"There's certainly a resemblance," Roux said. "But I hate to disappoint you. I never had the privilege of meeting either of the Kennedys."

He looked the journalist straight in the eye and lied, daring him to call him on it.

"That's a shame. But maybe this one is a little more familiar?"

Another picture.

This one was slightly out of focus, but Roux remembered the night well.

He'd forgotten a lot of the others in the photograph, but knew the man on the right—Paul Reynaud, the president of France. It had been taken a few months before the outbreak of World War II. Roux stood behind Reynaud's shoulder. He had been less cautious then, less concerned about being seen in public because the proliferation of cameras was nothing like it was today, and the chances of being caught and remembered from one image to the next were almost nil.

Only now Roux *had* been remembered, and the journalist had followed a trail of photographs into his past and found him impossibly unchanged despite the seventy years between the first and last picture.

"It could be the same man." Roux offered a noncommittal shrug. He needed something to throw the young

journalist off the trail, a conclusive spanner in the works
that would destroy his faith that it was Roux in the photograph.

"I'm absolutely sure it is, Mr. Roux. It's you, after all."
He produced another picture, a sepia-tinged photograph
of the Russian royal family. Roux was there again. "Do
I really need to show you more? I have them. Plenty of
them. Enough, I'm sure, to convince you."

"I'm not sure what you're trying to say," Roux told him.
"You can't possibly think these are all of me? They date
back nearly a hundred years. That's impossible."

"And yet that's you in each of those pictures, unable
to resist the allure of power, rubbing shoulders with the
rich and famous. As you say, there's more than a hundred years between some of these photographs and yet
there you are in all of them. And, most interestingly, you
haven't changed a bit. I would ask you what the secret of
your young skin is, but I'm assuming it's not some mois-
turizer." His smile was more of a wince.

"A good story, but for one fatal flaw. That's not me in
those pictures, no matter how similar the men are. With
the billions of people in the world, it's hardly surprising
that some of us wear recycled faces, is it? How could it
be me?"

"You're denying it?" the journalist asked, gathering
the pictures.

"I'm simply pointing out that you are mistaken."

"And that's your final word?"

Roux rubbed a hand over his face, a gesture that could
easily have been interpreted as having something to hide
rather than simple exhaustion. "I really don't think there's
anything else to say." He pushed himself to his feet, indicating their meeting was over. He wasn't about to sit and
debate the impossibility of longevity, never mind immor-

tality, with the young man when the only thing he risked was betraying himself with some careless word that would only strengthen his case.

"Then you'll have no objection to me running the story, then?"

"What story?" That brought him up sharply. He'd reacted just a little too quickly to the threat. An innocent man wouldn't have barked out those two words quite as fiercely. He forced himself to sound amused. "There is no story."

"Perhaps, perhaps not. We'll let the members of the public make up their own minds, shall we? Isn't that the joy of a free press?"

"I'm not sure I'd call making up some fanciful story anything more than irresponsible, Mr. Moerlen. It certainly isn't journalism."

The reporter inclined his head slightly, as though conceding the point. "I'm going to be in Paris for a couple of days. Think about it. I'll leave these copies of the photographs with you so you can go through them at your leisure. I do hope you will decide that you'd like to talk to me about this miracle, Mr. Roux. You have my number."

The man got to his feet and held out his hand.

Reluctantly, Roux shook it.

The more he made of the situation, the harder it would be to brush it aside as some bizarre flight of fancy. People didn't live forever. It was impossible. But then, so much about his life was impossible. He needed time to think about this. It would be easy to pull a few strings and make sure that the story was squashed before there was any danger of it being printed. No one made it to Roux's age without collecting an awful lot of favors owed in the checks and balances of life. It helped that the story sounded utterly preposterous.

He stood at the front door and watched as the young man drove away in the small Fiat, white crystals of fog gathering in the night. He could taste snow on the breeze. Maybe not tonight, or tomorrow, but soon, Roux thought. He usually liked this time of year because it was all about the end of things, something he'd experienced so much without having faced it himself.

As the fog folded around the journalist's car, Roux made his way to his study and started to make the calls.

2

"You absolute bastard!"

Roux had ignored Moerlen's calls and, when they finally appeared to stop, assumed he'd gotten the message: there wasn't a serious magazine or newspaper in the world that would touch the story. A few of the editors had humored Moerlen and admitted that yes, it was curious, wasn't it? But curious or not, it wasn't for them. A few that Roux knew personally had laughed in the young man's face.

Roux said nothing.

Instead, he allowed the journalist to vent his frustration over the phone. He was doing the man a favor, even if he didn't appreciate it. By letting him get it out of his system it minimized the chances of him doing something stupid. Sooner or later Moerlen would find some small circulation magazine that liked the unexplained and unexplainable, which would buy the story and might even run it, but no one took that kind of nonsense seriously.

"It's not going to work. You can't gag me, no matter

who you know. I'll find someone who will publish this story. The truth will come out."

"Look," Roux said patiently. "I don't know what you think you know, but believe me, you don't. There is no story to sell. Let it go. Get on with your life. Don't make an enemy of me, son," Roux said, deliberately patronizing the man on the other end of the line.

"You think you are so clever, don't you? You think that you have it all worked out. What you don't get is that the whole world will want to know your story. How can someone live for so long without aging? I'm not naive enough to think you signed some kind of pact with the devil, but something is going on. That is you in those photographs. I know it is. I'll prove it."

"I'm sorry that you've wasted time on this," Roux said, signaling an end to the conversation, but the man refused to go.

"Fine. I'll begin my story by telling everyone how I've been muzzled. That makes for a compelling beginning. How someone—you—didn't want this story out in the public domain. That just makes it more interesting, doesn't it? Think about it. The fact that the truth is being suppressed is more interesting than the truth itself. Why would you want this kept secret unless you had something to hide? You can try to ridicule me and make me look like a fool, but I won't be silenced. There are other ways to tell this story. This is the modern world now. Information wants to be free. There are bulletin boards and chat rooms that would devour this type of thing, giving it a life of its own. All I have to do is log in and start to tell the world everything I know. It's not about money anymore. It's about the truth. You've misjudged me, Mr. Roux, if you think that all I care about is money. I didn't turn up on your doorstep trying to blackmail you. I came looking for answers."

"And that was a mistake," Roux said, then hung up.

Moerlen was right; the world was changing, and changing faster than it had for decades before. It was already smaller than it had been even twenty years ago with the pernicious invasion of television, but now with so many people having access to computers and those machines somehow connecting like some giant message network, it was so much more dangerous for a man like him.

This was escalating too quickly. The risk now was that it would slip out of his control. There were strings he could pull, more favors he could call in, but once the story had a life of its own there was no way he could put that genie back in the bottle. And that was what those bulletin boards and chat rooms promised to do.

Which meant he had to find another way to stop the story.

He needed to speak to someone who understood this electronic world, and the very real damage that could be done if he were to be exposed. There was one obvious choice, but given that they hadn't talked for longer than Moerlen had been alive, it wasn't exactly an easy call to make. The last time they'd been together Garin Braden had tried to kill him. The same thing had happened the time before. A third time and he'd start to take it personally.

He dialed the number, but he was forwarded straight to voice mail.

"Call me," he said, then hung up.

There was nothing more to say.

Garin—his former pupil—would recognize his voice, and understand just how important it was that they talk simply because he'd swallowed his pride and reached out.

He thought about ignoring the situation and hoping the mess would just go away. The more he fought against it, the more obvious it was he had something to hide, after all. But what if it didn't go away? What if those damned photographs led to more journalists banging on his door, asking more and more questions he couldn't answer? He hadn't asked for this life, even if, looking around him at the riches he had assembled across the centuries, it might look like a blessing rather than a curse. All it would take was the wrong person digging deep enough and everything would begin to unravel. The last thing he wanted to do was to have to begin a new life somewhere else. It was getting harder and harder to do that in this era of powerful computers and international cooperation.

His world, and Garin's, was in danger of falling apart.

He punched a number on his phone again.

"Mr. Moerlen," he said before the man on the other end of the line had had a chance to say hello. "You are right, we should meet. I will be in Paris in a couple of hours."

"I'm so glad you've come to your senses, Mr. Roux. But things have changed since the last time we spoke."

"How so?" Roux asked, not liking the sound of this.

"Remuneration, Mr. Roux."

"Ah, so despite all of your protestations, this *is* about money, then? I'm disappointed."

"Don't be. I'm a child of the modern age. The modern age, as I'm sure you have noticed, is an expensive place to live. Let's make it the top of the Eiffel Tower shall we?"

Moerlen named a time and hung up.

Roux wondered how much this was going to cost him. It wasn't that he didn't have the money. He had plenty of money, but would it ever be enough to guarantee his privacy? Pay the blackmailer once and then what? Expect him to be good for his word and never turn up on the doorstep again looking for another handout? Blackmail was a dirty business. There could never be an end to it.

Which, unfortunately for Moerlen, meant it needed to end very differently.

IT WAS A long climb.

There were a dozen tourists already on the viewing platform by the time Roux reached it.

There was no sign of Patrice Moerlen.

Roux's plane had been refueled and would be ready to leave Orly Airport at a moment's notice if things went the way he assumed they would. He would need to distance himself from the city for a while. A glance at his watch, an eerily precise Patek Philippe chronograph, showed that he was almost five minutes early. He hated to be early for anything; time spent waiting around was time wasted. Perhaps it was because he had so much of it he hoarded it?

A couple of tourists glanced in his direction, no doubt wondering why he had made the dizzying climb up the iron stairs and wasn't leaning over the rail to take in the view across the city.

"Are you afraid of heights?" a small boy with a thick American accent asked him. "You can't fall out you know. You'd have to climb and jump because of the railings, so it's really safe."

Roux forced a smile.

"That's good to know."

The boy's mother took hold of his arm and pulled him away, muttering something about not talking to strangers.

Roux checked his watch again. Ninety seconds. Still no sign of Moerlen. And no sign of him on the stairs below, working his way up to the platform. This wasn't good. He couldn't control the situation. He didn't like it when he couldn't control the situation. The elevator doors opened behind him.

Another handful of tourists emerged, but the journalist wasn't among them.

As the last of them stepped onto the platform, his phone rang.

He still wasn't used to the fact that technology had advanced so quickly over the past few years that it was possible to carry a phone around wherever you were in the world, even if reception was patchy.

"Where are you?" he asked.

"I'm at the foot of the tower."

"I'm not in the mood for games, Mr. Moerlen. You said the observation platform," Roux said. "I am on the observation platform, you are not. How am I supposed to trust you if you can't even keep this simple agreement? This does not auger well for our relationship."

"What can I say? I changed my mind. I wanted to know how serious you were. Now I know."

"Serious? I'm trying to save you from wasting any more of your life, and in the process ending your career, but it looks like you are intent on leading me off on some wild-goose chase. I don't appreciate being treated like an idiot."

"Save me?" Moerlen had the temerity to laugh at him. "Save yourself, you mean. You misjudged me, Mr. Roux. It was never about the money. I've only ever been interested in the truth. And you've just given it to me. Goodbye."

Roux pressed against the viewing window, knowing there was no hope of being able to spot the damned journalist so far below.

People milled around like so many ants on the ground below. He'd read somewhere that if a person dropped a centime on its edge from this height it would cut through a man, splitting him in two. He had a problem. If he didn't do something about Moerlen now, he might not get the opportunity again before it was too late. He had to stop that story getting out. His privacy afforded him a certain standard of living. Exposed, his life could never be the same again. It really was as simple as that. Moerlen, consciously or not, had forced his hand.

Behind him, the elevator doors began to close. He moved quickly. Two strides, three, and he reached out, sliding his hand between the doors before they could shut. He stepped inside. The silence was punctuated by the occasional disapproving *tut* from the woman whose boy had spoken to him before.

Roux said nothing.

He waited out the short descent, then pushed his way through the doors before they were fully open, elbowing between the next wave of tourists eager to make their way up to the observation platform without the climb.

He couldn't see Moerlen; not that there was any guarantee the journalist had ever been there, no matter what he'd said. But if there was the slightest chance he was there, maybe watching from the safety of a nearby café to note how Roux reacted to his taunt, he had to try everything he could. If the guy wanted him to beg, then he'd beg. If he wanted to negotiate some exclusive deal to his story, then he'd negotiate it, but only if he could control it. That was what it was all about now—control.

He tried the journalist's number again, listening for some telltale ring and all the time he turned through three hundred and sixty degrees, scanning the faces around him. Moerlen didn't answer.

But Roux could hear a phone ringing.

He moved his own cell phone away from his ear and started to walk toward the sound.

He pushed through a family, barging between mother and father and sending the kids scattering. The commotion caused heads to turn. Roux saw one in particular, a reflexive glance followed by the fight or flight instinct kicking in.

The man ran.

"Wait!" Roux shouted.

More heads turned in his direction, everyone in the crowd thinking the call was for them.

The man didn't stop.

He ducked his head and quickened his pace, pushing through the gathered tourists as he aimed for the open spaces of the square and the streets beyond where he hoped to disappear.

Roux tried to keep up with him but people kept getting in the way, clustering around the shadow of the tower, seemingly oblivious to the rest of the world. He shouted again, his voice carrying over the heads of the tourists, but Moerlen had worked himself into open space and began to run.

He had no intention of talking.

Moerlen offered another frantic glance over his shoulder to be sure he was leaving Roux behind. There was nothing the old man could do. He couldn't keep up. In that moment, caught looking back, Moerlen's foot slipped and his ankle turned as he reached the road, stumbling on the curb. He couldn't stop himself as fear had him staggering out into the line of oncoming traffic.

A horn blared, harsh, panicked, but it was too late.

Bones and metal met in a collision. There could only ever be one outcome.

The car—a blue Peugeot—slammed on its brakes

and started to slide. The car behind it, slower to react, rammed into its trunk to a cacophony of crunching metal and breaking glass.

Moerlen was the only one who didn't make a sound.

But then, dead men had little to say.

Roux watched as people rushed toward the journalist, the first few to help while others gathered around, horrified. Roux heard someone call out that he was a doctor, the words parting the throng like the Red Sea to allow him through. Roux followed in his wake, knowing that the idiot was dead. It had never been meant to end this way. Yes, he had wanted him stopped, but he hadn't wanted him hurt.

A woman in a heavy knit cardigan knelt over Moerlen, her hand on his throat.

She looked up at the crowd.

There was a moment when she might have said anything else, when it could have played out differently, but then she told them, *"Il est mort."* And it was final.

Roux had known it from the angle of the fall, the way his body twisted on the black surface of the Parisian road.

This wasn't what he'd wanted. All he'd wanted was a quiet life, the journalist out of it. Peace. It wasn't a lot to ask, just to be left alone.

Roux heard the Doppler-effect sound of sirens approaching, still streets away. Someone had to have called for help. The crush of bodies eased, people moving back as if the man's condition might be contagious. The doctor knelt beside the body.

There was a briefcase lying in the middle of the road, having spun out of the dead man's grip.

The photographs were almost certainly still inside.

Moerlen had been emphatic that they weren't his only copies. It was irrelevant if they were or weren't. If the police opened that case and saw all of those versions of the old man's face, it could only lead to questions. Roux worked his way around the crowd to the briefcase and picked it up, careful not to draw attention to himself.

As the paramedics arrived, he slipped away through the slowly thinning crowd.

3

On a winter's night
The present

It was minus seven degrees, closer to minus fifteen with the windchill factored in.

The extreme conditions presented their own problems for filming, including static discharge ruining shot after shot. It was just bone-chillingly cold, and Annja Creed was going snow blind with the swirling flakes twisting and churning in the air as they turned the world to white.

They were outside the tent, standing in the last bluster of the storm. An hour ago it had been like Snowmageddon out there. Now, there was air between the flakes and she could see the high walls of the castle, meaning it was the perfect time for the establishing shot of the medieval site in the heart of winter.

Annja had visited Carcassonne before, more than once, but on her previous visits the weather had always been positively tropical in comparison.

"You ready to go again, Annja?" Philippe Allard, the cameraman, asked, hoisting his camera onto his shoulder.

"Let's do this," she said, moving back into position.

On her mark, she waited for the thumbs-up to say that she was good to go.

She took a deep breath, letting it leak out slowly in a mist that wafted up across her face and earning her a scowl from her cameraman. His thumb went up. Annja started talking to the camera as if she hadn't taken a three-hour break waiting for the worst of the storm to pass. An observant viewer might spot that the snow on the hillside was deeper, but their brains would quickly fill in the gaps and gloss over that inconsistency.

She knew that chunks of the footage would be cut, with other images overlaid on the soundtrack. They'd gathered plenty of fantastic material over the past couple of days. And honestly, once she was back in the studio, a fair amount of the commentary would end up being rerecorded because she was a perfectionist and couldn't stand to watch a segment that was any less than that. So yes, you put in the work on location, but you did it knowing that, when it was all edited together, some of it would end up on the cutting room floor. Subzero conditions or no.

"Overlooked by the medieval fortress, the Cité de Carcassonne, the land behind me, has been the site of a settlement since Neolithic times. The Romans were among the first to really capitalize on its strategic position, and occupied the same hilltop until the fall of the Western Empire and the incursion of the Visigoths." She missed a beat as the red light went off, and the cameraman lowered his lens.

"Something wrong, Philippe?"

"Don't take this the wrong way, but don't you think it's all a bit..." He shrugged.

"Weak?" Annja suggested. "Sloppy?" She inclined her head. "How about dull? Or, heaven forbid, boring?" She folded her arms in front of her and shifted her weight, waiting to hear what he had to say.

"Wordy," Philippe said eventually, making it sound like one of the greatest crimes that could possibly be perpetrated on TV.

She grinned. "Wordy?" Wordy she could cope with. Wordy was just another way of saying that she was talking too much and using long words. Sometimes long words were just fine. It wasn't like she was about to parade around in a bikini trying to sex-up history in the snow.

"Want to change places?" Her grin was sly. "I'm happy to have a go behind the camera. I'm sure Doug would approve." Doug Morrell was Annja's producer.

"Well, my mom always said I had a face for television." He grinned right back. "You know, what with the whole sun shining out of my ass thing, I'm definitely special."

"No arguments from me."

She held out her hand for the camera.

"Are you serious?"

"Why not? Consider it your audition tape."

"More like the Christmas gag reel."

Even so, Philippe handed over the camera and waited on the mark while Annja got the camera on her shoulder and started recording.

"Over my shoulder," he said, waving vaguely in the direction of the fortress, "you can see a prime example of intimidation architecture. The people who built this place really didn't like visitors, and wanted to make them work for it, giving them a long, steep hill to climb when they wanted to drop by for a friendly croissant." He grinned. "Unsurprisingly, baguette wielders who made it that far almost certainly ended up with a pot of black cof-

fee poured on their heads from the handy murder holes."
He bowed to Annja. "See? Food and murder. That's what
people want."

She shook her head. "Okay, okay, I get the point. You're
hungry. Let's wrap it up for today and go get something
to eat."

"And there was me thinking subtlety was dead."
Philippe took the camera from her.

"My treat. Go take a dip in the pool first. Warm up
and work the kinks out of your muscles and concentrate
on making yourself look pretty. I want to go for a drive."

Philippe raised an expressive eyebrow.

"I feel the need for speed," she said with a grin.

He didn't need telling twice.

Five minutes later the tent was broken down, the gear
stashed in its flight case and loaded into the trunk of
their rental car.

The banter didn't slow down during the drive back to
the hotel. One thing this local hire was good at was talking. Flirting, really. Philippe had that roguish charm that
all Frenchmen seemed to have, and an accent to die for.
Of course she was going to buy dinner. She was a modern
woman laying down a flirtatious gauntlet of her own. *All
work and no play makes Annja a dull girl*, she said to herself, sweeping down the narrow road into the town proper.

The snow had gathered on the surface, reducing traction.

Annja drove carefully, enjoying the process of driving stick on a road that really wanted her to work for the
privilege of driving down it.

She parked outside the hotel, and made a promise to
meet Philippe in an hour. He double tapped on the roof
to let her know he'd gotten the gear out of the trunk. She

caught a glimpse of him looking at her—trying not to be seen to be looking—as he went inside.

France certainly had its plus points.

Annja turned up the music, pushed herself farther into the driver's seat and opened up the engine.

She would have killed to be on a motorcycle instead of cooped up in a car, icy wind in her hair, red-lining it around the country roads... There was nothing like the freedom of a bike on open road, but for now the car would have to suffice. The local radio station was running an eighties marathon, which helped, offering up cheesy driving tunes. An hour in her own company would do her world of good. Jane Weidlin sang about driving in the rush hour. The juxtaposition was brilliant. Snowcapped hills and empty roads couldn't have been farther from the choking urban slow-death that was Manhattan's rush hour.

She drove with only the vaguest idea of where she was heading, but it wasn't as if it would be difficult to find her way back to the town. It was pretty much a case of all roads lead to Carcassonne around here. Worst case, she had the satnav app on her phone to fall back on, assuming she could get a signal in the mountains with the snow worsening again.

Twenty minutes from the hotel, she'd passed a grand total of four cars on the road, and seen the same number coming the other way.

That had changed less than a minute later.

A glance in her rearview mirror offered the glint of a silver car—a Mercedes—half a mile or so behind her. The driver didn't seem to be in a hurry, but the power of the big car was deceptive, the distance between them closing fast.

A signpost on the hard shoulder promised a right-hand fork that would work its way back around to Carcassonne, so she took it. It wasn't exactly hot-date territory, but tall, dark and brooding was better than room service for one.

The side road led her onto a second, narrower lane that hadn't been plowed, forcing her to slow down to stop the rear wheels fishtailing on the icy surface. Snow topped the old stone walls and high hedges lining the road. Annja dropped her speed again, down to thirty, tapping her fingers on the wheel in time with the beat of Simon Le Bon's vocal promising he was on the hunt, after her.

She joined in with the chorus, remembering another time in France, another wolf. The Beast of Gévaudan, right at the beginning of this whole mad life she was now living.

The road curved up ahead. There were no tracks in the virgin snow. The sound of it crunching under her tires was a constant undertone beneath the music.

The snow-laden trees dumped their burden in a whisper ahead of her, and as the fine dusting settled, she saw a battered red tractor lumber across her line of sight. Even though her vehicle was going slowly, the sheet of ice under the snow meant that Annja wasn't going to be able to stop in time. She felt the wheels lose their grip and the car start to slide. Thinking fast, she turned into the slide, pushing the rental up onto the grass at the edge of the road, the passenger's side scraping through the leaves of the hedge, barely inches from the unforgiving impact of the wall.

Even so, there was precious little room to spare, and if the driver of the tractor didn't do likewise she'd end up forced into the wall.

Annja gritted her teeth, wrestling with the wheel as it wanted to turn relentlessly back toward the oncoming tractor.

The music cut out as she lost the signal.

The only sound inside the car was the scrape of leaves against the fender.

The tractor moved over to the side, leaving Annja just enough room to squeeze through without wrecking the rental. The hood shivered under the impact of another snow dump from overhanging trees. She nearly jumped out of her skin. Her reactions were good. Better than good. She had an almost preternatural control of her body, and even in the unfamiliar car, driving an unfamiliar stick shift, she was able to ramp it up less than an inch from the wall, and scrape along the hedge lining it, without totaling the car, and come out on the other side.

That was close, she thought.

Too close.

She eased on the brakes and came to gradual stop twenty feet down the road, and turned in her seat to see if the farmer was okay. He seemed to have taken the near-collision in his stride, not that she could see his face.

Maybe it was an everyday occurrence? After all, the tractor looked plenty beat-up.

And as far as Annja knew, maybe it was.

The tractor rumbled on its way relentlessly.

It disappeared out of sight, greeted by the sound of a blaring horn. The Mercedes. It was considerably wider than her rental car, and wasn't going to have a lot of success getting around the tractor. She guessed that this was what counted as congestion in this part of the world.

Annja drove even slower for the next couple of miles, bringing the needle down under the twenty mark, and keeping her eyes fixed firmly on the road ahead, expecting the unexpected to be lurking just around the bend. The snowfall thickened in the air ahead. The wipers were hypnotic, swinging back and forth, back and forth, but as fast as they went they couldn't cope with the gathering swirl of the snowstorm.

A quick glance at the dashboard clock promised she'd have just about enough time to sneak a shower before she hooked up with Philippe for dinner.

She didn't see another vehicle until the huge castle was in view on the horizon, a blur in the white. The lane began to widen. It was only then that she realized just how tightly she'd been gripping the wheel.

Annja glanced in the rearview mirror. The silver Mercedes had managed to work its way around the tractor and was back on her tail. She could see the thin-faced driver leaning into the steering column, and a brute of a man crushed into the passenger seat beside him. The Mercedes drew up close behind her as she reached the next junction. She took advantage of the moment to study the two men in her mirror.

The driver revved his engine, meeting her gaze in the mirror. Annja didn't look away. She was in that kind of mood.

She used the blinkers to signal a right and eased out, taking the road back toward Carcassonne.

The Mercedes followed.

Of course, it was the logical way to go, back into the town. That didn't mean they were following her.

The snowplows had been out on this stretch of road, making the going decidedly less treacherous.

After a hundred yards, she pulled over to the side of the road, allowing the Mercedes to overtake her, but even as it did, she knew it was just as easy to follow someone from in front as it was from behind. She watched the Mercedes disappear into the swirling white of the snow.

There was something really off about the whole encounter.

4

The call came out of the blue.

Garin listened to the voice on the other end of the line, unsure whom he was talking to and incredibly curious as to how he had managed to get hold of his private number. Both problems were tempered by the fact that the man had a job that he was interested in. It wasn't every day a gig turned up that piqued his interest, and this time it wasn't all about the money.

"Obviously, given the nature of the artifacts I am looking to acquire, this is a sensitive undertaking," the voice said. "But I have been led to understand that you are the man for the job."

"Well, I'd say that rather depends on a combination of things, but right now I'm listening, which puts you ahead of the game. So, let's put the bush over there and stop beating about it, shall we?"

"By all means."

"What you are looking for?" After the lure of the cloak-and-dagger approach, the worst thing that could happen now was that voice would spoil everything by asking for something mundane. There was nothing more disappointing. There was no joy in locating something bland, even if it involved a great deal of money. It was all about how you valued time, and sure, Garin had more of it than most, but his time was the most precious commodity he possessed, meaning giving it up had to be worth something. And even then he might be inclined to refuse. No, the thrill of the chase, the great hunt, the glittering prize... they were all part of the package. If one of them were missing from a job, the likelihood of him getting out of bed to deal with it were poor.

"The initial task is a relatively simple retrieval job. I would like you to locate the private papers of Guillaume Manchon, a court scribe at the church court in Rouen for the years 1430 and '31."

Manchon? The name rang a distant bell, but that was nothing next to the Klaxon the date and place set off in his head. The year 1431 was burned in his memory; it was the end and the beginning of all things. It was the date of Joan of Arc's trial and execution and the beginning of the curse that saw him walking this earth more than five hundred years later.

"You have my attention," he said, which was true. Anything that pointed back in that direction was intriguing.

"I had rather hoped I might. Alas, the papers are no longer there, so you will need to be, ah...creative. Guillaume made his notes in French, and they were later translated into Latin with five copies made. The French original and three of the transcribed Latin copies are in private collections, and unfortunately getting access to them is next to impossible."

"So by retrieval you mean theft?" Garin decided to come straight out with it. Breaking the law wasn't a deal breaker for a man like Garin Braden. More often than not a brief flirtation with the dark side only added to the thrill.

"Ah, no, no. Actually, I want you to find me one of the missing copies."

"How can you be so sure that they still exist? Do you have a lead on one of them? Evidence, perhaps, that there is another copy that hasn't been destroyed?"

"Sadly, no. I am laboring purely under the apprehension that what is lost can be found, and that you are the right man to track them down."

"Remind me again who recommended me?"

"Remind? I didn't actually say a first time. Suffice it to say it was a most impeccable source or I wouldn't be talking to you now."

"That's really not saying very much, is it?"

"And yet it speaks volumes, if you care to think about it for a moment."

Garin wasn't so sure.

"Okay, let's assume this mysterious benefactor knows his stuff and that I am indeed the man for the job. Why do you want these papers? What's so fascinating? What makes them special, apart from the fact they're nearly six hundred years old obviously?" More often than not, the answer to that question was more money than sense, with the buyer willing to throw cash at some mythical El Dorado.

"Please, don't take me for a fool, Mr. Braden. I am sure that you know full well why a scholar such as myself would be interested in documents created in Rouen in that particular year."

"Do I?"

"Put it this way—if you don't, then I will have to reconsider the recommendation, and believe that I have made a gross error in judgment."

"So these documents relate to the trial of Joan of Arc?"

He could almost hear the man's smirk as he said, "That's more like it. No need to be coy. As I said, these papers are just the first of several artifacts I am seeking. In the interests of full disclosure, I will email a complete list once we have agreed upon a fee for your services."

Garin's mind raced to an extortionate figure; after all, if the man was as determined to get hold of these artifacts as he sounded, he was ripe for a little extortion. "Three million, plus expenses," he said, plucking the number out of thin air. He expected the man to counter with a lower offer and a back-and-forth of offers and counters to follow. It didn't.

"Dollars or euros?"

"Euros," he said without missing a heartbeat. "And this is purely for the papers. Anything else I turn up is extra." It was a fishing expedition, of course. The hook baited, he wanted to see just how desperate the man was to get his hands on these lost words. "If I can't find them, you don't pay me. Fair?"

"Of course."

The man hung up without another word.

Garin was glad that the caller could not see the smile that had spread across his face.

He wasn't smiling because he was looking forward to the challenge of the hunt, though that would normally be the case. Garin wasn't the kind of man who chased legends. He left that sort of thing to Annja Creed. He wasn't interested in history's monsters. He had gone toe-to-toe with more than his fair share of them. No, he was smiling because he knew the exact location of one of the two missing transcriptions of Guillaume Manchon's papers.

They were currently locked up safe and sound in a vault in Roux's house.

Sometimes it was just too easy.

5

By the time Annja had left the hotel with her cameraman, the sun had started to sink in the sky. The late-afternoon chill had turned into full-on cold.

She couldn't dislodge the thought that the two men in the Mercedes had been following her. Had it been Brooklyn instead of the South of France she would have been worried about carjacking, or that insurance scam where people deliberately rammed into you for the claim. But without them mysteriously reappearing on her tail, there was nothing for her to actually worry about.

"Are you okay?" Philippe asked as they drove away from the restaurant. The food had been good, rustic farmhouse fare. Good, plain, healthy, but tasty, too. Farm fresh. It had been his recommendation. She was always happy to take advantage of local knowledge when it came to food, stay off the tourist track, keep it cheap, keep it wholesome. "You seem distracted."

"It's all good," she promised. "Just thinking."

"Sounds dangerous."

She chuckled at that. "Isn't it always?"

They were heading back to the site to take a few night shots with the castle lit up in the distance. It was always good to hit the atmospheric stuff when the sun was down. It added to the mystique.

Philippe kept talking, telling more stories about growing up in the area and days on the farmhouse where his grandma would stain her toes purple crushing grapes and his grandfather would nurture cheese that smelled almost exactly the same as his grandma's purple feet. Annja smiled, jealous of the trappings of a normal childhood. Every few minutes she'd glance in the rearview mirror, only for her heart to skip a beat if she spotted the shape of a car behind them, silver or not. She had to snap out of it; she was jumping at silver ghosts.

The spot they'd been filming at earlier was covered in three inches of fresh snowfall, though mercifully the night was clear and crisp, not so much as a flurry to be seen. What had worked during the day wasn't as suitable for the night shot, and she'd never intentionally put herself in the exact same position—that would only serve to make the segment look like some weird time-lapse photography experiment. They moved around, looking for a better angle where the spotlights accentuated the harsh old stones and served as a great reminder of just how old the fortress was.

"Inside could work," Philippe suggested. "A different aspect, very mean and moody. It would give the shoot an air of foreboding." He opened his case as he talked, pulling out the camera and beginning the prep work before they started shooting properly.

"I get what you're saying, but a distance shot, looking up at me with the wall rising to tower over me and really highlight the insignificance of man in this harsh winter landscape, could look pretty impressive."

"You're the boss," he said, hoisting the camera onto his shoulder.

Annja skimmed through her rough notes, familiarizing herself with the facts even though she'd read them dozens of times and knew them inside out. It was a compulsion. She could recite this stuff in her sleep. That was just the way her mind worked. She couldn't wipe it away even if she wanted to.

She swept her hair from her face, took a deep breath and gave him the nod.

The moment the red light glowed in the dark beside his face she was in her element. The spotlight on the side of the camera threw her features into stark relief, the perfect accompaniment for the tale of murder, witchcraft and heresy she was about to tell.

"In his book *Practica inquisitionis heretice pravitatis—Conduct of the Inquisition into Heretical Wickedness*—the Inquisitor Bernard Gui wrote a section related to sorcerers and diviners and the invokers of demons." She considered that for a moment. "His work proves beyond the shadow of any doubt that the Inquisition was concerned with the idea of witchcraft one hundred and sixty-five years before the publication of the *Malleus Maleficarum*, and refutes the notion that paganism in France had been suppressed by the year 1000..."

"Look out!" someone shouted.

Almost too late, Annja launched herself away from the wall, barely managing to shove Philippe aside as a huge piece of masonry hurtled down from far above, shattering on impact as it cracked the ancient flagstones. Philippe stumbled backward, desperately trying to cling to his camera even with his balance gone. Annja reacted faster, already looking up at the top of the wall, at a loss to un-

derstand how the huge slab could have fallen, and not seeing anyone on top of the wall who might have thrown it.

"Are you all right?"

She turned to see an older man in a wheelchair.

The woman pushing him had turned an unhealthy
shade of white.

Annja offered a wry smile. "Thanks to you," she said,
dusting herself off.

"I don't even know what possessed me to look up," he
said. "I was just enjoying listening to your recounting of
our ancient history. I assume it's for a news bulletin? Has
something happened?"

"Oh no," she said, realizing his misunderstanding. "I
work for an American cable TV show called *Chasing History's Monsters*. We're filming a segment about Bernard
Gui, the Inquisitor."

The man offered a polite smile that spoke volumes.
There was no reason why he should have heard of the
show, and despite his cultured English there was a strong
trace of Italian in his accent. She noticed that his left hand
was trembling, just a slight tremor. He saw the direction
of her gaze and offered a rueful smile. "My affliction," he
said, meaning the tremor, but it could equally have been
a reference to the macabre history of the place.

"I'm sorry," she said.

"It's perfectly all right, my dear. I'm just glad my big
mouth could save the day and that you and your colleague
are in one piece."

Before she could thank him, he craned his neck and
said something rapidly, in Italian, to the woman behind him. She turned him around without a word, and
as she wheeled him away, the old man offered the briefest of waves. Annja watched the woman struggle with
the wheelchair in the snow, following the tracks they'd

made a few moments earlier as they returned the way they'd come.

Philippe was still checking the lens and various attachments on his camera for damage when Annja went to help him back to his feet; she rather liked the fact he'd stayed down on his butt in the snow, more worried about the camera than he was about himself.

"Did it survive?" she asked.

"Looks like the spotlight's broken, meaning we can't shoot in the dark, but otherwise everything looks good. It could be worse. Still, it means we're not going to be getting anything else done tonight."

"Okay, let's draw a line under today and start from scratch tomorrow."

6

The call was unwelcome when it came, just as most telephone calls were, as far as the old man was concerned.

Roux sank into a large leather recliner. He had been doing his best to try to enjoy the old black-and-white movie on the huge flat-screen TV, which was the room's one and only concession to modern living. The buttery leather of the armchair was almost enough to transport him back the two hundred years to the time it had been made. *Casablanca* was quite possibly the greatest film ever made, and Ingrid Bergman the most beautiful woman ever to grace the silver screen. She was certainly one of the most beautiful women he had ever met, and he had met his share of beautiful women across the centuries. Even as fashions changed what people professed to be beautiful, there was never any mistaking true beauty. Of course, the fair lady had only ever seen him as an old man, but Roux had had the privilege of watching her age with grace and poise, and seen her slowly fade while he had remained the same.

That was the nature of his existence.

He'd been forced to drift out of her life before she noticed he wasn't aging as she had.

Although she would always be the lovely woman captured on celluloid.

The temptation to ignore the call was great. He hated to have his privacy invaded. He couldn't understand the obsession that the modern generation had with always being available. Time alone with one's thoughts was precious. He had an answering service. It would be easy enough to check any messages once the movie was over. But the caller was persistent, dialing again. And again when he ignored it a third time. It could, of course, be Annja. Or Garin—he always had impeccable timing.

Roux paused the image on the screen with Bogart and Bergman close to a kiss that might never happen.

He didn't recognize the number.

"Yes?" One word, not offering his name or number. There were few people who knew how to get hold of him. He wasn't in the habit of sharing his secrets, and he considered the sanctity of his own home the most precious secret of all.

"Have you heard from Annja?"

He didn't recognize the voice, despite the obvious familiarity the opening gambit suggested. "I'm sorry, who is this?" The old man had met a lot of people during his long life. Some, quite simply, didn't make enough impact to be worth remembering.

"My name? My name is Cauchon."

"What do you want?"

"Want? Nothing. I just thought you might want to be sure your precious Annja is safe, that is all. Consider it a public service."

The phone clicked and fell silent before it was replaced by the dial tone.

He didn't like it.

Forget the fact that the stranger had found his number, forget the fact that he knew his connection to Annja, which was hardly public knowledge. Why would someone call to ask if she was safe if not to goad him because the person knew for certain that she was anything but?

Roux punched in her number and waited for it to ring at the other end.

It seemed to go on forever.

Cauchon.

The name was in there somewhere, locked away in some dim, distant memory. No more than that. Truth be told, he'd made a habit of forgetting the names and voices of those people who, when it came right down to it, meant nothing.

It was harder to forget those who did.

"Hi," Annja's perpetually perky voice answered, and he felt a wave of relief even though he knew she was more than capable of looking after herself.

"Annja," he said, only to be interrupted by the rest of the message.

"Sorry, I can't take your call right now—you know what to do."

Voice mail.

The devil's own damned invention. Knowing that he could leave a message was no help.

He hung up.

She'd see that he'd called and would call him back. He didn't contact her unless it was important. That was the nature of their relationship. It wasn't about frivolity and social niceties. There were no "How are you doing?" calls or "Happy Birthday" moments.

Of course, now that he was rattled, there was no way he'd be able to concentrate on anything other than Annja, so there was no real point in pressing Play and waiting to see if this time maybe Bogie would get the girl.

His phone rang a few seconds later, jerking him back into reality.

Roux answered, half expecting it to be this Cauchon calling to mock him again. "Yes?"

"You called?" Annja said, sounding like she was right behind him. He felt like a weight was lifted off his shoulders. And again, he couldn't say why he'd been worried, not really; she was a force of nature was Annja Creed. He felt stupid for worrying.

"Ah, yes, sorry, my dear," he said, offering an easy deflection. "I must have dialed the wrong number. Fat fingers and all that."

"No worries," she said, then paused as if she was on the verge of saying something, but decided against it.

"Is everything all right?"

"Well, yes, I guess. I mean, nothing's actually wrong, but it probably depends on your definition of *all right*."

"Talk to me, Annja. Right now. Tell me what's going on." He didn't care if she could hear the edge in his voice.

"It was the weirdest thing. We were filming less than an hour ago…"

"Are you still in Carcassonne?"

"Yes. I was doing a piece to camera below the walls of the fortress, and somehow a huge chunk of masonry came crashing down. It could have been pretty nasty."

He closed his eyes. "But you aren't hurt?"

"We're fine. The camera took a battering, but we're not even talking cuts and bruises. It was a lucky escape."

Roux didn't say anything. His mind raced. Cauchon's call took on a darker meaning, taking it beyond the strange into threatening. It wasn't a coincidence. Live six hundred years and a person learns that there's no such thing. It's all cause and effect. He almost told her about the peculiar call, but there was no point in worrying her before he knew what the hell was going on.

"And you're sure it was an accident?"

"There was no one on the ramparts, if that's what you mean. Don't worry. It's not like I haven't done this before," she said. "Maybe I'll come up and visit you at the chateau when we've wrapped things up here. We'll spend Christmas in front of an open fire roasting chestnuts and toasting marshmallows or whatever the French do."

"Sounds lovely," he promised her.

She hung up.

He needed someone to try to trace where Cauchon's call originated, but no doubt it had run through a dozen satellite relays and masking services to make that all but impossible, but if anyone could do it, it was Garin.

7

"Roux, you old bastard, what an unexpected and, if I might say so, delightful pleasure," Garin said, laying it on thick. The universe worked in mysterious ways, he thought, smiling to himself. He'd been agonizing over what excuse to use as a pretext to call the old man, even going so far as to suggest a good old-fashioned Christmas dinner at the chateau, just the three of them. "What can I do you for?" *Apart from liberate Guillaume Manchon's papers from your vault*. Though, if he stole Guillaume Manchon's papers during a cozy visit, the wagging finger of suspicion would point toward him—but it always was. And Roux would forgive him; he always did.

They were peas in a pod—him and the old man. Partners in crime. They were, even without the blood bond, family. They needed each other. What was a little theft and profiteering against a backdrop as profound as that?

"I need your help," Roux answered.

Interesting, Garin thought. The old man never made a habit of asking for anything lest he be beholden to someone. He'd negotiate, blackmail or manipulate Garin into getting what he wanted before he would say *please*. This wasn't exactly uncharted territory, but it was seldom-ventured waters. He knew Roux well. There were a lot of things he was unable or unwilling to try to deal with, including technology and murder.

"So who do you want killed?" he laughed, only half joking.

"It's the exact opposite…"

"You want someone brought back to life? I'm good, but I'm not even that good."

"Shut up, Garin."

"Is that any way to ask for help?"

"I've already asked. I'm not asking twice. Now stop being an ass. I've just had a most peculiar telephone call…"

"A mouth breather? I hate those."

"I need you to see if you can trace the call."

"I'm assuming this won't be as simple as hitting last-number redial? You have tried that, right? I know you're not exactly down with the kids."

"I'm not an idiot."

"Time?"

"Twenty minutes ago, maybe a little less," Roux said. The old man was using that annoyingly matter-of-fact tone he always had when he was worried. That was the giveaway. There was no banter. No back and forth. He was genuinely worried. That meant Garin, in turn, was fascinated—because anything that worried the old man was worth digging into.

"On this number? Not the main line of the house?"

"This number. Can you do anything?"

"Probably. There are ways and means. Nothing's truly hidden in this modern world. I'm going to assume this wasn't a crank call, so what is it all about?"

"The caller wanted me to believe he had hurt Annja."

Garin fell silent for a moment. That changed things. Annja was neutral territory. They were both protective of her. She was the glue that kept their dysfunctional family together. The implications zipped through his mind like a runaway train. First, it wasn't impossible that someone had joined the dots and learned of the connection between the two of them. It wasn't a secret, but it wasn't public knowledge, either.

Then there was the fact the old man was paranoid and didn't share this number with anyone, including the phone company who serviced it, having used his charms a long time ago to seduce the operator and have the private number "lost." That meant the caller had gone to a hell of a lot of trouble to track down a number that to all intents and purposes hadn't existed for the best part of fifty years. Third, which was completely selfish in origin, if the mysterious caller knew about Annja, odds were that they'd found the connections between the old man and him. That made it personal. That was a world of inconvenience he'd rather avoid.

"I'm on my way," he said, realizing he'd just been given the key to the house.

"There really is no need to come running," Roux said. "Just find out where the call came from. If you want to impress me, find out who made the call. Let me know when you have any news."

The old man had hung up before Garin could bluster about how he was heading over no matter what he said. Of course, that didn't mean he had to sit on his hands.

Garin was good with machines. He understood their universal language in a sense that far surpassed his knowledge of most things in this life. Most, but not all. He smiled at the woman who stood in the bedroom doorway, shadows not leaving much to the imagination.

"I just have to make this call. I'll be right there. Why don't you get started without me?" She turned on her heel. He enjoyed how her curves were accentuated by the soft light. Simple things offered the greatest pleasures in life. That was a life lesson worth hundreds of years, right there.

Another was, why sit hunched over a computer trying to track a call when there was a delicious woman waiting to do unspeakable things to you in the bedroom?

He made the call.

The drowsy voice on the other end of the phone didn't sound pleased to hear from him. Garin looked at the clock and then remembered his favorite hacker was half a world away. Instantly making the time zone adjustments, he apologized and said, "Sorry. I figured you'd have the phone turned off if you were crashing."

"Garin," was all the hacker could manage for a several seconds.

"I've got a job for you."

"Usual rates?"

"Do it right and I'll throw in a nice bonus," Garin said, and started to fill him in on what he needed.

"Leave it with me," the hacker told him. "Assuming the caller tried to mask his whereabouts, I'll set about stripping away his anonymity. That's always the fun part with these guys. First, I'll send a crawler into the satellite stream and try to backtrack the signal. That should give us a rough location pretty quickly, then I'll start narrowing the focus. Give me a couple of hours. But you know the odds are it's a burner phone and there'll be nothing to find at the other end apart from the batch number."

"That's not a dead end. Batches go to shops, shops have

CCTV. Get me everything you can, starting with a location. I'll take it from there."

He hung up and made another call. He would need to have his plane ready within the hour. That gave him plenty of time to finish what he'd started in the other room and to shower before he left for the airport.

8

Cauchon pulled the SIM card from the phone and snapped it in two.

It was becoming increasingly difficult to keep the smile from his face. He had Roux exactly where he wanted him. For the time being, at least, and that was a fact worthy of celebration.

Roux would speak to the girl. She would tell him about the near-miss and the falling rocks at Carcassonne, and the old man would know it wasn't accidental. He would know that she had been lucky—lucky to have been warned just in the nick of time that she was in the path of the masonry, sent falling at his word. And for that moment Roux would know Cauchon had had her life in his hands and could easily have snuffed it out had he so wanted.

The change in the tone of Roux's voice as he'd mentioned Annja's name had been delicious. It was all the confirmation he had needed to know he was right. He had never intended to kill the young woman, just shake her up, and only then so that she could pass the scare on to the old man so he would realize his mysterious caller meant business.

The old man was going to pay.

Cauchon played his fingers across the row of SIM cards he had lined up on the table in front of him, each one still attached to the credit-card-size retainers.

He had no intention of making it easy for Roux. That would only serve to take the sport out of it. Cauchon knew Roux wouldn't turn to the police. That was an avenue that was never open to him. Far more likely was him taking matters into his own hands. Cauchon welcomed the idea. Let the old bastard fight back. Breaking him then would be so much more satisfying.

It didn't matter if the girl herself believed that the incident was actually an accident. No doubt Roux would disabuse her of that notion when he talked to her, and that would keep her looking over her shoulder, on edge. Uncomfortable.

Cauchon was banking on the belief that Roux was protective of her. He had plenty of reasons to believe he was right.

He watched the hands of the clock on the wall slowly turn.

He wanted to give the old man time to find out what had happened and then more time to think about the call, to let his words get under his skin. He wanted him to start worrying, to imagine what might happen next. He wanted him to be constantly worrying, doubting, looking at strangers and thinking, *Are you the one trying to get to me?*

And then he wanted to visit the man's worst nightmares upon him.

9

They drove back to the hotel in near-silence, Philippe constantly tuning the radio in search of a song that wasn't going to get on his nerves. Obviously it wasn't about the music. It didn't matter what he found. Nothing matched his mood. Annja resisted the temptation to lean over and kill the radio. She concentrated on the road, checking her rearview mirror a couple of times more than she normally would have.

As much as she didn't want to admit it, Roux's call had disturbed her. She knew he was always concerned about her well-being, but that the first thing he said was to question whether the incident at Carcassonne was an accident…that was a little paranoid, even for him. So she was watching, even if she wasn't sure what she was watching for. Of course it had crossed her mind that the falling masonry *could* have been something other than a freakish accident, especially as Roux had chosen that moment to call her. Annja had been in the old man's orbit enough not to believe in coincidence. He hadn't misdialed as he'd said.

He was checking up on her. And once her mind started down that path she knew it wasn't an accident.

She thought about the silver Mercedes.

Cause and effect? Or seeing patterns where there were none?

"What do you want to do about food?"

"I like the way you think." She grinned.

Philippe shrugged and started to fiddle with the radio again. "I'm French. We love good food and good company."

"And I sure could use a drink." Annja tried to stay focused, but her thoughts kept going back to her conversation with Roux.

"Now I'm liking the way you're thinking," Philippe murmured as he glanced out the side window. Clever. She could be friends with this one, she decided.

"I think we might even stretch it to sharing a bottle," she suggested.

It wasn't long before her mind was elsewhere though, as the horn of a car traveling toward them on the other side of the road blared, causing her to admit she'd drifted toward the middle of the road. Instinctively, she jerked to correct the drift, overcompensating and yanking the wheel too hard in the other direction, which had the seat belts bite hard into their shoulders.

"Whoa, there, speedy. I know you want me, but let's get to the bar in one piece, eh?"

"You wish," she snapped back, regretting it the moment the words left her mouth. She tightened her grip on the wheel and eased her foot off the accelerator. "Sorry, it's been a weird day."

"All the more reason to end it with a friend," Philippe said, and she realized he was right.

"I need to blow off some steam."

"I think I can help with that," the cameraman said with a wry smile.

"I'm sure you can."

10

Garin was in the air within the hour.

He leaned back in the seat as soon as he was able to switch to automatic pilot. He wouldn't normally have taken the stick himself. It was late, he'd been working hard all day, then playing harder, but there was something about being up in the clouds, surrounded on all sides by the stars, the lights blinking on the wings, the city laid out below in a landscape of molded light, that clung to the world. It was one of the most beautiful sights, so completely manmade, unlike many of the other spectacular things he'd seen in his life.

It was a sight he could never grow tired of.

Up here, away from the world, he could think.

His hacker had already come through with the information Roux was looking for, but he wasn't going to pass it on to the old man yet. Information was as good as currency. And given he wanted something in exchange for it, he wasn't about to say anything until they were face-to-face. Garin was good at reading people. That particular skill had made him a lot of money. He was also good at exploiting weaknesses and vulnerabilities. He fully intended to make himself indispensable to the old man and, once he was on the inside, pull the strings.

Garin was determined to get his hands on Guillaume Manchon's papers, but not simply to hand over to his mysterious client. He wanted to know what was in them himself. Knowledge. If it wasn't money, it was knowledge that greased the wheels in this life. And then he'd decide if they were worth more than the agreed sum, and just how desperately his buyer wanted them. It wasn't personal. It was purely business. Roux would understand one day.

Garin had been surprised at the ease with which the hacker had traced the source of the call and turned up the information the old man was looking for, but then, a location was worthless in this day and age when you could circumnavigate the globe in twenty-four hours. The caller would have moved. Potentially a long way. Even so, he'd paid the hacker a hefty bonus to keep on digging and see what else he could turn up.

Now he was more interested in his own questions, like what it was that had gotten Roux spooked about the call, and how it was connected to Annja and the medieval town of Carcassonne. Because there was always a connection. Nothing in life was random when it came to trouble—especially the kind of trouble Roux brought to the party.

It had been a while since Garin had last heard from Annja, but that was hardly a surprise, given that he was once again persona non grata thanks to a little greed on his part. He couldn't exactly remember what it was he was supposed to have done, but obviously it had offended her sensibilities. She didn't approve of the way he lived his life. He didn't take it to heart. But it would be best for both of them if she would just learn to shrug things off. Nothing was that important in the grand scheme. And it wasn't as if he actively set out to piss her off; that was just an unconsidered consequence of his actions. Surely the fact he didn't mean to do it should count for something?

He glanced at his watch. He was making good time.

The radio burst into life with a request from the airport.

The short hop had taken an hour, and the time had rushed by so quickly that he'd almost missed the twenty-minute descent and wound up bringing the jet down a little more sharply than intended. With no passengers to complain about the steep angle of descent and hitting the runway hard, he wasn't worried. He'd called ahead, so his car was already waiting for him in the parking lot.

He allowed himself a smug, satisfied smile; it felt good to be him.

Next stop, the chateau.

Once he was inside those doors, in Roux's inner sanctum, the rest would be child's play.

Garin lived for this kind of stuff.

Even after all these years, he enjoyed it when the apprentice could get one over on the master.

But then, it was all a game to him, and money was just a way of keeping score.

11

Roux never seemed surprised to see him.

It was as if he knew Garin wouldn't do as he was told.

The old man's expression was utterly unsurprised when he opened the door to find him on the doorstep.

"You have news?" Roux asked as he ushered him inside.

"Carcassonne," Garin said, pausing just long enough to make sure that he was well inside Roux's home before he said it. He had to make sure the old man couldn't just close the door in his face now that he had what he wanted. He wouldn't have put it past him. They had a peculiar relationship these days. Once upon a time Garin had been the student, Roux his mentor, master. He knew the old man better than anyone alive—better than himself probably. He knew he wasn't averse to using people to get what he wanted, then discarding them when he had it.

That one word shook the old man.

Without another word he led the way through passageways of priceless oil paintings and previously lost antiquities into his study. The wealth assembled in the house was beyond counting. Roux crossed the room, straight to the old freestanding globe beside his leather-inlaid desk, and opened the world up to get at the drinks inside.

"I take it you are thirsty?" Without waiting for an answer, he uncapped a bottle of brandy aged to the point of musky perfection. He handed a snifter to Garin and sat in the leather armchair beside the guttering coals of the open fireplace. Garin sniffed at the liquid, knowing it dated back to the time of Napoléon.

"All right, now that we're being all civilized, do you want to tell me what's so special about Carcassonne?" he asked.

"Annja's there," Roux said as though that answered everything.

"So?"

"So, think. I get an anonymous call asking if I've heard from her. When I eventually get hold of her, I find that she's had a near-miss with half a castle wall, and both the phone call and the near-catastrophe originate from Carcassonne."

"Okay, I'll give you that—two events, same town. So you think your caller fired a warning shot? But was it meant to kill her, or screw with you?"

"I don't know. Yet. But we have to work under the impression that option number one is true, and just hope the answer to number two is the reality we're actually facing."

"Motive? Why would someone want to kill Annja? Revenge?" There were any number of people she'd crossed in the past who could come looking for some kind of payback. It wasn't impossible even if it was improbable. But who, then, would tie her to Roux? That changed everything in Garin's mind. It surely meant the trail ran instead from him to her. They hadn't exactly broadcasted their relationship. Roux was the kind of man who lived his life in the shadows even if his protégé was one for living in the spotlight.

"Possibly, but I'm inclined to send the questions the other way. Who would want to draw me out by threatening her? Who would have the wherewithal to get hold of my phone number and orchestrate something like this?"

"It's not *that* hard to get hold of a telephone number. Telecommunications companies don't exactly have the most effective security systems in place, even given your special arrangements, so we can assume he bribed someone, or has an element of technological know-how. The thing is, it didn't take long to source the call, did it? So he can't be that clever."

"I suppose not," Roux said thoughtfully. He raised his snifter to his lips and took a slow swallow, then rolled the remaining brandy around the glass. "Of course, it would be a lot easier if the caller already knew the number, or knew someone who did."

Garin could feel the old man's stare burning into him.

"You can't really believe that I have anything to do with this?"

Roux said nothing.

"Do you really think so little of me?"

Roux said nothing.

"Seriously, this has nothing to do with me. I was in bed with a beautiful woman when you called. I would tell you who so you could corroborate this, but I didn't get around to getting her name. I've got nothing to do with this. Come on, Roux, we go back a long way. You know I wouldn't hurt Annja."

"No, but you'd screw with me, so if you knew she was never in danger?"

"She's one of us, Roux. She's just like you and me. It's the three of us against the world."

"Is it? Is that how you really see things? I thought it was, but after the Pass of the Moor's Last Sigh it's hard to believe you sometimes. I think the things you want are very different from the things we want."

"Okay, so I like the finer things in life. I would say that's not a crime, but obviously sometimes it is. But you *know* me. You know I'd never hurt her." It was true, and he was very delicately dancing around the fact that he'd come here with every intention of stealing from the old man. The objects of his nefarious intention were only a few feet away in his hidden vault. There was wealth beyond imagining in that vault, not just in monetary value, either. The old man was a hoarder. He had works of art and irreplaceable antiquities all around the house. He wasn't worried about prying eyes seeing those, so he didn't keep them under lock and key. It was only things that could lead back to who he really was that ended up in the vault. Secrets.

"You may be telling the truth," the old man said, but he didn't sound entirely convinced. Garin was a gambling man. He knew a safe bet when he saw one. Roux still thought he was behind the whole scheme. Old habits died the hardest. Garin had to force himself not to look over the old man's shoulder at the vault.

He could almost taste the money heading his way once he had his hands on Guillaume Manchon's papers. It would only become a tough choice if, after examining them, Garin found something incriminating in the writings that tied them back to Joan of Arc's execution, and that was almost certainly not the case, even if Manchon had recorded their names. Lots of Frenchmen had been called both Roux and Braden in the intervening years.

"Okay, worry about me if it makes you happy, but what do you want to do?" The old man shrugged for an instant, revealing the years that lay behind his eyes. "My instinct is to go and find her."

"Which, for argument's sake, if it were me behind the call, is exactly what I'd expect you to do, so you'd be walking right into the trap."

"But you've convinced me it isn't you," Roux said with irritating smugness. "So, if the caller is in Carcassonne, and Annja is in Carcassonne, that's exactly where I want to be."

"Okay, I'll give you that. But we don't know who's behind this. The number's dead, so it's either a burner phone or they've just destroyed the SIM card and we're going to be chasing shadows once we touch down."

"Then we make ourselves the bait to lure him out," Roux said. "If he wants me, I'll give him the chance to come at me and hope he makes a mistake."

"And you wonder why I think you have a death wish sometimes, old man? You have no idea who you're going up against, what he looks like, nothing."

"I'll recognize the sound of his voice."

"Great, let's hope he offers a nice convenient threat before he cuts your head off."

"So you'd rather sit here and wait to see how things play out?"

"Yes. Think, Roux. If this guy really has it out for you, he'll call you to taunt you again, won't he?"

"And what if the next time it's because Annja's dead?"

"Have you met that woman?"

Roux shook his head. "How do you live with a lifetime of regret when your lifetime might never end?"

"I hate you when you get like this."

"You mean when you know I am right?"

"Okay, fine. He'll call or he won't. He'll make another attempt at Annja or he won't. He'll be waiting for you, though, that's for sure. And that's like putting your head in the noose and taunting the damned hangman."

"Or perhaps, just perhaps, going to Carcassonne means we are in the safest place in the world, as he'd expect us to sit here and wait for his call and is lining up an attack on the house."

"Not if he knows you, old man."

"So you stay here, answer the phones, while I go out and risk my life for our mutual friend."

And there was an offer that was almost impossible for him to refuse: Roux out of the house, and him having the run of the place and all the time in the world to infiltrate the vault and liberate Guillaume Manchon's papers. The temptation was incredible. But he could hardly say yes. Instead, Garin moved to take control of the situation by seeming to agree with Roux.

"All right, all right. I'll make you a deal. If he hasn't called by the morning, we head to Carcassonne, okay? There's nothing we'd be able to do tonight, anyway, so a few hours aren't going to kill us. Get some rest. We'll head out at first light."

Roux agreed, but there was an obvious element of reluctance in his voice.

He made a show of looking at his watch, no doubt calculating how long it would take them to get there.

"We'll be there in no time at all. Don't fret, old man. It's not like a few hours will make a difference."

12

Morning.

Annja had had a restless sleep and the bottle of Pouilly-Fumé hadn't helped. She had a dry-wine hangover and needed to get some air.

It felt like weeks since she'd been out for a proper run, really pushing herself. She had her gear with her, including a good pair of running shoes, so she got dressed, pulled her hair into a ponytail, stretched the kinks out of her muscles in a warm-up, then hit the streets. She pounded the pavement for a predawn hour, nothing but the wind in her face and the bite of the icy air in her lungs to keep her company until the first birds started to sing.

And then she kept on running, glad she'd resisted the temptation that Philippe presented, even when the wine had been flowing. It was always a mistake to mix work and sex. Always.

The ice glistened on the road ahead of her as the sun rose.

There was nothing like being out before the rest of

the world woke up; it was like sharing a secret with the universe.

It was the best hour of the day, because it was just her and nature.

She kept on running, pushing herself to go faster as she reached the hills, and whenever she was presented with a choice of the hard way or an easy way, Annja chose the hard way every time. It felt like a metaphor for life as well as being a grueling workout.

Ninety minutes later she was in the shower, steam venting up out of the drain where the hot water hit the cold tiles, then she toweled herself dry, dressed and went down for breakfast.

The dining room wasn't busy. Half a dozen people were keeping very much to themselves. She stocked up on a continental breakfast—fruit, muesli, yoghurt and a wonderfully fresh brioche—before she headed out to the car.

The run had cleared her head and taken the edge off her stress, as it always did. Even so, she checked over her shoulder as she slid the key into the lock, looking for the Mercedes.

She was past the point of being afraid. Very little in life scared her these days—in part because Joan of Arc's mythical blade was only an arm's length away in the otherwhere, just waiting for her to reach for it, but more because of the way her own body had changed during the few years since she'd first reached out to take it. She wasn't the New Yorker she had been, and even back then she'd been a together, strong, independent woman. Now, though, the strength of the ages ran through her veins. She could run farther, faster, fight harder, and had lightning-fast reactions. Now she was a daunting foe for anyone. She'd handled the worst the world could throw at her, and came away from it feeling indestructible. Maybe this is how it feels to be bitten by a radioactive spider, she thought, grinning, as she slid into the driver's seat.

If the guys from the Mercedes were interested in her, then let them come. It was as simple as that. They'd regret it. People who tried to mess with her always did.

That was why she was in the car in the first place, taking control of the situation.

She was using herself as bait to lure them out—or discount them as an actual threat and put the dumb notion out of her mind once and for all.

Annja took the road out of town, heading into the countryside. It was still early, meaning it was what passed for early-morning rush hour in these parts.

She checked the mirror.

There was nothing back there.

It wasn't the possibility that they were watching her, but the fact that she had no idea of who they were that bugged her. She didn't like not knowing.

Annja was barely half a mile outside the town when she caught the glint of sunlight on silver behind her.

She smiled to herself, and muttered, "Come out, come out, whoever you are."

Even without being able to see the shape clearly, she knew it was the silver Mercedes, and with no other cars on the narrow road it caught up with her quickly. She slowed, imperceptibly at first, gradually allowing the Mercedes to close the gap and invite it to pass her. But that wasn't the intention of the Mercedes's driver, and she knew that. Annja would have felt more in control if she were behind the other car, if she was the hunter rather than the hunted in this game of cat-and-mouse. But beggars couldn't be choosers.

She eased her foot off the accelerator, but kept clear of the brake. She didn't want the flare of the brake lights to betray the fact she knew they were back there until it was obvious.

As they drew closer, they slowed, too, tucking in fifty yards behind her, matching her speed, a sure sign they were indeed following her and this wasn't just the most ridiculous case of the universe having fun at her expense.

The road ahead was straight as far as the eye could see, the pavement shimmering with frost haze where the sun reflected off the surface.

Her hands felt slick on the wheel. Her heart beating just that little bit faster, the thrill of the extra adrenaline pumping through her veins.

She pulled over to the side of the road, put the car into Neutral and released her seat belt. She didn't kill the engine, letting it idle.

She wasn't going anywhere until she knew what was going on.

If the Mercedes raced by, she'd just follow it. Simple as that.

The other car reduced its speed, no more than ten miles an hour, as it drove by. The passenger, the giant brute of a man, held her gaze without blinking as the driver pulled up in front of her car.

The passenger door opened and the big man climbed out.

Police? It was possible, but it was a nice car for an unmarked gendarmerie vehicle, which made it unlikely it was local law enforcement. She had come across enough of them all over the world to know when it was the law keeping an eye on her. It was a sixth sense now.

The man reached down for her door handle before she thought to lock it from inside. She reached for the button just as he tugged hard at the handle, as though brute force would be enough to beat her and the lock. When the door didn't open, he banged against the window with the side of his fist.

Annja took a breath. It was that moment, the single point between fight and flight. She inched the window down a crack.

"What do you want?"

"Miss Creed," the man said in a gruff voice, taking a step away from the car.

"Yes," she said.

"Get out of the car."

"No," she said, not making an argument of it, but simply stating that there was a line she wasn't stupid enough to cross just because he said so. "Not until you say please." She used humor to show she wasn't frightened, no matter how physically intimidating the giant was. And towering over the roof of the car, he was like a mountain more than a mere mortal.

"Please," he said, laboring over the word, like it was something unfamiliar to his lips. Annja saw by the way he clenched and unclenched his fists that he was pumping himself up for an explosive confrontation. She almost felt sorry for him. It wasn't as though he could know what he was letting himself in for. She was ready.

He used one ham hock of a hand to pull back the edge of his leather jacket to reveal the butt of a pistol tucked into the waistband of his jeans, removing all doubt as to his motivation. So much for the hope he was an over-zealous autograph hunter. The odds of a peaceful outcome whittled down to zero as the driver opened his door, emerging from the Mercedes to join his hulking companion.

She needed to act quickly.

Dealing with them one at a time was preferable to taking them on together. It was simple mathematics. She had seconds to make the parity count. Annja moved fast, unlocking her door and slamming it open, far harder than she needed to, forcing the mountain to stumble back a couple of paces. He actually moved pretty well for such a big man, which was disappointing. She slid out from behind the wheel, climbing out of the car just as he reached for his gun. In a fair fight he would have drawn down on Annja before she was halfway out of the car, but this wasn't a fair fight. Annja was fast. Even if he knew who she was, he had no idea just how fast she was.

Before he could raise the muzzle in her direction, she had reached into the otherwhere, her fingers curling around the familiar grip of her sword. Her entire body thrilled to the touch of the ancient blade, her blood resonating with the weapon on some primal level as she pulled it free of its resting place. Sunlight glinted from the keen steel edge that never dulled. She brought it down hard, slashing through the air in a savage arc that drove the mountain back two more steps, stunned by the impossibility of what had just happened.

It didn't matter how big he was, or how many bullets he had in his magazine, he was afraid. She had seen that look often enough in the past. The sword had a way of making big men shrink down to size.

She moved the blade through a kata, whipping her wrist about to control the vicious dance of steel.

The man released the first shot.

Annja was barely three steps away from him, but it was all the room she needed to bring the ancient sword to bear, deflecting the bullet off the flat blade and sending it whistling away harmlessly in a shower of sparks. The sound of the ricochet rang through the air, echoing over the fields on either side of them.

The second shot nicked the blade, lodging itself in the

body of the rental car behind her. He didn't have time for a third. Annja slashed the tip of the sword close to the mountain's great barrel of a chest, slicing through the leather jacket and parting the cotton T-shirt beneath without breaking his skin.

"See how easy it would be for me to gut you?" Annja said, completely matter-of-factly, her breathing deep, calm, controlled.

He stumbled back, stubbornly trying to fire again.

Annja shook her head. The blade, moving faster than the eye could possibly follow as more than a silver shimmer in the air, slapped against his gun hand, springing his fingers apart in a cry of pain.

The gun went flying, another shot drilling harmlessly into the ground.

She looked down at it, then up at the mountain, knowing he was nursing a couple of broken fingers. He wouldn't be firing a gun again in a hurry. At least, not with his right hand. He followed the direction of her gaze, looking down between his legs in time to see Annja's foot come up. He buckled as she made contact, doubling him up. It didn't matter how big a man was, how many steroids he pumped into his veins or how many reps he did in the gym. He couldn't strengthen that one very frail human weakness no matter how hard he tried. Her adversary fell to his knees howling with pain. Annja launched herself into a vicious roundhouse that connected with the side of his head and stepped back to watch as the mountain's face plowed into the dirt at her feet.

He was out cold.

"Stay right there," the driver said. He looked ruefully at his unconscious comrade, obviously glad he wasn't in his shoes. He had his own gun aimed squarely at the center of Annja's mass, but wasn't in a hurry to fire. He'd just seen what she was capable of. Why would he think his bullets had a better chance of finding their mark than the mountain's?

Annja held her sword in front of her, balanced lightly in her grasp, moving forward onto her toes. He was close enough she could hurl the blade at him, cleaving his head from his shoulders before he could get down behind the safety of the car. But killing him wouldn't give her any answers. And it wasn't her style.

"There was no need for that," he said, doing his best to sound reasonable. "We just want to talk to you."

"Of course you do," she said. "People always come up to me wanting to have a nice little chat with a gun in their hands."

"Look, I'm sorry. It wasn't meant to go down like this. If you'd just come with us, we could have done everything nice and calmly."

"And why on earth would I want to go with you? I think you better start talking fast."

"*Why*? Because we were asking nicely."

She shook her head. "You didn't ask at all. Your brute tried to strong-arm me. I'd hate to see what you call nasty. So, what do you want to talk to me about? I'm sure you've noticed that you have my undivided attention right now."

"Not me. I was only asked to pick you up."

"I'm already fed up with the way you answer questions. Who asked you to pick me up?"

"It doesn't matter who." He shrugged. "Not to me. I'm just doing my job."

"Ah, the good old staple. 'I'm just following orders,' is that it? I think I've heard that before somewhere."

"Look, there's no need to get hostile about this. I don't want *anyone* else to get hurt, especially me, okay? So why don't you just drop that *thing* and get into the car. We can just do what we've got to do and everyone can be happy."

"Happy? You seriously think I'm about to get into a car with you? What kind of happy pills have you been popping? Give me some answers and I'll *consider* following you in my car," she said, with no intention of following him. But if he believed her, maybe she'd get a few details.

The man on the ground started to groan. He didn't sound happy with life. She probably had a minute or two at most before she'd have to put him down again or things might get a little feisty. At least his gun was out of easy reach.

She started to walk toward the driver, inclining her head in invitation for the man to talk.

The only words that came out of his mouth were, "Drop the sword," and they were followed by the sound of his thumb fumbling with the safety on his gun.

"Seriously? You're thinking of trying that? I'm disappointed."

She took another step, but it was a mistake.

The man squeezed the trigger and the gun ripped out a roar that shattered the silence.

The world moved in slow motion for an instant.

A bird rose from the field behind him, giving out a cry of warning that had barely left its beak when the bullet hit her sword. Sparks flew as it rang off the metal, ricocheting into the car and sinking into the bodywork. There was another sound, a deep pop that made her think it had hit the engine block, which was a pain, but it hadn't hit her.

The man shook his head, not believing his eyes. She realized that he hadn't trusted the mountain to get a shot on target but, knowing his own should have buried itself in her heart, didn't know what to do next. She liked beating people's expectations.

"What can I say? I guess I got lucky. Want to try again?" Annja asked, taking another step closer.

The man had nowhere to go without leaving the safety of the car.

He was nervous and that made him dangerous. Annja wasn't about to drop her guard, even for an instant, no matter how quick her reactions. It didn't take a lot to squeeze a trigger, and the fact he was willing to take her life made him as dangerous as any killer she'd faced. She knew the second and third shots were coming. She could see it in his eyes. Dropping to one knee, Annja blocked a shot on the cross brace of the sword and another on the tip, sending it back the way it had come. The bullet shattered the glass of the window inches from where the driver stood, completely undermining any notion of safety he harbored.

"Next time I won't miss," Annja said, "so how about telling me who you are working for?"

There was no hiding his fear now.

He was far more afraid than she was.

"Or maybe you want to wait here for the police to arrive. I'm assuming they will, even somewhere this remote. When people hear gunshots, they call the police."

She completely ignored the fact that he was the one holding the gun.

She was in control here. They both knew it.

She watched the black eye of the muzzle waver as the gun trembled in his hand. Even if he tried to fire again, there was no way he'd hit her. As if on cue, she heard the sound of the siren in the distance.

"I assume you don't want to spend the rest of the day trying to explain to the police what's happened here, so if you won't tell me who you are working for, I think we're done."

The man nodded and placed the gun on the roof of the car, holding up his hands, palms out, where she could see them.

He stepped away from the car without taking his eyes off her.

She gave one last glance at the man still lying on the ground. Given more time she might have had more success with them, but such was life.

"Can I make a suggestion?" The man said nothing. "If I were you, I'd quit," she said. "You're really not cut out for this line of work. Two grown men beaten up by a girl." She shook her head and smiled.

She kept walking toward the Mercedes, making the man back up a couple of steps, before she sliced the tip of the sword into the black rubber of both front tires one after the other, deflating them with a hiss that had ended before she climbed back into her rental car.

Now she was relying on a little bit of luck when she turned the ignition, hoping the bullet hadn't done anything terminal when it had embedded itself under the hood.

The engine coughed, and died.

She tried it again.

It rumbled a second longer before it died.

Third time was the charm.

She checked on the driver in the side mirror. He wasn't going anywhere.

That was something at least.

But it didn't answer the one question she really wanted answered: Who had sent them after her?

13

The house was silent.

It was huge, with only Henshaw who lived on-site, but he had his quarters away from the guest rooms and the master suites. The main problem was alarms and security, but more often than not the old man didn't activate the internal sensors, at least for parts of the house. Though Garin was almost positive there were silent alarms in place around core areas of the house, including Roux's study.

Garin had retreated to his room, certain that many famous people had once visited here. Roux moved in many circles. Garin couldn't help but wonder who had lain on this bed before him, listening to the sounds of winter in the distance. It was close enough to Paris that the likes of Louis-Auguste, dauphin of France, and his young bride, Marie Antoinette, had very likely summered with the old man before the dark days of the revolution.

He didn't sleep.

He listened to the building, lying on the bed fully dressed. He heard the occasional groan and sigh of the old building moaning to itself, and old ghosts whispering away along its splendid corridors. Finally, he pushed himself off the bed. It was time—if not safe—to make his play.

Roux was a light sleeper, a habit he'd picked up from years of metaphorically dozing with one eye open, but Garin was light on his feet, and barring something stupid, like sending a priceless Ming dynasty vase tumbling, he wouldn't wake the old man.

Floorboards creaked with almost every step he took, no matter where he placed his feet. He carried his shoes in one hand, his laptop case in the other.

Each time he made even the slightest sound he paused, waiting in case there was any sign of an echoing call from somewhere else within the house, even though he knew that it was the erratic nature of a disturbance that was more likely to rouse a sleeper than the steady sound of footsteps on old boards. A red light pulsed slowly and regularly at the far end of the passage—the alarm's motion sensor. With no siren blaring, it seemed safe to assume it wasn't set. He crept onward, keeping his breathing slow, steady, aiming for a Zen-like state of calm that put him at one with the hallway. But he was excited. He couldn't help himself. There was a thrill that went with this kind of thing, snooping around in the old man's secrets. That was just the way he was. Garin carried on down the hallway, keeping his footsteps to the edge of the treads as he reached the stairs, and descended.

It was all he could do not to give a slight sigh of relief when he reached the bottom without an alarm betraying his nocturnal perambulations. Now all he had to do was to enter the vault, get Manchon's papers and get back to bed before Roux roused himself.

Easy.

He placed his shoes carefully on a chair in the hallway and made his way back into the study, pausing to listen at the door before he eased it slowly open.

The last embers of the fire had burned down to an amber glow that still clung to the crumbling coals. Moonlight shone in through the French windows, casting abstract shadows over the room.

Garin placed his bag on the desk, easing it open, and retrieved the laptop. He opened the lid. The machine had been in sleep mode rather than turned off, so there was no chime of the operating system starting up. He quickly dimmed the screen so the glare didn't show through the window, giving him away to any security the old man had prowling the grounds. The heavy oak would be enough to muffle almost any sound he made in the room, but that didn't stop him from taking exaggerated care as he prepared himself. He didn't have an excuse for being in the study. If Roux walked in, the best he could manage was that he couldn't sleep so he'd come down to do some work. It was unlikely the old man would fall for it.

Best not to get caught then, he thought, examining the spot on the back wall that would reveal the vault.

He fished a cable out of his bag and slid one end of it into the microcoupling on the laptop, before placing the sensitive electromagnetic reader on the other end onto the wall itself.

Once he had done that, he ran the hack from the terminal and sat back waiting for the machine to do its thing.

Digits cycled through the boxes on the screen, at first faster than the eye could possibly see, each change indicating the sending and receiving of an electrical pulse between the computer and the safe as it raced through the dizzying permutations eight digits offered, searching out the slightest difference that would indicate it had found the correct number in the sequence.

By the time the third number had been locked onto the screen, Garin was absolutely certain he knew the combination. The old man was predictable. A smile played across his lips.

05301431.

A date that was seared across both of their lives.

The date of Saint Joan's execution.

He tapped the eight digits into the keypad.

The wall opened with an electronic click as the lock disengaged.

The way he figured it he had less than an hour to similarly open the vault and then get back to his room before he was caught. It wasn't as if the old man would have been thoughtful enough to have Guillaume Manchon's papers neatly stacked in a pile and put to one side conveniently for him to find. That would have been too easy.

But Garin was a resourceful thief.

It was one of his better qualities.

14

Garin had disappeared by the time that morning came.

Roux thought at first he'd simply gone for a run in the grounds, but then he saw his erstwhile squire's car was missing from the drive.

It shouldn't have surprised him. Garin Braden had been disappointing him one way or another for centuries. He should have guessed there was another reason for his late-night visit than simply concern for Annja. There was nothing he'd said to Roux that couldn't have been said over the telephone, which meant he had another purpose for coming.

He almost missed it, because nothing in the study had been moved, but when he went through the security tapes, he got to watch firsthand as Garin robbed him.

Most of the documents and treasures he kept inside the vault were more of a sentimental or academic nature than having any intrinsic value.

He followed the usual procedure, then entered the vault.

The room, given the kinds of things it had been designed to protect, was airtight.

At first glance it was next to impossible to see what, exactly, had been taken.

The jewels he had acquired from King Louis XIV were still in the black velvet pouch that had kept them safe since the day he'd stolen them, and the gun he'd liberated from the German SS officer who'd thought that he possessed the power to do anything he liked likewise was nestled in its place. There were so many incredible items in the vault, each with a history that defied simple categorization on a museum's shelves. So many seemingly innocuous treasures that were little more than trifles to the human eye possessed such significance to the eye of time. And, as far as he could tell, they were all still where they had been left.

It would take ages to check each one on his inventory.

But why would Garin steal a memento?

He wouldn't.

That wasn't his style.

There were other antiquities in the vault, arguably more precious, even if they looked less glamorous. There were a stack of notebooks and papers, ledgers, journals, diaries, everything that he had ever accumulated that could possibly be used to pick a path between who Roux was now and who he had been. They were tied up in ribbons, each color signified a century and decade within it—hardly the most elaborate filing system, but it sufficed. One of the ribbons, the purple of the fifteenth century, was loose.

The old man rubbed at his jawline, feeling the rough stubble where his beard was already thickening, and took down the bundle. Surely Garin knew he would have allowed him to examine any of these papers, and that the only secrets they represented were the ones that down the years had protected them from witch hunts and claims of heresy?

He should have burned them all, of course, but he could never bring himself to do it.

Roux had few secrets from the man. How could he have? They'd shared so much of this life together, the only two men in the world who could confide in each other as the world aged around them, leaving them untouched. And yet he had chosen to take them? To break in here in the middle of the night and disappear before dawn, trying to cover his tracks?

It couldn't be good.

He knew Garin better than he knew himself; there was only ever one motive for him to do something like this, to betray the pair of them so completely: money.

He had a buyer, almost certainly, but for what?

And just how much damage could the papers do out in the world once they were sold?

Without knowing exactly what was missing, it was difficult to tell, but most of the material in here was primary source research. Handwritten notes of scribes and eyewitnesses to incredible moments of history—like the burning of Joan of Arc at the stake in Rouen.

He felt foolish. Garin was a scorpion. It was in his nature to sting, no matter how much love there was between them. He took what he wanted without giving a second thought to anyone else. If it meant so much to Garin to risk their often-strained relationship, then there was nothing he could have done to stop him short of handing the papers over himself, with his blessing. And that would have taken the fun out of it for Garin. That was just who he was. No, what hurt was that he had used Annja and his concern for her as a cover for his crime.

As always it was only ever about what Garin wanted.

And what Garin wanted, Garin took.

He took the opened bundle of papers and cradled them

carefully in his hands, intending to check them off against the inventory, but once in the study the first thing he did was call Annja.

The call went straight to voice mail.

That only made him all the more nervous.

He needed to know she was safe, primarily, but he wanted to know if she'd seen anything, marked anyone taking an unnatural interest in her beyond the usual autograph hunters. That meant that he was looking for one single piece of information: Had the anonymous caller made contact?

He'd only kept the call from Annja because it had felt like the right thing to do the previous night. Now, in the cold light of day, he was starting to doubt his own judgment.

"It's Roux," he said. "Please call me when you get this. I'm on my way to join you. I'll be there in a few hours."

Using the intercom on the main phone, he summoned Henshaw. The man appeared in a matter of seconds, as though materializing from thin air. "Henshaw, is there a way we can redirect calls from the line in the study to my cell phone while I am on the road?"

"Yes," was the man's reply, taking the phone from the cradle and punching in a code.

It took him all of three seconds.

"It is done, sir."

"Excellent. Please prepare an overnight bag. I shall be leaving the chateau soon. Call ahead to make sure my plane is ready, would you?"

"Yes, sir." The faithful servant nodded.

"That will be all."

"Very well, sir. Safe travels."

"We can but hope, but they rarely ever are," Roux said.

15

The sun had barely kissed the horizon when Garin reached his plane. It was a short return hop. Let Roux go chasing after Annja and meddle in her life. Besides, she was a big girl. And he had another, more pressing engagement with a buyer who was about to pay an awful lot of money for the papers he'd liberated from Roux's vault. An obscene amount of money, really, given what they actually were, which only made the deal sweeter.

Before he ran through safety procedures, he made a call to the interested party, assuring him that he had come into possession of the merchandise, and that he was ready to make the trade. The price had just gone up, however, by another mil, for expenses incurred, which was a fat lie, but the kind of fat lie a person could get away with when he held all the cards. Unsurprisingly, given the hour, no one was there to take the call.

"I've got what you were looking for, but now that I have, we need to revisit the price," was all he had said before he hung up.

He checked his watch. The buyer would call back soon

enough; Garin knew the man was desperate. And when the buyer did contact him, Garin would be back in the comfort of his own home, reveling in the fact the score card read Garin +1, the rest of the universe 0. With luck, it would be months before the old man even realized something was missing. It wasn't as if he had the need to go into the vault every day.

But then, his absence would set the old man to thinking.

Nothing good ever came from the old man thinking.

But maybe he should have been doing more of that himself?

He knew absolutely nothing about his client.

Not quite true. He knew a single string of numbers—the account code for the wire transfer that had deposited the funds to secure his fee. That was enough of an act of faith for Garin to trust the mysterious buyer to hold up his end of the bargain.

It would have been enough in normal circumstances, but Roux had got him thinking now, second-guessing himself. These papers were almost as old as he was, and recorded an event he'd witnessed firsthand.

So why these papers?

Why ask him to find them?

Why go after one of the missing copies instead of stealing one of the known ones?

Unless his buyer knew Garin had easy access to them—knew about Roux.

No.

Unlikely.

Sometimes a spade was just a spade.

He made another call.

"I've got another number for you," he said when his hacker answered the phone. No preamble. No pleasantries.

"Shoot," the hacker said.

Garin reeled off the digits.

No need to discuss rates. This particular kind of transaction was about as commonplace as walking into a supermarket and picking up a loaf of bread or a liter of milk.

"How quickly do you need it? There's been a lot of traffic on the net, and I may have to bump some stuff to get in if you need it in a hurry."

"Definition of a hurry—I'm going to be in the air for the next hour, and if you can have something for me by the time I land there'll be a bonus in it for you."

"I'll see what I can do."

Garin knew he'd come up with the goods; the hacker had never let him down before, and no reason to think he was about to start now.

He took off in the plane, rising to altitude smoothly. There was a simple joy in flight. It put him up with the angels. Sometimes it was incredible to think how the world had changed even over a few short decades that something as wondrous as flight could become so utterly normal.

But the joy of the flight was second to the thought of the money waiting at the other end.

Sometimes Garin Braden was a simple soul.

Even if he already had more money than most people could spend in three or four lifetimes, even if he was richer than Croesus, that didn't mean he had enough.

He could *never* have enough.

That was a lesson he'd learned a long time ago.

There were people in this world simple enough to believe that being able to pay the bills was enough, or being able to go out for a meal any time they wanted to was more than enough. There were others who believed that enough meant being able to change their car whenever they felt the urge, but Garin wasn't one of them. Garin wanted to be able to buy *anything* that took his fancy, whether he needed it or not. Even the plane he flew now was bought on a whim.

And still he didn't have enough.

It was all about staying on top.

His buyer was determined to possess Manchon's papers, as it opened the way to something else he was determined to get. And if he wasn't determined enough to pay the extra premium, then maybe Garin would hang on to the papers and see if he could unlock the mystery himself.

16

Annja was frustrated.

She didn't like being in the dark.

Those two thugs had been working for someone. They might not come after her again, but that didn't mean that their boss wouldn't send others to make up for their failure.

Which—and she wasn't about to admit it aloud—was exactly what she was hoping for. That way maybe she'd find out who the organ grinder was, even if she had to take care of a few more monkeys.

The sirens faded, then fell silent behind her.

She sped away, ignoring her cell phone when it started to ring.

Whoever it was could wait.

She had no doubt that the two men wouldn't be going anywhere before the police arrived, meaning it wouldn't be long before they were gracing an interview room somewhere in the vicinity, answering some uncomfortable questions. What were they going to say? A crazy woman pulled a sword out of nowhere and used it to deflect bullets meant to kill her? The police would laugh in their faces, and then they'd be drug tested before they were shipped off to the psychiatric unit, white jackets on standby.

None of what had just happened would make the front page of the tabloids.

She realized that she was traveling well over the speed limit, knuckles white from gripping the wheel too tightly, and eased the pressure on the accelerator, watching the needle drift and slowly count down the numbers. It was only when she was closing in on thirty that she relaxed her grip on the wheel.

Annja fished out her phone and glanced briefly at the screen. Roux was listed as the missed call. She pulled over as best she could, then pressed redial with her thumb to return the call.

He answered before the first cycle of the ring tone had finished.

"You called?" That was an event in itself. She could go for weeks, sometimes even months, without hearing from him. Now he'd called twice in as many days.

"Are you still in Carcassonne?"

"For a couple of days at least. Why? Is something going on?"

She listened to the moment of silence stretch on just a little too long.

"Roux?"

"I'm coming to see you."

"Why? Is something wrong?"

"Maybe. Or maybe not. It could just be in my head. But it'll set my mind at ease to be there. I'm going to ask you a question now, girl, and I want an honest answer. Has anything else peculiar happened to you since we last spoke?"

"You mean apart from a couple of guys pulling a gun on me?"

"What? When?" There was a genuine alarm in his voice.

She kept it matter-of-fact. "About five minutes ago. It didn't go well for them, and now they're talking to the gendarmerie. I'm long gone. It's all good."

"Go to your hotel room and wait there until I arrive. Something's happening here, and I don't like it. I really don't like it."

"I've got work to do."

"Your life could be in danger."

"It has been ever since you first walked into it, my friend. I'm still here."

"Please," he said.

It wasn't often he used the word *please*.

His usual method for showing just how much he cared was blind indifference.

She didn't like the new Roux.

"Okay, what aren't you telling me?" Another pause. "And remember, you're a terrible liar. No matter how good you think you are at it, I always know when you're trying to hide something, so spit it out."

"You know how I feel about coincidences," he said, which was no answer at all.

"There are none."

"Right. That masonry falling wasn't an accident. Ancient masonry doesn't just happen to work itself free after hundreds of years the very moment you are standing beneath it. It just doesn't happen. And now two men held you up at gunpoint?"

"I think, technically, it was more a case of me holding them up by the end of it," she corrected him.

"I don't care. Stop making light of it. They are connected."

"And you know this because…?" Because he was still holding something back from her. She knew it.

"I had a phone call. No more than a few minutes after the rock nearly killed you. Someone called to taunt me."

"Who?"

"He called himself Cauchon. The name should mean something. I know it should. But for the life of me, I can't work out why. The only thing I know for sure is that the call originated in Carcassonne."

"Are you sure about that?"

"Positive."

"Because…?"

"Because Garin doesn't make mistakes with this stuff."

"Please don't tell me he's about to descend on me, too."

"No, he's not. The call was made from a burner phone in Carcassonne."

"Not my goons," she said. "They weren't running the show."

"No. I don't think this is about you. I think it's about me."

He hung up, promising Annja he would be with her in a couple of hours, and she agreed to sit tight.

But if this was all about Roux, then coming to Carcassonne put the old man in the line of fire.

Was this what Cauchon wanted?

Almost certainly, Annja thought. If he actually had a vendetta against the old man, he was using her as bait to lure Roux here.

She'd lied to the old man, though; she had no intention of hiding in her hotel room.

She had an appointment with the curator of the museum.

17

"Thank you so much for seeing me," Annja said as she held out her hand in greeting.

The curator made a show of looking at his watch, as if to reinforce just how important his time was, and just how close she'd cut it. She'd met plenty of men like him before—officious jerks basically—but she plastered on a smile as she hurried toward him.

His suit, neatly cut and definitely not off the rack, looked sharp, and his starched white shirt and fancy tie no doubt bespoke of some significance or loyalty to an ancient house or cause no one but he remembered. His hair thinned prematurely, showing a pink scalp around a prominent widow's peak.

He looked like a man who was aging before his time.

"Miss Creed," he said, taking her hand. His hand was like a dead fish in hers. This was going to be more difficult than she'd hoped.

If she wasn't careful this segment for the show was just going to end up a puff piece that would have Doug threatening to keep her desk-bound for months and have that bimbo Kerstie in her bikini strutting all over the next great story.

"Annja," she said, flashing him her widest smile, "please." Though the odds of a blast of full-on Annja Creed charm at its brightest was unlikely to do the trick, she wasn't about to walk away without giving this one shot her absolute all.

It took him a heartbeat to respond, but he replied with a thin weak smile of his own. "Armand," he said, the ice barely broken.

He led the way through the museum, sweeping along the corridors, clearly master of this particular domain.

He sidestepped a party of schoolchildren that a single teacher was struggling to control, but then it was mission impossible.

Armand *tut-tutted* as he walked, giving the children a withering look that shrunk them to the size of ants. The teacher looked mortified.

"So, I am led to believe you want to talk to me about Bernard Gui?" he said, opening the door to his office. He ushered her inside before she could answer.

"That's correct," Annja replied. "Or more specifically about his book on the conduct of the Inquisition."

"Practica inquisitionis heretice privitatis," the curator recited, giving it its full and original title. *"Conduct of the Inquisition into Heretical Wickedness.* We only have a facsimile copy here, I'm afraid."

"Even so, you boast some of the world's premier resources when it comes to the inquisitor, and, if I understand correctly, there is additional material relating to the writing of that book?"

"Ah, of course. Yes, we do indeed have a copy of the original handwritten draft of the final chapter in our possession."

"Would it be possible for me to take a look at it?"

"Of course, though I regret to say that we do not have a complete translation of the document. If you had said that was what you were interested in, I would have made arrangements for a Latin scholar to join us."

Clearly, he assumed she was just a pretty face to go in front of the camera. It would be amusing to disabuse him of that notion. While she didn't claim to be fluent, she had more than a passing fair acquaintance with the dead language, and had read enough ecclesiastical documents to be confident in her abilities to get by.

"That's fine. I'm sure we'll cope between us." She smiled.

"Out of curiosity, may I ask why you are interested in this particular document?"

"As I explained on the phone, I'm doing a segment for my show, *Chasing History's Monsters*. This isn't the first piece I've done about the Inquisition, but I wanted to go back to the root of its involvement in witchcraft."

He raised a curious eyebrow. "Then aren't you better consulting the *Malleus Maleficarum*? Surely that will have more to say about witchcraft than the writings of Bernard Gui?"

"It does, absolutely, but if the contents of that final chapter are as I suspect, it will prove that some of the assumptions in the *Malleus Maleficarum* may have been incorrect."

"One book contradicting another? Hardly seems like gripping television."

"You'd be surprised. Think about it this way, Bernard Gui wrote his book more than a hundred and sixty years before the other one. What I'm hoping is that there's confirmation in there about the state of suspected witchcraft during his time, or perhaps more pertinently, the lack of it."

"Lack of it?"

"If Gui says that there was little or no evidence of such practices during his day, then isn't it reasonable to posit that witchcraft and devil worship are as much a product of the Inquisition as a target for it?"

"Ah, so you think they looked for it where none existed? Interesting, but perhaps dangerous from a scholarly perspective to come up with theories before you have examined the evidence," he said.

He was right, of course, and she knew it. "Confirmation bias." She nodded. "Yes, I'll admit I want this story to be true, but I won't manufacture evidence to support the supposition." There was more than enough material to do a segment without it, but it was the meat of what she wanted the episode to be about. And then she wanted to link back to the atrocities of modern day, showing how monsters of all stripe will manufacture their truths if it helps them get away with murder.

"Then perhaps the best thing to do would be to take a look at it."

He got back to his feet, but as Annja rose to join him he gestured to her seat.

"Please," he said. "Make yourself comfortable. I will bring it to you. There is no need to trouble yourself."

She could hardly insist otherwise, but documents as precious as this should be kept in controlled environments, not brought out for casual inspection in a room like this where they would be exposed to all sorts of potential contaminants. And, admittedly, she'd been hoping to have a bit of a poke around in the archives. There had been times when she had stumbled across things, connections long since lost, simply because she'd seen the label on a neighboring box that had filled her mind with all kinds of possibilities and sparked the idea that had led down an unexpected alley to something wonderful.

She would have to make do with browsing the shelves here while he was gone.

Most of the titles were in French, but she was intrigued to see copies of Plutarch's *Lives* and Suetonius's *Twelve Caesars* in Latin.

At first, it seemed like an odd collection of books, especially given that the man hadn't revealed he was able to read the language, but on closer inspection it became obvious that the books clearly hadn't been read. An inscription on the title page of the first of them showed that it had been a gift.

Hearing footsteps approaching, she returned it to its rightful place in the stack.

She had only just taken her seat when the door opened.

The curator entered, carrying a leather-bound ledger.

She assumed it wasn't Gui's last chapter, which surely wouldn't have been bound. "Problem?" she asked. The look on his face was answer enough. Of course there was a problem.

He set the ledger on his desk, and sat before he spoke. "I am afraid someone else must be using it at the moment."

He was lying to her—or to himself.

"You mean it's not where it should be?" she suggested. She wanted to give him the chance to voice his own fears rather than have her put words into his mouth.

"I'm sure we will be able to locate it for you, assuming you can call back again later in the week?"

The man was in denial. Documents like this didn't just go missing. There were processes in place to stop that from happening. The identity of everyone who examined the chapter would be carefully documented somewhere—

she assumed in the ledger he had brought with him, the archival boxes signed for, then checked and double-checked when they were reshelved. That these measures had failed almost certainly meant someone had stolen the papers.

"I'm only supposed to be here for another day or two, but perhaps it would be possible for me to contact the person who has signed it out, to arrange a quick look? I'm sure they wouldn't mind."

"I'm afraid…" He stumbled to find the words, all the coldness he had shown earlier melting away as he struggled to keep the sense of panic from his voice.

He was failing badly.

He didn't need to say anything else. Those two words spoke volumes. There was a pleading look in his eyes.

"I'm sure you'll be able to recover it before it's noticed," she said.

"Yes, yes," he said, nodding a little too rapidly. "I'm sure. After all, it can't be far."

"Do you know who last looked at it?" Annja asked.

The man nodded, opening the ledger. She watched as he ran his finger down column after column of signatures, looking for the entry he needed to find.

"Here, and for some reason it hasn't been signed back in."

"A misunderstanding, then," she offered.

"Let's hope so." He breathed a heavy sigh of relief.

She read the name over his shoulder.

Roux.

18

Roux was frustrated.

Annja wasn't at the hotel.

He'd asked her to do one thing for him.

He tried her number, but as usual it went to voice mail.

The valet found a parking space for his car close to the entrance of the hotel and carried his bag in for him while Roux waited in the reception area drinking a thick black coffee. He had no intention of checking into a room until he'd seen Annja. There was no guarantee either one of them would be staying here. He hadn't heard from Cauchon again. That didn't set his mind at ease, either. The man was out there, somewhere. It was only a matter of time before he made contact, either by phone or by arranging another almost-accident.

Even as the thought crossed his mind, his phone vibrated on the tabletop in front of him. He snatched it up, but before he could say anything Annja cut across him.

"Where are you?"

"Me? I am at your hotel. The more pertinent question would be where are *you*?"

"It doesn't matter where I am."

"Au contraire."

"Have you checked in?"

"I was waiting for you."

"Don't use your name when you check in." She hung up on him.

He hadn't been planning to; he seldom did when he traveled, often enjoying the anonymity of a Smith or Jones if he wasn't in the mood for some fun with a Derrida, Foucault or Comte.

He had no idea if she was already on the way, or what had been bothering her. He couldn't do much more than wait. She'd get here when she got here. He pulled out a passport and credit card from his bag, choosing Jean Joseph Mounier, a politician and judge from Bonaparte's day he'd had the pleasure of punching square in the jaw once upon a time, and returned to the receptionist to book into a room.

The receptionist offered a practiced smile, not recognizing the name.

In a place like this his normal habit was to ask for the best room they had, but that would have been following predictable patterns, and the last thing he wanted to do was be predictable right now, so he booked two rooms, a suite on the upper floor, and a single closer to the ground, small but adequate for his needs. The receptionist didn't bat an eye at his request, returning with four keys for him, two for each room.

He booked them for a week, even though he was hoping the stay in Carcassonne would be a short one. Memory was a tricky thing. It made you forget the worst of times, so when it came time to do horrible things all over again, to experience the worst life had to offer, you did it willingly. He really couldn't remember when anything had affected him like this. But then, he'd experienced threats and betrayal in less than twenty-four hours. How was he supposed to react?

The receptionist offered to get a bellman to show him to his room, but Roux shook his head, assuring her he could make his own way there. He had no intention of leaving the small room until Annja arrived. Then they'd reassess the situation. He sent her a text with the room number and waited, lying on the bed, feet crossed at the ankles, hands behind his head.

He hated waiting. There was nothing in the world worse than that. It didn't matter what you were up against. Once you knew, you could act, fight, but when you were waiting you were helpless, and waiting had taken up so much of his life lately.

He needed to take control of it again.

His phone beeped. An incoming text. Annja.

She was only a couple of minutes away, but he shouldn't open the door to anyone, not even the police, until she had spoken to him.

It meant things were starting to get interesting.

19

Cauchon watched the video feed again and again, still not completely believing the evidence of his own eyes.

The tiny hidden surveillance cams he'd paid to have fitted to the front and rear of the Mercedes had paid dividends beyond imagining. They were better than eyes and ears. They couldn't be fooled. He saw exactly what went down when his men had to deal with Annja Creed. In an ideal world he would have been there himself, but now he was glad he had been nowhere near the scene; and, of course, there was always the risk she might remember him. It was too soon to show his hand. He wasn't about to risk losing everything.

He clicked frames backward and forward, trying to work out how she could possibly have achieved the trick—because that's what it had to be, surely?

In the flicker of a frame her hands went from being empty and unthreatening to gripping a wicked sword drawn out of thin air, like one of the great illusionists conjuring it from nowhere.

He watched it again and again and again, unable to

zoom in any tighter on the image, which lost focus as he tried to adjust it.

He lost count of how many times he had flicked the image backward and forward; now she had it, now she didn't. A hundred, a thousand? It hadn't taken more than a couple viewings to grasp the truth, that somehow, some impossible how, this was no conjuring trick.

This was something *more* than that.

Something altogether more *wonderful*.

This was proof of greatness.

This was proof of witchcraft, and in his mind there was no greater heresy.

He had held his suspicions for so long that he felt a sense of euphoria at the evidence unfolding there on the screen, everything he had ever suspected, confirmed, and so much more besides.

For years he traveled the world in search of substantive evidence, of fact, of something that would prove beyond the shadow of any doubt and stand up to the most rigorous scrutiny, that witchcraft was real, but every single time he had been disappointed. Every avenue he followed had led to hoaxes and scams set up to relieve the gullible of their hard-earned money or to prey on the emotionally vulnerable.

He had dreamed of finding the divine among the mundane.

He had dreaded the presence of evil to be lurking in every shadow, but the only evil he ever encountered was man-made, greed and avarice, the allure of fame.

Until now.

Until Annja Creed.

In her, he had found more than he had dared hoped.

Even the sword matched the descriptions he'd been able to find from contemporary accounts.

He was sure of it now. Sure that the proof was his. There could be no doubt.

An agent of the devil possessed Annja Creed and that agent bore the name of Joan.

He had chosen his own name well.

20

"Are you going to tell me what all this cloak and dagger stuff is about?" Roux asked.

Annja had finally arrived at the hotel.

Time was elastic at the best of times, but at the worst it seemed to stretch into infinity. He had taken the gun from his overnight bag and slipped it under his pillow, not that he expected trouble or that he was particularly comfortable with guns. That was more Garin's territory. Even so, his hand had reached for it instinctively as she tapped on the door. It was only the sound of her voice, muted by the door between them, that stopped him from drawing it from under the pillow.

"I was hoping you'd tell me," she said bluntly.

He inclined his head, furrowing his brow. It was hardly the picture of innocence, even when he said, "I've got no idea what you're talking about, girl."

"Really? I find that incredibly hard to believe. I know you don't answer to me. Why would you? But just this once, try telling the truth."

"Be careful, Annja. What you say can't be unsaid.

There are no 'take-backs' in life. I am not in the habit of lying to you."

"Then tell me about your last visit to Carcassonne."

He thought about it for a moment, trying to recall the last time he'd set foot inside the cursed fortress. It had been a long time ago. He had been a different man, almost literally. "My last visit?" He shook his head. "That was more than a hundred years ago. What do you expect me to remember? Not very much."

Annja said nothing.

She sat on the edge of the bed and looked him straight in the eye.

"I'm going to ask you again," she said, sounding more like an interrogator than a friend. "Tell me about your last visit. The one you made more recently, not some visit from a century ago. Think in terms of the past month or so."

"Month or so? I haven't been here in years and years, girl."

"So you didn't visit the museum and fail to return a precious artifact?"

He shook his head.

"Well, someone did, and signed your name."

"My name?"

She nodded.

"What did they steal?"

"The final chapter of *Practica inquisitionis heretice privatitatis*, handwritten by Bernard Gui."

Roux's mind was racing, making a logical connection he'd missed when he'd been obsessing over what Garin had stolen. He had a collection of Gui's writings in his vault. Was that what Garin had taken?

"Garin," he said.

"What about him?"

"It's got his sticky fingers all over it," Roux muttered,

and filled her in on the events of the past twenty-four hours, leaving nothing out, not the call, not Garin's visit, not the theft from his vault.

She didn't seem that surprised

"And you think he took Gui's papers from the museum?"

"Who else? And typical of him to use my name to cover his tracks. I assume he produced some kind of credentials to get away with the theft. And like it or not, Garin does nothing without strong motivation, if not good reason, so to steal multiple documents, I fear we'll never see them again."

"Money."

"It must mean that he has a buyer."

Annja shook her head. "Surely he wouldn't steal from you *just* for money."

"I think that's the only reason why he'd do it, my dear," Roux said. "Money is the strongest motivator of all in the mind of Garin Braden. But that means that someone must have offered enough money to make it worth his while. And enough in this instance is a small fortune. That limits the possibilities."

The old man knew he would forgive him in time, just as he had forgiven him in the past. Garin could no more change his nature than a shark could or a lion. But it would be much harder to forgive him for robbing him of his good name. The last thing Roux wanted was to be constantly looking over his shoulder for the police. Scrutiny by the law was bound to bring up questions he couldn't or wouldn't answer.

"We've got to find him," he said. "But first we have to deal with Cauchon."

"Cauchon?" Annja said.

"What?"

"That name."

"What about it? I know I should know it. But…" He held up his hands helplessly.

"You should know it. It should be burned onto your soul."

And he remembered it then.

Cauchon.

It was the name of the man who had signed Joan of Arc's death warrant.

21

The call came through as he had been about to land.

The temptation was to answer it straightaway, despite the need to keep his wits about him, but that would have made him seem desperate. Desperation in negotiation was weakness. So he would let the phone ring, make the man wait. He was going to do this on his own terms. Garin patted the bundle on the copilot's seat to reassure himself that the papers were still there.

The flight hadn't been long enough for him to give them more than a cursory glance, but it was enough to realize that there was far more hidden in those few pages of writing than he could decipher. To a certain kind of collector this account was priceless, which added a few zeroes to any transaction as far as Garin was concerned.

Once the plane had come to a standstill, he made the call.

It was answered on the third ring.

"I've got the first thing on your list," he said.

"Where are you?"

Garin read the instruments, and just for the hell of it

gave his location in longitude and latitude. He glanced out of the windshield at the plowed runway and the banks of snow on either side of the black line that stretched all the way to the airport's small terminal. Men moved across the apron, working hard to clear more of the snow. None were heading in his direction.

"I'll arrange for someone to meet you within the hour," the man said. "Stay where you are."

"Not so hasty, my wealthy friend," Garin replied, enjoying this part of the conversation. "The price has gone up. I am thinking in the region of an extra fifteen percent in relation to the finder's fee, then half a mil bonus for the speed of the operation."

"I'm not in the habit of bargaining, Mr. Braden. I am a man of my word."

"I have what you want. It's called supply and demand. I control the line of supply, so I can demand whatever price the market will stand. In other words, take it or leave it. I'm sure that I can find another buyer for the papers." If he squeezed an extra five percent out of the deal, he would feel like he had pulled one over on the other man. That made the whole exercise that little bit sweeter. Ten percent and he would have been robbing him blind.

Which made the man's response all the more surprising.

"Fine," he said. "But I will send a car to pick you up. I am going to have to inspect the merchandise myself before I transfer the cash."

"That's reasonable," Garin said, patting the bundle again. "Believe me, you won't be disappointed. The package is in mint condition." His thinking was that he'd just opened the door to a cash cow, and now was the time to negotiate on some of the other documents to satisfy the collector's fetish.

"I am not a man who enjoys disappointment, Mr. Braden, so let us both hope that I am not."

With that, the call ended.

Garin felt a cold shiver chase up the ladder of his spine one vertebrae at a time.

His red Ferrari was parked a few hundred yards from the hangar where he kept the Gulfstream, and a couple of mechanics who'd be in place to check her as he taxied her in. It wouldn't take him long to get anywhere in the immediate vicinity—or technically in Europe, should the caller demand it.

He jabbed at the phone again, trying to reconnect with his mysterious buyer, but the call went straight to voice mail. Garin assumed he was on a call to his proxy, making arrangements for the inspection. Garin had no choice but to wait it out. The driver would appear eventually, and there were worse places to wait than in a luxury jet.

He didn't have to wait long.

A black limousine swept into view, executed a wide turn, then drove quickly toward the open doors of the hangar, pulling up to a stop right across the doorway. A woman clambered out of the driver's seat. Even from this distance he liked what he saw as she came walking toward the Gulfstream. He lowered the steps, ready to allow her to board. She was dressed in a tailored suit, designer, Italian and probably worth as much as the car she was driving. It clung tantalizingly to every inch of her body.

He watched her all the way to the stairs. The closer she came, the better she looked. His buyer at least had exquisite taste in companions. Good to know.

She boarded, knocking on the frame of the Gulfstream's door before setting foot inside, calling out, "Mr. Braden?" as she did.

She had a smile that lit up her sun-kissed skin.

"That's me." He smiled back, rising to shake her hand.

"I'm Monique," she said.

"Do you want to do it here?" Garin asked, enjoying the deliberately provocative double entendre.

"No, Mr. Braden. Your chariot awaits." She nodded in the general direction of the hangar doors and the waiting limo.

He gathered together the bundle of papers, tying the ribbon, and followed her back down the stairs. He liked to walk a few steps behind beautiful women for the view. A person could always learn a lot about a woman from the way she walked when she knew she was being watched. Monique descended with her shoulders back and head held high. In control. Strong. Not unlike Annja. He thought about offering a cheesy line, just for the amusement factor. Sometimes it was fun to play, but without knowing just how far they had to drive, or how tight she was with the buyer, mixing business with pleasure would be stupid.

But that didn't stop him from enjoying the view.

"So, tell me, how long do I get to enjoy the pleasure of your company?"

She held the rear door open for him. It was a nice reversal of the gender stereotype, the gallant lady and all that, even if he would have preferred to ride up front with her.

"Around thirty minutes at this time of day, so sit back and make yourself at home. We have an excellent bar. Feel free to help yourself to anything that takes your fancy."

"Thanks," he said, sure she was playing the game and flirting right back at him. As tempting as it was, he didn't rise to the bait and kept things strictly professional. Playing it straight was positively boring.

She closed the door. The mechanism was almost silent, save for a reassuring click. Precision engineering. He re-evaluated the cost of the car against her suit.

Garin sank back into the leather seat. The windows were tinted and, he suspected, armored. Interesting. He gazed out of the window as they pulled away from the hangar and followed the parking lot around to the road that would take them out of the airfield, past the parking lot and a hollowed-out 747 that had been converted into an overnight hostel for travelers.

He felt like celebrating even though the business was far from concluded.

He'd played the game perfectly so far.

Even so, he resisted the temptation to help himself to a drink.

Maybe on the ride home.

"We should reach the hotel before my employer," she said. "But he is en route."

"Hotel?" For some reason Garin had been expecting a clandestine meeting somewhere far away from prying eyes. But a hotel was practical, even if it was disappointing. Hotels also kept records, which meant he had another way of finding out exactly who he was dealing with. He smiled to himself.

"That's correct. I take it you weren't informed of your destination? He maintains a suite there."

"Not a word. All very hush-hush."

She smiled at him through the rearview mirror. "I just do what I'm told to do," she said, and he caught a glimpse of her eyes watching him in the rearview mirror. "And in your case, I was told to make sure that you were kept entertained."

"What a hardship," Garin said. The thought of spending a little time with a beautiful woman was never a bad thing. Well, almost never. He just wanted this business concluded, then he'd think about blowing off some steam, maybe a visit to the racetrack with some paid companions to dip into his new wealth.

The car cruised to a sedate halt outside the plushest hotel in the city—exclusive, expensive, home to the beautiful people.

Monique entrusted the keys to a doorman who looked down at the tip she'd crumpled into his hand as if all of his Christmases had come at once.

Garin followed her inside.

They took the elevator straight to the penthouse suite where she produced a swipe card that allowed them to gain access.

"Hello," Monique called. There was no reply. "Looks like we're on our own for a little while. I can check in with him to see how long he'll be if you like?"

"There's no need," Garin said as he took a look around the room. If there had been any lingering doubts as to the depth of his buyer's pockets, they were banished by the room. If he could afford to maintain a place like this, which had to have run upward of three or four grand a night, then the man had a good line of credit, at the very least.

"We can have that drink while we wait," Garin offered. She hesitated. "Remember, you're meant to entertain me, and I really hate to drink alone."

"I really shouldn't," she said.

"I would consider myself unentertained if you forced me to drink alone. I'm not sure that your employer would be too happy about that, would he?" Garin offered a cheeky grin.

"Just one, then," she said. "But only because I wouldn't want to think you were unentertained."

"You are teasing me, aren't you?"

"Just a little bit. Perhaps *bored* would be a better word?"

"Ah, but I'm never bored," Garin said. "Just thirsty."

"What can I get you?"

"Scotch," he said, spying a familiar-looking bottle on a drinks tray.

She poured a generous measure, ice cubes clinking together as she handed the glass to him. She made herself a gin and tonic. A lot more tonic went into the glass than gin. No ice for her, but she speared a slice of lemon that had already been cut and laid out.

"So, I can't pretend I'm not curious. What's your boss like?" he asked. "Is he good to work for?"

"He is a powerful man."

"Which doesn't answer the question."

"But it's the best answer you are going to get, Mr. Braden."

"Well, if you ever get tired of the cloak and dagger, I'm always on the lookout for good people."

"I really don't think he'd be very happy to hear that you were trying to steal me from him," Monique said.

"Well, *steal* is such a vulgar word. *Entice*, more like."

"I'm not sure the size of your vocabulary will make a lot of difference if he decides that you are disrespecting him."

"Oh, rest assured, I'd never disrespect a man of such obvious wealth. You make friends with rich people if you are smart. But it's out there. I won't mention it again. But if you were to reach out to me after we've finished our little piece of business here I wouldn't say no."

"I'm sure you wouldn't," she said, and took a drink, her eyes glancing away for a moment.

He took a pull at the whisky, feeling the heat on his tongue before it slipped to the back of his throat. He swallowed. The liquid burned his chest as it slid down, a familiar warming that held him like an old friend. He held the glass up to the light and watched the ice cubes drift through the amber liquid.

"Only the best," he said.

"Would you expect anything less? My employer doesn't do things in half measures. His belief is that if you want the best in life you have to be prepared to pay for it, and that goes for everything."

It was hard to disagree. Garin had the same philosophy. He took another mouthful, holding it in his mouth a little longer this time, allowing the fire to melt in his mouth before swallowing.

"Does that include you?" he asked, pushing his luck.

"I certainly don't come cheap."

"And what exactly do you do for him apart from pick strangers up from the airport in a fancy car?"

"Whatever I'm asked to do," she said, and settled down in chair opposite him. Her legs stretched out in front of her, impossibly long. She swirled the ice in her glass and he listened to the steady *clink, clink, clink* as if it was building into a rhythm, like a song or a heartbeat.

The sound seemed to mean something to him, or was it the smell, or the heat?

Clink, clink, clink.

His thoughts tumbled as he tried to hang on to a single thread of thought, wanting it to make sense, but it was getting hotter in the room, and the *clink, clink, clink* was less like a heartbeat now and more like the banging of a drum. Incessant. Driving.

He loosened his collar, feeling uncomfortable.

The room swam around him as Garin reached out to place his glass on a marble-topped table. He misjudged it. The drink splashed over the side in slow motion, the glass tumbling to the plush carpet, the ice cubes falling out like a pair of dice.

He needed to get to the bathroom as quickly as he could.

When he tried to get to his feet his legs refused to hold him. He leaned on the arm of the chair, struggling to find his balance.

"I think you should sit back down, Mr. Braden. I wouldn't want you to have an accident," Monique said. Her voice sounded strange, her words echoing.

"What's…?" His tongue struggled to wrap itself around the next word, his lips numb as he worked his jaw.

He clung to the arm of the chair, stubbornly refusing to collapse, but it was a losing battle. The bathroom door seemed to be moving closer, swimming toward him across the silk carpet, but he couldn't tell if his feet were moving or if he was pitching headfirst toward it.

She'd slipped him something in his drink.

He tried to curse his own stupidity, but was incapable of doing even that.

Somehow he managed to reach the door, his palm sweating as it grabbed for the knob, slipping as it opened at his touch. Instead of the hoped-for bathroom he fell into a bedroom that seemed far too white, a brilliant white that dazzled him apart from the vicious splash of arterial red on the bed and the wall beyond it.

He tried to focus, tried to hold on to his grip on consciousness, even though he knew he was failing.

All he could see was the shape on the bed and the splatter of blood.

22

"It's done," was all the voice said before killing the call.

Two words.

Small words, but so very important.

There was no more that needed to be said, no need for small talk.

She would be on her way to join him now that she had everything he needed.

Patience was a virtue.

But getting what you wanted was so much more satisfying than being patient.

It had taken so very long to locate everything he needed, but now all of the pieces in the puzzle were beginning to come together, the long game he'd been playing paying out. He was determined to enjoy each and every little victory now. This was what it was all about.

He put the phone on the desk in front of him.

How long would it take for her to reach him?

Too long for his liking obviously, he thought wryly. Knowing how long he'd waited for this moment, a few more minutes couldn't hurt.

He felt the familiar pain in his legs even though he knew that it was no more than a memory; it had been a long time since there had been any significant feeling down there. His lower limbs were little more than an ornament, their presence an elaborate charade meant to make him feel close to normal. Not that he would ever feel normal again.

He had spent years watching military advances into the field of exoskeletal frames, willing the breakthrough to come, dreaming of walking on his own two feet again. The time would come, but not yet, and maybe not even in his lifetime.

There were times when he had wished that the surgeons had just cut them off instead of fighting to keep them intact. Their very presence meant he clung to hope despite the torment hope entailed.

Now, though, he had a mission of his own.

He hated having to rely on other people to do the work for him, but he would find his own reward. All he had to do was to continue with the work of the man whose name he had adopted.

On the table in front of him lay a copy of the document.

He ran his fingers down the paper, realizing that while this might not be as significant as the moment that the other Cauchon had added his name to the warrant that led to Joan of Arc's execution, this was his moment and that meant savoring it. He had no doubt now. It was fated. He was going finish what Cauchon had started six centuries ago.

He picked up his pen and unscrewed the cap.

There were no witnesses to what he was doing.

That didn't matter.

He wasn't looking for fame or immortality; his writing would not be stored in museums and libraries beyond the next generation.

This was about ending things—one thread that had been dangling for centuries, another for considerably less time but promised the sweet succor of vengeance. He ached for satisfaction.

Cauchon took a deep breath, the nib of the pen still a hairsbreadth from the paper, then added a name into the space where the Maid of Orleans's name would once have been.

His hand trembled.

He steeled himself.

This was not the time for doubt or hesitation.

He wrote the name that belonged there.

Annja Creed.

23

"What have you done this time, Garin?" Roux said. There was no mock-exasperation in his voice. There was only cold fear. He rubbed at the white bristles of hair along his jawline. "I thought this Cauchon had worked out our connection, and convinced myself that he was using you to get to me. I was wrong. This proves that. I don't know how, but he knows about what you are, Annja. He knows who you are."

Annja sat on the edge of the bed, trying to take it all in. "But how...?"

She looked at the old man, but he couldn't look her in the eye.

Did he know something else that he wasn't telling her? Was some secret from his past about to come back to haunt him, to haunt both of them?

Could someone really have stumbled across the truth about what she had become?

"Do you think there are others?" she asked.

"Others? I don't follow."

"Like you and Garin. Like me?"

His expression didn't change. He shook his head slowly in denial, but Annja was sure that the thought had flashed across his mind. Had he ever considered the possibility before?

Why would they be the only ones like this in the world?

If it was possible for people like Garin and Roux to defy time, held here for some higher purpose, then why couldn't there be others?

"We have to find him and stop this," Roux said. "He's still here, I'm sure of that." He was thinking on his feet. "He will have been watching you. He must have been, to make that call. We can only assume he won't leave until he's finished whatever it is he's planning to do. So we have to make sure that we stop him."

"Easier said than done. Where do we start?"

"We have one obvious link to him—the two men who tried to kidnap you," he said finally. "If he doesn't come to us, we go to him. Through them."

"You must have forgotten about the whole police custody thing. There's no way that the gendarmerie is just going to let them walk away because we want them to."

"Who said anything about walking away? We're going to walk in there."

"You mean spring them?" Annja asked, not quite sure she was following the old man's thought processes. Every now and then he acted like the law just didn't apply to him. It took her a moment to switch gears sometimes and remember that. "I'm not sure I want to know." The one thing she was absolutely sure of was that no matter what she said, Roux would go ahead and do whatever he wanted.

It was something they had in common.

"So, we just show up at the police station and ask to speak to a couple of gunmen they're holding in custody?"

"I can do anything I set my mind to, young lady," he

said, flashing her a dangerous grin. "All we need are the right credentials, and they can always be arranged for a price."

"Credentials?"

"In this case, a business card, a good suit and a dose of confidence that will border on arrogance, as if I'm used to people prostrating themselves at my feet and saying yes to my every whim. Our boys will no doubt be sitting there hoping that Cauchon has hired a top-notch lawyer for them rather than throw them to the wolves. I shall be their advocate."

Annja shook her head. "You've been spending far too much time with Garin." She laughed before realizing just what she was saying. It was enough to kill the conversation stone dead. She checked her watch. Philippe, her on-site cameraman, would be waiting for her. As much as she wanted to get swept away with the chase, the adventure that came with keeping company with Garin and Roux, she still had a job to do, no matter who might be watching.

As long as she stayed in public places, no one was going to try anything.

And if she wandered off the beaten track, she was more than ready to protect herself.

In fact, she was kind of hoping that someone *would* try something.

Annja left Roux making calls, barely getting a raised hand in acknowledgment as she walked away. She needed to pick up some things from her room before she hit the road. There was still plenty of daylight left. She called Philippe as she hurried along the corridor, and was fumbling in her pocket for her room key by the time he took the call.

"Where are you?"

"I'll be with you in a couple of minutes," she said,

avoiding answering the question. He wouldn't appreciate the fact she was back in the hotel while he was working. She'd worked out that much about him already. "Have you managed to get the shots you need?"

"Pretty much," he said. "But I should warn you, my throat is starting to long for an ice-cold beer, so if you want to get this bit finished before I give in to the siren song, you better hurry." He was grinning as he talked, pretending to be indignant, and hamming up the French reputation.

"You better tell me where you are, then."

"I'm outside the cathedral, but I'll be finished what I want to do here in ten minutes, fifteen tops."

"I'll be there," she said.

She hung up, slipped the phone back into her pocket and unlocked the room. It had an old-fashioned charm. She liked that the floors weren't quite even, that the walls weren't quite straight, the corners not quite square. The building might not be as ancient as the city walls, but it was old and it belonged there. It had the kind of gravitas you couldn't manufacture with new builds.

A breeze fluttered the curtains as she closed the door.

An instant too late, she realized there was someone in the room.

She tried to turn, reaching into the otherwhere for the sword as she moved, but the crushing weight of a body slammed her against the wall before she could close her hand around it. She felt the searing stab of pain as rough plaster gouged into her cheek. An involuntary cry escaped her lips as she was pinned, unable to move, a huge muscular arm pressing into her nape, a hip into the small of her back.

She smelled a cheap cologne that was doing a poor job of masking stale sweat.

She tried to speak, but that only increased the pressure on her body, until she felt a scratch on her arm.

Annja threw everything she had into trying to push the man away, but he was incredibly strong. A brute. She realized just how vulnerable she could be without her sword.

As darkness began to swirl around her, all she could think of was Roux.

24

It turned out to be easier than Roux had hoped.

It hadn't taken long to pick out a decent suit that hung well enough that it could be mistaken for a made-to-|measure garment if a person wasn't sophisticated enough to know better. It still cost more than the average policeman's monthly salary and looked like it did. That was what mattered. The clothes maketh the man. In this case, one of wealth and taste—a successful man who meant business. The manager of the store had been only too happy to come to his hotel room with a selection once he had been given his measurements over the phone, and in less than two hours Roux was ready to play his hand.

What had taken a while was getting the names of the two men being held in custody. But he'd worked his magic, contacting an old flirtation at Interpol who called in a couple of favors to access the information for him in return for a promised dinner next time he was in town. Of course, there was always a risk that the local law enforcement officers would get huffy because some distant agency was muscling in on their turf, but huffy or not, they gave up the names. Garin would have been able to do it, and probably faster, but right now Roux wasn't inclined to offer him the time of day, let alone ask for his help.

He strode up the steps of the police station, pausing on the threshold to adjust his suit, before approaching the desk sergeant.

"I'm here to see my clients," Roux stated, putting his gilt-edged business card on the desk in front of the uniformed man. "Marcel Dugarry and Étienne Rameaux."

The desk sergeant looked him up and down slowly, taking in the sharp suit and the crisp white shirt as well as the ridiculously expensive diamond studded cuff links that completed the ensemble, then returned his attention to the card again.

"You got here quickly," he said.

"As I am sure you appreciate, my clients get the best treatment money can buy."

The officer snorted and made a note in his ledger. "One minute," he said, picking up the telephone on the desk beside him.

He talked quickly to a colleague somewhere else in the station, and a moment later a sallow-eyed man emerged through a combination pass-locked door.

"Mr. Reyes?" the young plainclothes officer said.

Roux inclined his head.

"Follow me, please," he said. He seemed polite enough, but give him enough time down here swimming amid the detritus of humanity, and all of his smoothness would rub off and leave a jagged disdain for officers of the court who represented the men they had in custody. It was inevitable. The legal eagles were the enemy of the honest cop, twisting words and truths, looking for any technicalities they could wrangle out of a situation to get guilty men off. He didn't say another word as he led Roux down the institutionally grim corridor, stopping at the fourth door.

He opened it and stepped aside to allow Roux to enter.

"There will be someone outside at all times," he said. "Just knock when you're ready to come out."

"I know the procedure," Roux said. He waited until the door had closed before taking a seat on the other side of a steel table across from the man who was sitting there. He had no idea which of the two thugs he was dealing with, but judging a book by its cover, he didn't think he was dealing with the brains of the operation.

"Who the hell are you?" the man asked.

"I am your salvation," Roux replied.

"Huh?"

"I've been asked to get you out of here," Roux said, which wasn't entirely a lie. Annja had probably said something like that during the conversation, even if not explicitly using the words *spring them* as a request but rather as a question.

"Yeah?" His eyes had brightened, though now it was a case of the lights being on but no sign of anyone at home. He shuffled in his chair, pulling himself upright.

"I need to make sure that you've got your story straight."

The man nodded. "Sure. Yeah. Of course. Are you going to spring Étienne, too? Or just me?"

"What do you think? Would I be sent to get you out of here and leave him to take the rap?"

"Right, yeah, of course. Leave no man behind."

"Indeed. I need to get you both out of here if I'm going to make this all go away."

"You think you can do that?"

"I know I can," Roux said.

"Right, so what do you want me to say? Anything you need saying, just give me the script."

"Before we start, I need you to tell me what you've told the police so far."

He'd found one of the easiest ways to gain a man's trust was to get him to repeat whatever story he had trotted out—truth or lies, it didn't really matter. It was the sharing that did. It built a bridge between them, made them feel complicit. Roux was confident he would be able to tell truth from fiction, particularly when he had spoken with the second man. There was bound to be some common ground in their stories that would come together as a reasonable recollection of the sequence of events.

If Annja was right about how far away the police were when she left them standing by their car, they hadn't had time to concoct an elaborate story. And going back to that book-cover judgment, this guy didn't seem as if he was all that creative.

Roux sat back and listened as the man rambled on without making eye contact.

Every now and then he looked up at Roux for a reassurance that he hadn't told them anything he shouldn't have.

"So who is the woman?" Roux asked.

"Her name is Creed. Annja Creed. She's supposed to be some kind of television personality. I've never seen her on anything, though, so she can't be all that famous."

Roux wasn't surprised. Dugarry looked like the kind of man who preferred sport, action movies and porn, though not necessarily in that order.

"And you say that she attacked you?"

"Yeah, the crazy woman pulled a kind of sword out of nowhere like she was a magician or something."

"And you pulled a gun on her in self-defense? Is that what you're saying?"

"Self-defense, that's it, man, right there, that's it." Dugarry nodded just a little too rapidly, a smile starting to spread across his face to reveal a missing tooth.

"And that's what you've told the police?"

More nods.

"So how did you know her name?"

"What do you mean?"

"I mean, if she attacked you, and you were acting in self-defense, how did you find out what her name was?"

The man's face went blank again. He was clearly so used to telling lies that the truth wasn't always easy to find when he went looking for it.

"Did you tell the police that you knew her name?"

He paused again, perhaps trying to play the whole of the conversation back inside his head.

"I don't think so," he said at last.

"So Cauchon told you what to do?" he said, providing the answers, but making it sound like a question rather than a statement. The nod came easily to the man.

It had been a long shot.

Dugarry could have denied having anything to do with Cauchon. He might even have known him by a different name, but Roux had gotten lucky.

The thug glanced toward the door, then leaned in to make sure that no one could overhear what he was saying. "I didn't think he would send anyone to get us out of here," he confided.

"How many times have you worked for him?"

"A few. Usually just collecting things, carrying packages, you know?"

"Did you ever look at what was inside?"

The man shook his head rapidly. "Never," he said. "We were paid enough not to."

"What about this time?"

"We were just supposed to pick her up and take her to Cauchon."

"Whether she wanted to go or not?"

"Whatever force was needed, that was what he said. Just get her there alive."

"Where were you supposed to take her?"

"We were to call him when we had her, and he'd tell us where we needed to go."

"And the police have the phone?"

Another nod. Roux admitted that he'd been fortunate to get access to Dugarry without any trouble, but the odds of him getting a look at the phone were pretty slim. Thinking on his feet, he gambled. "That's a shame. Cauchon uses a variety of cell phones as I'm sure you can appreciate. I could have warned him to destroy the one used for this job if I knew the number."

"Oh, that's easy," Dugarry said, and rattled off a string of digits. The thug smiled. "I'm good with numbers."

25

Pain tore through Annja's shoulders as she tried to move.

Her wrists were bound together behind her back and her ankles were tied together, too. The ground was cold and hard beneath her. In the near-darkness she had no means of knowing where she was.

She tried to move, but all she did was make the pain worse.

"There's no point in struggling."

It was a woman's voice.

Annja tried to twist her head to get a look at her.

All she could make out was a dull light in the corner of her eye and a shape behind it. Just a shape. It was impossible to get a good look at her captor.

"What do you want?" she asked, feeling the numb heat of pain on one side of her face from where she'd been slammed against the wall. There was no way it had been the woman who had taken her out, which meant someone else was hiding in the darkness. "If it's money you're after..."

The woman laughed. "Money? How little you understand... This has nothing to do with money," she said.

"What, then?"

"That's not for me to say. I am simply doing my job. I
was told to keep you here until the time is right."

"Right for what?"

The woman didn't answer. Annja heard the click of
heels on the hard stone floor. She put the woman from
her mind. Right now, she would be better served spending her time trying to work out where she was, rather than
worrying about why she was there.

The floor was cold and damp against her face. There
was a familiar smell. It took her a while to identify the
chill mustiness. Her eyes became gradually more accus-
tomed to the meager light. In it, she saw the evidence that
confirmed her suspicions.

"A crypt," Annja murmured, without realizing she'd
spoken the thought aloud.

"Most perceptive," the woman said.

The light began to move. It was an oil-filled lantern.
The woman placed it on top of a large sarcophagus close
to where Annja lay.

Annja tried to move her head again. She managed to
get a better view of the blonde standing in front of her.
Early thirties, maybe, but the light wasn't flattering. She
was well toned but not muscular, which confirmed that
she wasn't the unwashed mountain of muscle that had
caught up with her in the hotel room.

She pushed against the pain, and by sheer force of will
managed to get into a sitting position, propped up against
the wall; only it wasn't a wall, it was a stone sarcophagus.
The carvings dug into her spine. Annja tried to move her
shoulders, working the muscles against the discomfort.

It didn't help. If anything, she only succeeded in making it hurt worse.

"I sincerely hope my friend was a little rough with you," the woman said.

Annja managed a bleak smile. "I like it a little rough," she said. "How long was I out?"

"Four hours, nearly five. You must have the constitution of a horse. That dose should have put you down for the best part of a day. Unless he managed to mess that up, too." The woman's gaze flicked to one side for an instant, an involuntary motion. Annja knew that there was something there. She peered into the shadows. Between two sarcophagi lay a darkness that was even blacker than the shadows. It ended in a heavy work boot.

"Is he dead?" she asked.

"I should hope so." She made the shape of a gun with her fingers and thumb and mimed putting a bullet through his brain.

Did this woman really value life so cheaply?

Annja's blade had tasted blood often enough, but that didn't mean that she would ever kill if there was an alternative. All life was precious.

"And me? Am I just another loose end to be put out of my misery?"

"You? Oh no, not at all. You are *far* more important than that. I am sure my brother will tell you all about it when you meet him."

"Brother?"

"Enough with the questions. This isn't a quiz show. One more and I'll tape your mouth shut. You're almost as bad as your friend."

"What friend?"

"The pretty one. Garin."

"Have you killed him, too?"

"Killed him? Certainly not, why would I? He's vital to what's happening. He's been most helpful."

Annja thought of everything Roux had told her about the midnight visit and the theft from the vault and muttered, "I'll kill him."

"That's entirely up to you, but not until we're finished with him."

26

Garin woke with an irresistible urge to vomit.

His head was on fire.

The blood inside his skull pounded so fiercely against the bone walls he couldn't bring himself to move.

The slightest roll set off a drill inside his head.

Garin squeezed his eyes shut tight to drive it away.

The only light, a thin gauze, came from the doorway that had to lead into the bathroom.

His mind was full of jumbled memories that made no sense and had no order.

There had been a blonde woman, that much he remembered. But any more than that he struggled to hold on to.

His mouth was dry, but the lingering taste of whiskey convinced him she'd slipped something into his drink.

"Monique," he said, testing the word in his mouth. It came out as little more than a mumble.

Then he was hit with the last thing that had filled his mind before it had given up its grip on consciousness.

Garin fought against the nausea as he saw the shape of the body sprawled on the bed.

He had let his guard down, and the woman had taken advantage of the moment.

No.

She had engineered it.

It took a second for him to realize that she most certainly had taken the papers, and more pertinently, he had been tricked out of his finder's fee.

Not good.

He cursed himself for an idiot, even though there was only a corpse to hear him.

He needed to get out of there before anyone came up to the suite. If anyone found him in here with a body he was in danger, which, of course, was exactly why she'd left him alone with the corpse in the first place.

He was such an idiot sometimes.

He managed to get to his feet, shaky and unsteady, one hand to his forehead—finger and thumb pressing against his temples to hold back the throbbing that increased in intensity as he moved upright—the other against the wall to keep from falling. After a heartbeat or two the intense wave of nausea started to pass.

He opened his eyes again to take a proper look at the body on the bed.

There was something familiar about the man.

More than familiar.

Garin knew him.

Eventually a name came to his lips, a name he had not heard for at least a couple of years. Jake Thornton. Thornton had been in a line of business that Garin took an interest in—the trafficking of relics and mementos of the past—though the dead man had been more interested in stealing them from museums and galleries than digging them out of the ground.

But what was he doing here?

And more importantly, how had he ended up dead?

More and more questions tumbled into Garin's mind, each one arriving with all the clarity of a nail being driven home.

Twenty-four hours ago this had seemed like a straightforward kind of job, good money for minimal exertion. The money had blinded him. Staring at the bed, he figured Thornton had made the same kind of mistake.

He splashed water on his face and looked at the drawn and drained features that stared back at him in the mirror.

He was starting to feel more like himself, but he had the overwhelming urge to sleep, convinced that it would all feel better when he woke up. Sleep wouldn't change the fact that there was a corpse on the bed. A corpse he had a connection to. But before he left, he would get rid of whatever traces there were that would lead the authorities to know that he had been in the room.

Garin used the towel from the bathroom to wipe every surface he could remember touching, trying his best to retrace his steps. But it was almost impossible through the drugged haze of memory to recall everything he'd come into contact with since following Monique into the room. There was only one glass on the table in the living area, the other had been washed and replaced on the tray. It didn't take much to realize that the woman had already erased every bit of her presence. With a last glance over his shoulder, he left and closed the door behind him.

He slipped the do not disturb sign on the doorknob and headed for the elevator.

The short trip down to the lobby was barely long enough to compose himself, get his breathing in order, calm his jittery nerves, with all of the questions playing over and over inside his head.

He needed to think, go back over what he knew, see if

he could piece together the component parts: Who could have wanted those documents badly enough to kill for them? Next up, why? Why was Jake Thornton lying dead in that room while Garin was still alive? Was that just because he was meant to be the patsy, or had Thornton retrieved something with extra significance to their scheme? Or had he just become too greedy and paid the price?

The answers would have to wait, at least until he'd gotten out of the hotel.

Admittedly there were cameras, and almost certainly the woman had booked the room in his name. Her mysterious boss wouldn't have brought the bodies to his own door. There was too much that would connect Garin to the room, and not a lot he could do about any of it.

The elevator door slid open.

He took a first step onto the plush red carpet that covered the lobby.

He focused on the glass doors that exited onto the street, not making eye contact with anyone as he made his way across the foyer. He stepped aside as bellmen carried luggage in from the taxi that stood outside.

A woman struggled to keep in check a young child who was clearly overtired, but she didn't even seem to notice him.

The door opened almost silently as he approached, the air that rushed in feeling warm against the chill of the air-conditioned lobby.

The doorman looked up from his conversation with the taxi driver and gave him a smile.

"Good evening, Mr. Braden," he said. "Would you like me to get your car?"

So much for anonymity. The man knew his name. He'd been set up good and proper. "My car?" He was about to say that he hadn't brought his car, but thought better of it.

"Yes, sir. Your lady friend dropped it off for you a little while ago. I trust you are enjoying your stay." He reached inside his pocket and pulled out a set of keys.

"Absolutely," Garin said, wondering just how deep a hole she had left him in.

The doorman not only knew his name, but could put him in the hotel where Thornton's body was slowly decaying. Sooner or later he'd be tied to the man's murder. He needed to know who was behind everything before then if he stood a chance of wriggling out of this mess.

He knew that there was only one person who'd be able to help him, but given that he'd just robbed him, he didn't imagine Roux would be very forthcoming. Life was funny like that sometimes.

27

Roux was having a hard time keeping the smile from his face as he left the police station.

He'd promised Cauchon's goon that he would make a few calls, and that he should just relax, enjoy the solitude of his surroundings, because he'd be getting out of there before too long. He enjoyed lying to the man. He had no intention of helping either thug, even if they had given him the first solid clue he could follow back to Cauchon. He couldn't afford to waste the opportunity he'd just been handed. If Cauchon got wind of the fact that Roux had the number, he would destroy the SIM card, and that would be that, another dead end.

As soon as he was back at the hotel, he tried to call Annja's room, but there was no reply.

There was something going on here. He didn't really understand it, but there was no denying the danger that Annja was being dragged into because of him.

He tried her cell phone, but it went straight to voice mail.

"Call me," he said, and ended the call, frustrated. He tossed the phone onto the bed.

He needed to do *something*. The only problem was he didn't really know what.

He hoped that Annja would be able to help.

Part of him wanted to call the only person he was sure would know someone who could trace the call, but he couldn't bear to even *think* his name right now, let alone hear his voice. He would do this without Garin. Somehow. There were always alternatives. He just had to find them.

Ten minutes later Roux was still pacing the small room trying to work out his next move. Even though he had checked his cell phone every couple of minutes there was still no sign of Annja returning his call. His anxiety was broken at the sound of the courtesy phone at the side of the bed. He snatched up the receiver.

"Annja?"

"Philippe."

"That's no help at all. I don't know a Philippe," Roux said, realizing how cranky he sounded.

"Annja's cameraman," the other man said. "I was hoping she might be with you. I saw you together in the lobby earlier. I had to bribe the receptionist to put me through to you. She wouldn't give me your room number."

Roux hadn't noticed him. He was getting sloppy in his old age.

He didn't make a habit of befriending Annja's colleagues. Distance was the best method to retain his privacy. That was something he valued above everything else, which was why he could not understand how Cauchon—whoever he really was—knew so much about him. Although, this wasn't the first time someone had gotten too close to him. The memory of the young journalist twenty years ago still haunted him sometimes. He hadn't wanted him dead; he had just wanted to be left alone. It shouldn't be a lot to ask of the world.

"Are you telling me that you don't know where she is?"

"Annja was supposed to meet me at the cathedral. She said she was on her way so I hung around for almost an hour, but she didn't show. I tried her phone, but she didn't answer and she hasn't replied to the message I left on her voice mail."

Roux didn't like anything about that. "Where would she go?"

"I have no idea," the Frenchman admitted. "But it doesn't seem to be out of character. She gets the whiff of something interesting and off she runs without giving a second thought to anyone else."

"Sorry. I haven't seen her," Roux said. "I'm waiting for her to call back. I'll let you know when she does."

"Great. I'm in room 221."

Roux replaced the receiver and listened to the noise of movement in the hallway: people opening and closing doors; housekeepers starting their daily routine, pushing cleaning carts along the corridor. They were the sounds of normality, the world going on as if nothing had changed, but it had. Annja hadn't just gone off chasing another story. He knew her better than that. She might not have heeded his warning and still left the hotel, but she would have kept her phone with her so they could remain in touch. That thing was glued to her hip. If she wasn't answering her phone, it was because she was in trouble.

Suddenly he felt absolutely helpless to do anything about it.

His cell phone rang while he was staring at it, willing it to ring. He grabbed it, praying that it was her, but it wasn't. It was the last person in the world he wanted to speak to.

"Garin," he said flatly. He should have just ignored

the call, let it go through to voice mail. He wasn't ready to talk to the man yet.

"Roux," said the voice at the other end of the phone. "I think I might be in trouble."

28

Annja listened as the blonde woman walked away from her.

She took the opportunity to try to work her hands free, but the plastic ties that bound her wrists bit into her flesh, cutting deep into her skin until they were slick with her blood.

She fought against the pain, but the restraints showed no sign of giving way.

Annja shuffled along the ground, sliding her back against the crypt, feeling for the edge of the stone in the hope of using it to burn through plastic, working it back and forth quickly.

Beads of sweat started to form on her forehead as she concentrated, worrying the plastic against the stone. No matter how furiously she worked the tie, there was no sign of the tension changing.

She gritted her teeth and squeezed her eyes against the fierce burning sensation and tried again, the sound of her own heartbeat thundering in her ears, blocking out everything else.

Annja concentrated so hard on freeing herself, only

one thought was on her mind: being able to call her sword from its resting place.

She closed her eyes.

Breathed deeply.

She had no doubt that the woman would be no match for her in a fair fight, with or without the sword, but she wanted the sword. She wanted to close her fingers around the hilt and feel its reassuring strength in her hand, to feel its energy sing in her blood, the thrill of it bringing her truly alive again.

Annja screamed, unable to remain silent as the air was expelled from her lungs and her ribs exploded with pain.

She opened her eyes to see the woman standing over her.

She had been so caught up in the effort to free herself that she hadn't even heard her return.

"You're going to have to work harder than that to get out of those," the woman said, her voice dripping with smug loathing.

Annja resisted as her captor put her hand on her head and pushed Annja onto her side. She went down. The woman yanked her arms back agonizingly in the joints to examine her efforts. She felt a sudden surge of pain as the woman tightened the plastic ties, burying them deep in Annja's bloody wrists.

Annja gritted her teeth, bracing herself as best she could against the added tension.

The woman was stronger than she looked, and as long as she had her hands tied, there was nothing that Annja could do apart from wait. She'd tell her why she was here eventually, and what her brother had in mind for her. Until then she would just have to stay calm, conserve her strength and gather her wits. She needed to learn as much as she could about where she was and what was

going on in the hope that anything she did find out might
be useful later.

"You won't have too much longer to wait," the woman
said, as if she could read her mind. "We'll be leaving here
soon enough."

"Where are you taking me?"

"Does it matter?"

"It might. You tell me."

The woman laughed. "Oh, the naiveté. Let me just
squash that hope right now. It won't make *any* difference
to what happens to you. I'm going to have to leave you for
a while now, but please, don't waste your time trying to
escape. Even if you did manage to somehow work yourself free of those ties, there's no way out of this place. One
door, one key, and believe me, I'll be locking the door behind me when I go. I should be back before the lamp runs
out. Unfortunately for you, I won't be gone long enough
for you to dig a tunnel." She smiled. "And just in case it
had crossed your mind, no one will be able to hear you,
no matter how loud you scream."

"People will be looking for me."

"The same people we are looking for, so let them come.
It only makes our job easier. Besides, let's be honest. No
matter how hard they look, they are *never* going to find
you down here."

Annja listened to the sound of heels on the stairs,
counting the steps as the woman climbed.

Ten steps, then a pause as she opened a door.

The groan spoke of centuries of accumulated rust on
hinges.

Even the sound of the key turning in the lock echoed
in that quiet chamber, the bolt dropping into place with
a heavy clunk.

The flame in the lantern flickered for an instant as the air moved, then settled down to a steady burn once again.

It was all Annja could concentrate on.

It helped to drive the other questions out of her head, allowing her to concentrate on the very first one: How was she going to get her hands free?

29

"Roux?" There was silence.

Garin assumed that the old man had hung up on him.

He had made some lame excuse to the doorman about leaving his keycard behind in the room, and turned around and gone back inside. At least while he was there he could delay the discovery of the body, until the smell became a problem. He needed to come up with a plan for dealing with the disposal of a corpse. The one thing on his side was that he was a creative thinker. He knew people. Get rid of the body. That had to be his course of action. If he could pull that off, then there was a chance that he'd get away with a murder he hadn't committed.

"What do you want?" Roux replied eventually. "Haven't you taken enough from me already?"

Garin didn't have a plausible lie, and wasn't about to pretend he hadn't been the one who'd broken into the old man's vault. The fact was that lies came more easily to his lips than the truth, but this time he was going to have to be straight with the old man.

"I'm sorry," was all he could say.

"Sorry? That's a first. But I'm disappointed, Garin. All you had to do was ask. You know I would have given you whatever you needed, so 'sorry' isn't going to cut it this time," Roux said. "I want everything back. Everything you took."

"That's just the thing…"

"You've sold it? Obviously you have. What could I have been thinking to ask such a silly question? I hope you made enough money to make betraying me worthwhile."

"I'll get the documents back. I promise you. I'll get everything back. But I need to get out of here first. And I need you to help me do that." He had expected to hear more venom in Roux's voice. There was no doubt the old man was angry, but there was something else, something that he was more concerned about.

There was only ever one thing more important than berating Garin for doing something venal and stupid, and that was Annja.

"Who did you sell the papers to?" Roux demanded.

"It doesn't matter," Garin replied, still unable to admit just how badly he'd screwed up.

"Believe me, it matters. It matters because on the same day that you break into my vault there's a threat on Annja's life. It matters because she discovered *someone* had signed out documents here in Carcassonne in my name. And now she's gone missing. There has to be a connection between those documents and what has happened to her. That's why it matters, Garin."

"Missing? What do you mean, missing?"

"I mean missing. What else would I mean? She was supposed to meet her cameraman, and she didn't turn up."

Garin listened as the old man told him about her encounter with the thugs Dugarry and Rameaux, how he had paid them a visit in the local lockup and that he had managed to get the phone number of their boss, Cauchon.

He had to admire the old man's tenacity. He was a terrier when he was chasing something.

"But that doesn't mean that there's any connection with the man who wanted those documents," Garin argued. "Sometimes a coincidence really is just that."

"And yet here you are calling me to say you need my help. Let me guess, your little transaction didn't go smoothly, did it? I assume you aren't wanting advice on how to invest your windfall? Did your buyer know these papers were in my vault? Or was that just blind luck?"

"You're right, it didn't go well," Garin confessed. He'd already figured out that there was more going on than just the theft of a few ancient documents.

You didn't need to be a rocket scientist, he thought, to work that out when people started drugging you and trying to frame you for murder. The problem was he couldn't bring himself to talk about it. It would have been easier face-to-face. Right now Roux needed his help and he needed Roux's help, and Annja almost certainly needed both of them.

That's what was tempering the old man's anger. He would have to make things right later. Saving Annja would be a start.

"Give me the number. I'll get my guy on to it. If you're right and Cauchon doesn't know you have it, there's a chance he hasn't covered his tracks. Where are you at the moment?"

"Carcassonne," Roux said, giving him the name of his hotel.

"Room number?" Garin asked. It came as no surprise that the old man was already there. It was almost certainly the same hotel that Annja was staying at.

"Room 301, but I'll be heading out for a while."

"You have a lead?"

"No. I'm going to check Annja's room. If there's nothing there, I'll take a walk from here to where she was supposed to meet her cameraman." And almost as an afterthought, he added, "So, you called me. You didn't do that for fun. What's your problem?"

Garin glanced through the open bedroom door at the body on the bed and knew that Roux was right; there had to be a connection. And if that was right, it meant that Annja could be in real danger.

"You know what? It can wait," he said. "I've got a couple of things to take care of here, but then I'll come over to you."

"Call me as soon as you have news. Anything at all. And just because we are working together doesn't mean I have forgiven you, Garin. Don't mistake my concern for Annja as anything but that."

"Wouldn't have it any other way, old man," Garin said, and finished the call.

He had more calls to make.

First things first; he needed a cleaner.

30

The documents were more than he could have hoped for.

The man who called himself Cauchon pored over the papers he had spread out on the desk in front of him.

He had assumed that he would find at least a hint that there was real evidence of witchcraft buried somewhere among the material that had, as of yet, never seen the light of day. He felt a grim sense of satisfaction in having framed Roux for the theft of material, even though it had meant that the dealer who had impersonated him—Jake Thornton—lay dead in a hotel room. At least his corpse was serving a second purpose, in setting up Roux's cohort. Garin Braden was going to have his hands full trying to worm his way out of the mess he'd woken up to, assuming Monique had not disappointed him. It was highly unlikely Braden would be in a position to interfere before his endgame was played out.

And then his time would come.

All good things come to those who wait.

Hiring a man like Garin Braden to steal those papers from under the nose of a man he knew so well had been inspired—it drove a wedge between them. Cauchon reveled in it.

They would all pay in the end, but in the meantime he would draw enjoyment from their torment.

Bernard Gui had been only too aware that there had been a form of witchcraft that had existed long before it had first been recorded in the suspicions and revelations of the Inquisition. That magic was far more dangerous than the hedge magic of cures and curses. The writings showed no evidence of devil worship however, there was something else, and if he could follow its trail he would use it to his advantage.

What he had was proof that it was possible to rid the woman, Annja Creed, of the spirit that possessed her. Then she could be a true martyr.

Her death would mark the beginning of his new Inquisition.

There had been so many years of planning, so many years of preparation, waiting for more than just the stars to align, but now he had the key to it all and he was going to use it.

There were other items he needed to locate before the last pieces could fall into place, but by the grace of God he had already obtained most of them.

In a box on the floor beside him he had accumulated possessions and documents touched by the men who had condemned Joan of Arc.

Even with the amount he had so far, he might be able to make the attempt. All he needed now was something that had belonged to Joan herself, something that had once been close to her.

Since he had the girl, he knew that he would be able to make Roux dance to his tune. The old man would do *anything* if he thought that it would lead to Annja Creed's release. More fool him. He was also sure that if he gave Roux the opportunity, he would make the suggestion himself: he would exchange his life for hers rather than see her suffer. The thought alone was delicious in itself.

His sister would truly enjoy that.

There were times when he worried that perhaps Monique enjoyed inflicting suffering on others a little too much. She had relished the opportunity to deal out pain and death. It had been her idea to kill what she called their loose ends. They were expendable. Cauchon was only too aware how dependent he was on his sister.

Roux had to have realized that Annja was missing by now, and it had to have been driving him out of his mind that he couldn't find her. Come nightfall Cauchon would make sure Creed was sedated before they moved her. Monique was certain that she would be able to handle it on her own, no matter how doubtful he was. There were some things he could not do himself.

He looked out of the window at the world and wondered if it sensed what was about to happen. If it could feel the importance of tomorrow and the beginning of his New Inquisition.

This time it wasn't about which god people believed in.

It was so much more fundamental than that.

He knew where he could find the last piece in the puzzle. Roux was going to be the man to get it for him.

The most important thing now was not to rush. This was a time for patience, for choosing the right moment when the broken old man would do anything for him.

31

Garin wrapped the body in the bed linen and waited for the cleaner and a team to arrive.

It hadn't been as easy to organize as he had hoped. It wasn't as if a person could just look them up on the internet and check their ratings. But he was resourceful. He made a call to a guy named Hunter, thousands of miles away in the States, who connected through four different fixers to the kind of cleaner he was looking for, who were over the border in Zaragoza. That meant several hours before they could get to him. He didn't have a choice. Better to go with someone he could trust than take a risk on trying to do it himself, and these guys came on Hunter's recommendation. That meant they were good at what they did. In the grand scheme of things, a couple of hours wasn't so bad—certainly better than no help at all.

Roux's voice echoed inside his head, the unspoken accusation that this was all his fault, that he was the one who had brought this to their doors.

The accusation had no foundation in reality. Garin

hadn't precipitated this. The worst he had done was not turn his back on an offer of easy money.

Roux had received the call about the first threat on Annja's life, not him.

The old man was at the center of this, even if he could not see it.

Garin had played his part. He was prepared to admit that, and he intended to put that right, but playing his part was a damned sight different from taking the blame for everything.

He heard the movement in the hall before he heard the tap on the door.

"Housekeeping," said the voice from the other side.

Garin checked his watch.

It had barely been an hour and a half since he had made the call. It was hard to believe that they could be there already, given the distance from Zaragoza, but it wasn't impossible, he supposed.

He closed the door to the bedroom just in case it wasn't them and went to answer the knock. Two men, far too burly to be regular hotel staff, waited on the other side.

"Mr. Braden?"

He nodded.

"We understand that you have something in your room that needs to be removed?" one of them said. The other scoped the corridor, making sure no one was coming. He leaned against a laundry cart. They had come prepared.

Garin stepped aside to let them through without another word.

"If you could direct us to the item?" the first man said.

Garin nodded toward the bedroom and made sure that the door to the hallway was closed before they reached it. He wasn't about to risk the slightest chance of a tourist or a member of the staff getting even a glimpse of what lay on the other side.

"You might want to be somewhere else while we do this. It's going to take a little time and it's not particularly pleasant."

"How long?"

"A couple of hours, maybe more. By the time we're done you won't be able to tell that anyone has been in the room, at least not with the naked eye. We'll cleanse the room, scrub it down to be sure nothing will turn up under UV light, either."

"What about the bedding?"

The silent man reached inside the linen cart and pulled out a set of the hotel's bed linen complete with a new duvet.

"We'll dispose of the soiled sheets."

The man ignored the bundle that wrapped the body, still lying in the middle of the bed. The mattress beneath was stained red and it seemed unlikely that they would be able to do anything about that.

"It will be more difficult to get the blood out of the mattress. Ideally we'd take it off-site, too, but we'll scrub it down, flip it and buy some time. With luck it'll be weeks before the staff turns the mattress. By then dozens of people will have come and gone. The wall and the headboard shouldn't be too much trouble."

He talked as if the disposal of the body was the least of his problems. For that reason and that reason alone, Garin was convinced the man knew what he was talking about.

There was nothing to keep him there.

The best thing he could do was get out of their way and let them get on with their job.

"We'll close the door behind us," the man assured him. "Unfortunately, there will be a lingering smell of chemicals for a few hours, so we'll leave the window open, but I'll make sure that the do not disturb sign stays on the door. Trust us, everything will be fine."

There was no talk about what would happen after they took the body away; that wasn't his concern, and frankly, the less he knew, the better.

There was no talk about payment, either.

This was about favors being called in and repaid up and down the line through a network of people who offered specialist services, where a cash value could not be placed on a service. These were professionals, just like him. It was going to cost a lot of people a lot of favors in the long run, but contrary to what the song said, the best things in life weren't free.

He left them to it.

He took the elevator back down to the lobby and headed out to get his car from the valet who brought it around from the hotel garage for him. As he passed through the doors, the valet stood beside the red Ferrari he had left behind at the airport.

"Your keys, sir," he said, holding out a set of keys by the leather fob with the iconic Ferrari badge on it.

There was no doubt that they were his keys.

She'd worked fast when he was drugged up. Faster than he would have thought possible, unless he'd been under longer than he believed.

"Thanks," he said, slipping his hand in his pocket for a folded bill. He handed it to the valet, who slid it into his own without giving it a glance. A moment later he was behind the wheel and roaring away from the hotel without really knowing where he was heading, not even completely sure where he was. He was loath to admit it, but he had been distracted by his abductor's beauty, which no

doubt was part of her plan. Yet again he was left to pon-
der the wisdom of trusting in beauty.

Garin had been driving for a few minutes before he
noticed that there was something off about the car, something different about how it handled.

He pulled over to the side of the road and took a look
around to try to understand what it was.

When he figured out what was missing, he couldn't
help but laugh at just how devious the woman had been,
and in truth how incredibly careful she had to have made
her plans.

He climbed out of the car to take a look at the license
plate to confirm that it was the same as his own car.

It was.

But this wasn't *his* car.

It was the same make, the same model, but it wasn't his.

She'd worked out the con to the minutest detail, determined to ensure that he was implicated in Jake Thornton's
murder, including putting on plates that would incrimi-
nate him.

But he'd slipped away before the noose had closed.

He had to assume she'd made an anonymous call to
tip off the police, or was going to soon. He could only
hope the law wouldn't arrive in the middle of the cleanup.

Garin climbed back into the car, sure it was hot. He
needed to switch vehicles, but he couldn't just ditch a
flame-red Ferrari in the middle of nowhere. First he
needed to swap the plates out with some other vehicle—
thankfully Monaco was a billionaire's playground. There
were plenty of supercars lining the strip and the seafront,
and he left the vehicle in its natural habitat, where one
more Ferrari wouldn't set off any alarm bells.

He didn't go back to get his own car, but hopped a

bus to the airport and went inside the terminal to the car rental desk, emerging with the keys for a tank of a 4x4.

The urge to skip the country was strong, just drive south, hit the border and keep going, but he couldn't do that while Annja was still in trouble. Especially when there was just a tiny part of it that was his fault.

If Garin kept to the speed limits on the winding country roads, Carcassonne was a little over five hours away.

He had no intention of keeping to the speed limits.

32

Roux was itching to get out of the hotel room.

He was wasting far too much of his life in places like this, walking up and down a cramped room little bigger than a prison cell, even if it was better furnished.

The cameraman hadn't shed any more light on Annja's whereabouts, and Garin's call was worrying away at him. There was more going on here than he was seeing. He clenched his fist and unclenched it, but the exercise did nothing for the frustration he felt building. He needed to do something. He couldn't waste the day just *waiting*.

Roux grabbed his coat and headed out, checking his phone instinctively before he slipped it into his pocket. The caller ID was empty. No calls. No messages. No texts. No Annja.

He obtained a city map from the rack in reception and stepped out into the street, feeling the icy air hit his lungs as traffic swarmed past.

He took a minute to pick the best route to the cathedral and struck out, folding the map and slipping it into his pocket as he walked.

It felt good to be moving after being cooped up inside.

There was every likelihood that he was being watched. Cauchon knew too much about Roux not to have eyes and ears on him. Let the man watch. Let his spies report back. He wasn't going to hide from him in some hotel room. Now he was going to take the fight to the mystery man. It would help to know the underlying cause behind Cauchon's obsession with him, which had to have something to do with the papers Garin had stolen from his vault and the papers that had been liberated from the museum here.

While he wasn't sure exactly which journal was missing, he knew the time of its writing, and that it tracked back to the death of Joan. He didn't know the documents word for word, but was familiar with almost all of the secrets they contained, because they were his secrets. He had been there. He had lived through those dark days. If Cauchon had even the vaguest concept of the secrets he'd managed to procure, he could be a very dangerous opponent.

Roux used shop windows and car windshields to see if anyone was following, deliberately doubling back to retrace his steps and move counterintuitively against the flow of bodies, always checking the reflections to see if anyone followed him. To the casual observer his actions might have appeared erratic and more than a little strange, but Roux didn't care about that. He wanted to flush out his tail. Get them to show themselves, to make a mistake. He'd happily face anyone head-on. He'd had showdowns before, even gone up against ArmaLites and AK-47s with nothing but his bare hands, and come out alive. And if he got to take one of them down, put a few questions to Cauchon bare-knuckle-style, then he'd happily take the opportunity to get a little exercise and learn more about this incarnation of the man.

Twice he thought he had spotted someone tailing him, but both came to nothing. They were just heading in the same general direction, attracted by items in shop windows that made them pause for a while before moving on again.

He was becoming paranoid.

He needed to shake himself out of it.

There was nothing on the route that seemed out of the ordinary, nothing that might have attracted Annja for more than a moment. She wasn't a fashion-obsessed kind of girl. She was only happy when she was getting her hands dirty. Once the cathedral came into view he knew that there was no point going any farther. Philippe, her cameraman, would have seen her once she was this close to the site. He wouldn't have missed her in the crowds.

As he turned to retrace his steps and return to the hotel, his phone rang.

He checked the caller ID.

It wasn't Annja.

"Garin." He said it fast, like he wanted the call over before it had begun so that he could free the line up in case Annja was trying to get through. "I gather you have taken care of your business?"

"It's under control. It got a bit hairy there for a while, but I'll join you shortly. I should be at your hotel within the hour."

"And the number I gave you?"

"My guy's on it. So far, he's confirmed that the last time it was used was in Carcassonne, in the past twenty-four hours, but it's inactive now so there's no telling if he's moved on or is still in the area until he puts the battery back into the handset. He knows what he's doing, in other words."

"Nothing that helps, then." Roux wasn't sure what he

had expected, but being able to pinpoint Cauchon's base of operations from a cell phone number would have been a good start.

"When you say Carcassonne, is there any chance of narrowing that down? I don't know how these things work, triangulating cell phone towers and such, but everything you see on the internet these days seems to talk about a surveillance society and these cell phones of ours being nothing more than electronic tags tracking our every movement."

"Pretty much, but our boy is covering his tracks—or at least making it difficult for us. My guy's monitoring the number. The second the phone comes online, he'll let me know."

"And in the meantime we do nothing?"

"In the meantime we do what we do best, we make trouble. If Cauchon is as keen to speak to you as I think he is, he'll make contact. He'll want to goad you. We'll be ready for him."

"Not much of a plan, Garin." Sometimes it felt like he was talking to a small child who always made light of everything.

"If you don't want my help, I'll just turn around and head back home."

Roux bit his tongue. He wanted to say, *Yes, do that, do exactly that*, but instead he said, "I think you owe Annja more than that."

"It's always about Annja," Garin said after a few seconds of silence. "Have you noticed that? It's never about us anymore. The only time we talk is about her."

"We ran out of things to say to each other about two hundred years ago," Roux said, and this time Garin did laugh.

"Probably. Look. You're right. I owe her more than

that. And given everything else, my part in it—which I didn't realize at the time—I owe you more, too. So no, I'm not going to head back home. I'm going to be with you in an hour and we're going to put an end to this threat once and for all. You, me and Annja. The three slightly cranky musketeers."

"That's one way of describing us," the old man said, and ended the call. Garin could always infuriate him. All he had to do most days was open his mouth and he'd manage it. But so many times that same infuriating man had turned out to be the solution to problems that were beyond Roux. Like it or not, they made a good team.

A horn sounded.

Roux took a step backward, not noticing that he had been so close to the edge of the sidewalk.

A woman on a scooter smiled at him, blond hair flowing from the back of her helmet, then blew him a kiss.

He smiled back, not knowing if his cheeks were flushed with embarrassment at almost walking into the road or at attracting the attention of a beautiful woman.

He watched as the woman rode away, her hair getting caught in her own slipstream as it trailed behind her. For a moment he wondered if he knew her, if that airborne kiss had been meant to remind him somehow, but the glimpse of her face had been so fleeting he couldn't possibly place her from this lifetime or any other.

33

Moving the oil burner behind her back wasn't easy. Annja worked it around so she could lift it with her hands, but before she'd taken half a dozen steps the heat from the wick was burning her skin.

She gritted her teeth against the pain, only just managing to lower it to the ground without dropping it in the process.

That would have been a disaster.

Her heart raced, as she couldn't help but imagine all of the potential consequences of the thing smashing.

The worst was that it was only a short step away from what she was contemplating.

The wooden door at the top of the short flight of stone steps felt dry enough that she might just get away with the crazy notion she had: smashing the lantern against it.

If she got really lucky, the oil-fueled flame would be enough to start it burning. But to undermine its integrity enough that she could batter her way out? It was a long shot.

And for all that to happen before the woman returned? Perhaps impossible.

In the absence of any windows she had no idea how much time had actually passed since the woman had left. Annja didn't even know what time of day it was. She hadn't been able to hear any telltale sounds coming or going from the other side of the door, even when she'd kicked against it with her heel trying to get someone's attention.

She was beneath some kind of church—that much was obvious—quite probably not in use. Her assumption, heavy on the irony, was that she was in the crypt of the cathedral where she'd been supposed to meet Philippe. The idea forced a bitter laugh from her.

When it finished, she heard the sound of a key being rattled into the lock.

She strained again at the ties, hoping that the heat from the lantern might have weakened them. They showed no sign of breaking no matter how hard she pulled at them. The plastic was uncomfortably hot from where the lantern had burned at it. Given a few minutes longer she would have tried to melt the ties, but knew that chances were the plastic would just fuse with the blood and abraded skin beneath them rather than snap. That was the kind of luck she was having today.

Annja scrambled back to her feet, ready to face the woman.

She had no intention of letting her look down at her.

Even with her hands behind her back she knew that she had a chance no matter how slight. If the woman had wanted her dead, she would have killed her by now. The fact that she'd taken the trouble to drug her and transport her to this subterranean crypt boded well for her opportunity to survive. As long as that hadn't changed in the intervening hours.

Annja backed away as the woman descended the short flight of steps.

It was a ploy to appear subservient, deferential. In other words, make sure the woman didn't see her as a threat. She needed to draw her into the room and work enough space to get past her if she could bowl her over bodily.

"Good to see you up and about," the woman said, pausing when she saw that the lantern had been moved from the sarcophagus. She nodded slightly, but made no comment as she bent to pick it up.

Instinctively, Annja knew that this was chance to strike. It wasn't much of a disadvantage, but the woman was off balance and off guard. It was as good as it was going to get.

She took two quick steps and swung her right leg hard, in a high arc, before the woman knew what was happening.

The point of her toe made contact beneath the blonde woman's jaw, snapping her head back and sending her sprawling to the ground.

She hit the stones hard, losing control of the lantern. The momentum sent it crashing against the side of the sarcophagus.

Fuel splashed against the stone and spread in a pool across the floor.

There was a moment's breath, a deep and profound silence, before the flame chased across its surface with a whoosh, sucking the air to the flame.

The fire blazed, forming a barrier between them.

Annja was on the wrong side of it.

The woman struggled to get to her knees, disorientated by the blow.

She shook her head, trying to gather her wits, leaned forward, hands flat on the cold stone, and spit out a mouthful of blood.

Annja took her chance while she still could.

There was no time to go around the flames; instead, she had to run through the fire, gambling that it wouldn't catch onto her clothes. Burning fabric wouldn't be easy to put off with her hands tied behind her back.

She launched herself forward, five rapid steps and she was through and on the other side, rushing awkwardly toward the stairs, her bound hands making it difficult to run properly.

Her foot came down on the first step just as the woman's hand snaked out to grab her ankle, fingers taking a grip too tight to shake off.

It was enough for Annja to lose her balance.

She stumbled forward with no hope of saving herself from falling even as she twisted sideways, trying to take the brunt of the impact on her shoulder instead of her face. Even so, the pain of impact was jarring. Annja cried out as she hit stone. She gasped for air that was rapidly filling with smoke.

In an instant the woman was on top of her, her weight pressing down, and then Annja felt the sharp sting on the back of her neck.

She fought to dislodge the woman, but even as she did so the strength started to seep away from her struggle. She heard words—they could have been hers, they could have been her attacker's. They were just a slurred mumble that she couldn't understand.

Annja barely felt the kick that the woman planted in her ribs.

34

Roux waited in the lobby.

There was no point in going up to his room while he waited for Garin. Besides, he'd be happy never to set foot in that monastic cell again if he had anything to say about it. He was tempted to go up to the suite, but ordered black coffee and stared out through the glass doors while the drink grew cold on the table in front of him. Twice a server approached to see if he needed anything else; he shook his head to say, *No thanks*, before she could ask.

Eventually Garin appeared in the doorway as the first fat flakes of a new snowfall filled the air.

"No luggage?"

"Traveling light."

"Any more news?" Roux asked.

"Nothing yet. I take it that he hasn't reached out to you."

Roux shook his head.

"Let's head up to the room. We can talk without worrying about being overhead." He knew procedure. The museum would have alerted the police to the theft from their archives, and given them his name as the last known signatory, meaning he was a person of interest. Eventually someone was going to come looking for him if they weren't already.

"Devious." Garin chuckled appreciatively when they were in his room. It wasn't quite the reaction Roux had been expecting.

"Is that what you really think?"

"Of course. Look at it this way. He got you to blame me and put the blame squarely at your door at the same time. I'd say that was pretty devious. And pulling it off without half the world realizing it was missing...brilliant."

"It wasn't you?"

"Not this time, boss," Garin said, shaking his head.

"Pity."

"Sorry to disappoint."

"That's twice. I'm not used to you apologizing. It's really quite disconcerting. Maybe now would be a good time for you to tell me what happened to you and why you decided to steal from me."

"It's no big deal, really. Nothing out of the ordinary. I was approached by a broker to ask if I could locate some historical documents for his client in exchange for a very generous fee. It was supposed to be the first of a few objects the client had his eye on, and given that I knew exactly where it was, it felt like an easy buck."

"I hope it was worth it."

Garin shook his head. "I didn't see a cent outside of the retainer. Some people just don't like to pay. Shame, because I'd enjoyed the haggling."

"What did you take?"

"Papers recording Joan's burning, documented by Guillaume Manchon, a court scribe at the church court in Rouen at the time."

Roux knew them well.

They mentioned him by name.

It wasn't good, but it could have been worse. He remembered Manchon, a particularly disagreeable runt of a man who had wormed himself into favor with Cauchon and delighted in the burning of the young woman. He'd been sure she'd been possessed by a whole host of demons. It was really quite pathetic. But that didn't stop it from being dangerous.

"You actually handed them over without getting the cash up front? You're slacking." It was Roux's turn to laugh. "I take it there was a woman involved?"

"How did you guess?"

"I know you, my friend," Roux said, and for a moment it was as if all of the betrayals between them had never happened. "Any idea who she was?"

"Not a clue. She certainly wasn't the person I spoke to on the phone. He certainly wasn't a beautiful blonde."

"Beautiful blonde?" Roux's mind raced, making connections.

It was another of those coincidences that could be a coincidence but absolutely wasn't. He knew that deep down in his ancient bones. One day a beautiful blonde is outwitting Garin, the next another drives by on a scooter blowing him a kiss? They had to be one and the same.

"I may have seen her," he said, "which confirms my suspicions that it's all connected."

Garin shook his head. "How long has it taken you to work that out? Both of us getting phone calls from people we don't know, the only person that we both know well going missing? Absolutely it's all connected. Every single thing that's happened is connected. It's a web. Every strand, from the museum to the library to the falling masonry to us getting here, all strands of the same dark web.

I'll bet I can even tell you who they got to pull off that robbery at the museum and how he set you up to take the blame."

"Who?"

"Jake Thornton."

"Should I know the name?"

"He's a thief who likes to try his hand at robbing institutions. He also likes to think of himself as a bit of a high-end cat burglar, or did at least."

"Do you know where we can get hold of him?"

"By séance."

"What?"

"That problem, I mentioned? Being framed for murder. Thornton's corpse was on the bed in the hotel suite where I was expecting to meet my buyer. I was drugged, and pretty effectively framed, right down to them stealing a Ferrari the same color as mine and putting my plates on it, and making sure the valet knew my name. Like I said, a little problem. I called in the cleaners and left them to it. I'm assuming his body's long gone now and there's nothing left in the room to tie me to the crime—and no actual evidence of a crime for that matter." They had both seen enough death over the years, but that didn't mean that they were completely immune to it.

"And Annja is missing," Roux said, not finishing the thought. It went in an obvious direction. Neither of them wanted to follow it.

"So what's the plan?"

"We don't have one."

"That's not ideal." Garin chuckled mirthlessly. "We could tap into the hotel CCTV system to see if we can spot Annja leaving the hotel, but it's not like this place is wired, eyes everywhere. It's an ancient settlement. It's going to be filled with blind spots even if we get in."

"But it's a good start. Can you get the equipment you need in a place like this?"

Garin smiled smugly. "With these fingers I can work magic, my friend. Even in a place like this. All I need is a laptop and an internet connection."

"Fair enough," the old man agreed.

Garin picked up the phone at the side of the bed and spoke to someone at the reception desk. Within a couple of minutes he had the directions to the nearest computer store and was heading out the door.

"I'll be back in twenty minutes," he said. "Why don't you order from room service? I'm starving." He closed the door behind him without waiting for a response, leaving Roux alone in the room.

35

Annja felt the bruises even before she was completely awake.

Her body bounced up and down on the unforgiving metal floor as the vehicle rocked and rolled on its suspension.

The ties binding her wrists had been supported by another set around her ankles and there was a gag across her mouth. She could taste the wad of cloth that had been stuffed in behind the gag to make sure she couldn't be heard. Swimming back toward consciousness, it felt like she was drowning on the material, choking and gagging as she tried to suck down precious air. It took her a moment to master the panic and focus on breathing in slowly, calmly, through her nose.

She had no idea of where she was or what their destination might be.

The rear doors had small windows at the top. They'd been whitewashed, but still let in a faint glow of light that kept the darkness at bay. She couldn't see anything through them, though. The most she could glean was that it was daylight outside—not that she knew if it was the same day, the next day or any day of any week. Gravity pulled her toward the doors as the vehicle jounced and shuddered up a rough track, climbing.

It was already cold in the pickup, but there was no mistaking the fact that the temperature was dropping as they traveled.

In her head she tried to visualize a map of the region in her mind, thinking about the hills and twisting roads. It gave her something to concentrate on as she tried to fight her way out of the drug-fog that still lingered inside her head.

Whatever she had been injected with wasn't doing her any good. She felt slow, lethargic and like she didn't really have control of her limbs. Having that stuff pumped into her veins twice within a matter of hours was not good at all.

There was an empty pit in her stomach where the hunger gnawed away.

She tried to ignore all of it, all of those different sensory inputs and distractions, as the map came into focus.

How far could the woman have taken her in an hour or two, assuming that was how long she'd been out?

Could she have reached any mountains?

Of course she could.

In that time they could have made it into the Pyrenees.

They could have been crossing into Spain or Andorra.

So why take her into the mountains?

What could be gained from that?

Apart from finding a nice secluded spot well off the beaten track to dump a body where it wouldn't be discovered for months?

Annja didn't like it, but it made a grim kind of sense.

But if the woman had wanted to kill her, she could

have done it back at the church, put her corpse inside one of those old sarcophagi, and it would have taken years, if ever, before someone stumbled on it. So no, it was something else.

Every time she tried to move to ease the slowly mounting pain in the muscles around her shoulders, Annja felt the plastic dig deeper into the raw wounds, and that just made the pain worse. There was no point in trying to fight against the restraints. They weren't going to break. If she'd been awake when they'd cuffed her, maybe. There was a way to brace your wrists against each other so when you pulled down hard and sharp the ties broke, but not from behind your back. So now she was just going to have to hope that the kidnappers gave her the opportunity to make a run for it.

The truck braked suddenly. She heard the tires spit gravel, spraying against the underside of the vehicle, the clattering chips of stone against the metal sounding like a hailstorm inside. Up front, the driver killed the engine and the world fell silent. She heard the cab door open and slam shut and the crunch of feet on deep snow moving around the side of the truck.

She closed her eyes and slumped, giving her best imitation of someone still doped up.

A key slipped into the lock and turned.

The back doors swung open together, letting in a sudden wash of light.

Annja squeezed her eyes shut against the invasive sun; even so it seeped through her eyelids, stinging.

"Time to move, sleepyhead," the woman said, leaning into the back of the truck.

Annja had no plans to make this easy for her.

She lay motionless, waiting for the other woman to make her move.

The woman reached in and took hold of Annja's ankle.

Annja moaned, like someone trying to claw her way back to consciousness, not resisting. She kept herself as limp as possible, expecting the woman to try to drag her out.

Instead—and so much better than she'd dared hope—she felt the tension suddenly go as the ties binding her ankles were cut.

The woman muttered to herself all the time, but Annja couldn't make out what she was saying.

"If you think I'm going to carry you inside, you can think again," she said finally, so Annja had to assume she was talking to her.

The chilly air filled the back of the truck quickly, bringing the temperature down fast. She was beyond cold, even in the thick fleece she was wearing. Without it, the cold would have been unbearable. She let out a groan, faking the slow return to consciousness, gambling that the woman wouldn't stick her with another syringe. She didn't. She reached toward Annja and yanked the gag away from her mouth and pulled out the wadding. Obviously they were somewhere remote enough she didn't care about noise anymore.

"What the hell did you do to me?" Annja moaned, struggling to raise her head.

"Ah, so you are still with us. Pity." The woman ignored the question. "It'll take you a few minutes to come around, quite a while longer to clear your head completely."

"What did you hit me with?"

"The same stuff they use to tranquilize elephants," she said, holding another syringe where Annja could see it. "You should think yourself lucky my brother wants you alive. It would have been so easy to get the dose wrong."

"Why are you doing this?" Annja asked, just to keep her talking.

"You'll know soon enough," she said, but there was something in her voice, a quality to it, a vagueness, that made Annja doubt that she knew herself. If her brother was keeping her in the dark, did that mean he didn't trust her? Was that an angle she could work? If she was reading the woman right, she'd have been just as happy to kill Annja as deliver her alive, so she was going to need all the angles she could work to get out of this situation.

But at the end of the day she knew that all she had to do was to keep calm and wait for when her hands were free, and if that didn't come, reach into the otherwhere with both hands tied and draw down on her abductors. No matter how dangerous they thought they were, she was infinitely more dangerous to them.

Annja levered herself into a sitting position, using her feet now that they were free. Changing positions relieved some of the excruciating pain.

The woman took a step away from the vehicle, revealing the sweeping mountain vista that lay behind her.

High snowcapped peaks seemed to crowd around them, reflecting the last of the day's dying light.

Annja scanned the landscape, trying to pick out any signs of humanity.

There was nothing but nature, still wild and unconquered, as far as the eye could see.

"Okay, princess, move it," the woman said, motioning for Annja to climb out. She still clutched the syringe in her right hand, brandishing it like a knife. Annja had no intention of taking a third shot.

Her chance would come.

She slid to the edge and set her feet down slowly until they settled on crisp snow that crunched under her weight.

As she stood upright, her legs buckled, struggling after being cooped up for so long. The woman caught her and hauled her up to her feet.

She dragged Annja a couple of steps.

Annja in turn dragged her feet.

"Any chance you could do something with my wrists?" she asked, pushing her luck.

"I know what you can do. Believe me, there's no way in hell I'm going to let you pull that sword of yours, even if I had a gun in my hand." So the grunts had reported back what had happened when they'd ambushed her. So much for the element of surprise.

She pushed Annja forward, making her walk around the side of the truck.

Annja crunched through the snow, feeling the ice just beneath the surface.

There were tracks in the snow, meaning the truck wasn't the first vehicle to make the climb up the mountainside. They ended at an SUV that was parked beside a farmhouse, its gray slate roof covered with several inches of snow. The SUV's tracks had only just begun to be filled by the latest snowfall.

With the sun dropped, the temperature was falling fast. She wished she'd put on her ski jacket instead of just the fleece. The wind swirled snow up and down in the air, driving it against the wall of the farmhouse in a steep drift.

The building had been cut into the mountainside, a feat of engineering in itself.

It was hard to imagine why anyone would go to such an effort to build a home here given the inhospitable terrain.

There were lights on inside, but that didn't make the place feel any more welcoming than the ice and snow of the mountainside.

"Keep moving," the woman said, pushing her in the back. "I'd hate to think that I'd brought you out here only for you to die of hypothermia."

Through one of the bay windows Annja saw the flickering red glow of an open fire. A man sat beside it, talking on the telephone.

There was something familiar about him, even if his face was distorted in the firelight of the bubbled glass.

Annja paused midstep, trying to remember where she'd seen him before, knowing that she had, and hoping that remembering would be the key to unlock his motivations for dragging her out here as his prisoner. Another shove in the back got her moving again.

The man looked up from his telephone call.

In that instant, as they locked eyes, she realized where she'd seen him.

When she had met him before she'd made the mistake of thinking he was insignificant, someone who had just happened to have been in the wrong place at the wrong time.

Now she knew different.

Now she knew one piece of the puzzle.

36

Garin didn't need twenty minutes.

He returned with a new laptop and a couple of bags brimming with additional purchases.

It took longer to install the software and get the machine up and running.

"I need a shower," he said, heading toward the bathroom, treating the hotel room as if it was his own.

"What about that?" Roux nodded toward the laptop.

"It will take a while for all this stuff to load," Garin assured him, disappearing into the small bathroom. Thirty seconds later the spray of the shower was running.

Roux felt as if he had reaped the whirlwind and its name was Garin Braden.

He glanced at the screen, with no idea of what was happening. Again all he could do was wait.

After another minute he could hear Garin singing to himself.

His cell phone rang. It was a blocked number. He snatched it up, knowing it couldn't be Annja. That only left one alternative.

"Yes?"

"Mr. Roux, so good to speak to you again."

"Cauchon," Roux said. "You've had your fun. How about you tell me what this is all about? Man-to-man. There is no need to involve anyone else. Let's keep this between us. Whatever you want, we can work this out."

"I really don't think we can."

"What do you want from me?"

"Honestly? I want you to suffer. Are you suffering? It sounds as though you are. I hadn't expected it to be this easy, but then every man has his pressure points, and if you know where to apply pressure he's always going to break."

"What have you done with Annja?"

"Ah, the delightful Miss Creed. She's safe. For now."

"Where?"

"Don't take me for a fool, old man. She's safe and that's all you need to know."

"Just let her go. I'll give you whatever it is you want."

Garin emerged from the bathroom, wrapped in nothing more than a towel. Roux gestured to the phone, and mouthed, *It's him.*

Garin eased himself into the high-backed leather chair in front of the laptop, his fingers flying over the keyboard as he punched instructions into the command line.

"What could you possibly offer me?" Cauchon mused, enjoying himself. "Perhaps something for my collection?"

"Like the papers you had Garin steal from my house?"

"Very much like that, yes."

"Name it, and it's yours."

There was silence on the other end of the line.

"I can't help you if you don't tell me what you want."

"A reliable source tells me there's a piece of armor…" Cauchon's voice trailed off again, and even without him uttering another word Roux knew what he was talking about. There was more than one piece of armor in his collection, but there was only one piece that was related to Joan of Arc.

"I don't know what you're talking about." He tried the lie, but Garin was better at that than he was. He knew his voice wasn't convincing. His inflections changed subtly, as if his soul refused to let him get away with the false-hood, which was ironic given the thousands of lies he'd told in his lifetime.

He looked across at Garin, who was still frantically hammering the keys of the laptop.

Cauchon laughed, a sound that seemed mean, bitter, cynical. There was a degree of cruelty in his voice that the man made no effort to mask. It was obvious he was enjoying having Roux dangling on a hook, the old man a worm ready to be lowered into the water.

"Did you really just try to lie to me? With the girl's life on the line? Is there no level you won't fall to? Don't do it again, old man. We both know what we are talking about. And before you get any bright ideas to try to palm off a fake on me, I will recognize the original. Anything less, the woman dies. And that's just the beginning. I have so many ways of hurting you, not least of which is expos-ing your secrets."

"It will take me a few days," Roux said, knowing he needed hours, not days, and all he was doing was stalling for time. Cauchon would know that, too, but if it bought him a couple of days it was worth it.

"Really? To return to your home, secure the item and return here with my prize? A couple of days?"

"As you've pointed out, I'm an old man," Roux said. It sounded like a reasonable excuse, but the truth was the armor wasn't in his vault. It was hidden somewhere far safer.

"Fine. Two days," Cauchon said. "I will call you at your hotel. I will only dial the number once. If you don't answer, you know what happens."

The call ended.

Garin frowned. "Not enough time to narrow it down. I took a chance, tried a shortcut, assuming that he was in the vicinity of Carcassonne, and hoped that it would cut down the search time and give us a chance to pinpoint his location. No dice."

"So it was a waste of time?"

"I didn't say that. I managed to get a rough fix on him, maybe within a twenty-mile radius, but that was as much as I could manage."

"Where?" Roux asked.

Garin swung the laptop around so he could see the map of Southern France that filled the screen. He jabbed a finger at a circle that covered much of the border between France and Spain.

"The Pyrenees?" he said.

"I started off with the wrong assumption. It cost us. I'm sorry. I didn't think he'd have moved. Not now that we are here. I thought he'd want to be on top of us, having a laugh at our expense."

"Is there nothing else you can do to narrow it down?"

"I've got a lock on the number he used to dial in, but given his MO, he'll have ditched that SIM card already. One card, one call."

"So, our best hope still lies in him using the number I got from his thug Dugarry. And if Cauchon knows the man's been picked up by the police he could have destroyed that connection, too."

"The alternative is to give him what he wants," Garin said, putting it out there.

Roux didn't like it; he said nothing.

Garin didn't know about the piece of armor.

He had kept it secret all these years, one of the few he had kept from him, and wasn't sure that he was ready to share it. Deep down, he just didn't *trust* his companion.

"Come on, Roux. Be straight with me. He wanted something from you, I heard that much. Are you going to tell me what?"

"No," Roux said.

There was no point in trying to pretend that he didn't know what Garin was talking about. Better to simply refuse to answer.

"You don't think that telling me what he's after will help?"

"No. He's a collector. He wants something else to add to his hoard."

"And you're not going to tell me what?"

"Not yet," Roux said. "Think of it as a need-to-know basis. I'll tell you when I think you need to know."

The younger man shrugged but didn't try to argue. "However you want to play it. This is your show. I'm just along for the ride. We get Annja back safe. That's all that matters, right?"

Roux nodded. For now, at least, he had Garin where he wanted him. He just hoped that he'd be able to keep him there for the duration.

"So what now?"

"You stay here," Roux said. "If you manage to get a fix on him, call me."

"Are you heading back to your house?"

"Not yet. There's something I need to do first. I'll need to take your car after I've picked up a few things."

Garin reached inside the pocket of the jacket that he had dropped on the bed and threw the bunch of keys to him. Roux caught them in one hand and tested their weight. No matter how much he tried to think about alternatives, he knew that he had to do this. He had kept that piece of metal hidden from the eyes of the world for centuries, but maybe this was the reason for that. If he could trade it for Annja's life, then surely it was a small price to pay, no matter the potential long-term consequences.

What he didn't like was the fact that the ancient piece of metal was closer to Cauchon than he was just then.

"You might want to put some clothes on," he said to Garin, pocketing the keys.

"I'm hoping to surprise the maid."

"I'm sure you will." Roux shook his head and left the younger man to it.

37

"You?" Annja said when she was finally led into the room where the man was finishing his telephone conversation.

There was a passing resemblance between him and the woman who had brought her to this remote place—obviously brother and sister, even if he was fifteen, maybe twenty, years older.

"Expecting someone taller?" the man asked in English, laughing bleakly as she was pushed farther into the room.

He moved a control on the arm of his wheelchair to turn it so that he faced her.

Through the window she hadn't seen the chair, and thought he was merely sitting to make the call. But as she stepped through the door and saw the wheelchair, she recognized him as the man who'd saved her from the falling masonry with his warning cry. She'd assumed that he'd been there by coincidence, caught up in her near-disaster by chance, but he'd been there to watch.

His sister had been with him, pushing the wheelchair, which meant they had a third man in their team, someone to set the masonry in motion—assuming his sister hadn't set some sort of remote charge in the stone to blow it free of the wall.

"Indeed, me."

"I know you. You were there. At the church."

The man's face twisted into a cruel smile. "Indeed I was. And believe me, I wouldn't have missed it for the world. From where I was sitting, it looked as though you had a lucky escape. You might even say someone must have been watching over you."

"So, was it just meant to shake me up, or do you want me dead? Rock falls, ambushes on the country roads. Not exactly subtle."

"But effective. You are here now, after all. But to answer your first question, was it meant to shake you up? Not really. Do I want you dead? Again, not really. It's more what you represent, what makes you more than just Annja Creed, television personality. That aspect, I cannot deny, yes, indeed, I do want to see that destroyed. But before that, I want to humble an arrogant old man. You might know him. He calls himself Roux. We have unfinished business."

"The old man shouldn't give you any trouble," the blonde woman said.

"Never underestimate old men, Monique, particularly one as old as Roux. You live that long, you learn a trick or two about surviving, isn't that right, Miss Creed?"

"He's clever, if that's what you mean," Annja said, deliberately ignoring the gibe about Roux's age. She made a show of trying to free herself from the restraints again, giving them something else to think about. It earned her a cuff across the back of the head from Monique.

"I'm going to ask you to do me a favor, Miss Creed. Please don't take me for a fool. It's one thing I really cannot abide. We both know who Roux is, or perhaps I should say *what* he is. The same, I suspect, goes for his partner in crime, Garin Braden, though I have not confirmed the link as yet."

"Garin?" She hadn't meant to say his name aloud. Fatigue and the lingering drug-fugue still fogged her brain.

"Are you going to pretend that you don't know him, either? How precious. Perhaps you would like to see a few photographs to jog your memory. I'm sure we've got a few shots of the two of you together if that would help? You do make quite a handsome couple. I assume you are lovers. There is something very intimate about the way you interact. Would he cry for you? Put roses on your grave?"

Annja said nothing.

Anger built inside her. There was no release for it. She stared at the man in the chair, knowing that even if her hands were free, even if she had the comforting familiarity of the sword in them, she couldn't strike him down. His sister, on the other hand, yes, she could hurt her. They had a date with pain.

"What do you want with me?" Annja asked, barely masking the frustration in her voice.

"Patience. All good things come to she who waits."

"Humor me."

He inclined his head slightly to the right, as if weighing the notion, then straightened in the chair. "Why should I? Why should I make your time here any more tolerable than it needs to be? I will be honest with you, Miss Creed. I have no reason to take your life. For all I care you can walk away from here once I have cast out the demon that possesses you. That is all I care about. Alas, I have to admit that I cannot guarantee your survival. But you are young. You are strong. You might indeed live to see the ritual completed."

She couldn't possibly have heard him correctly.

Demon? Possession? She was dealing with a madman. That changed everything. "Demon? What are you talking about?"

"Am I talking to the creature inside your skin? Or is it still you? Demons wear many faces, many of them comely. They survive because of their beauty. They lure in the innocent and take refuge in their skin. We both know there is an entity hiding itself within you, and that it hides itself well, but we've seen the evidence with our own eyes, how when under threat you can conjure weapons out of thin air, how you are impervious to bullets. None of that is natural, Miss Creed, we both know that. But soon I will have the last item I need to be able to rid you of this thing, you have my word. The ritual will not be painless. I wish that it could be, but to liberate the flesh of its demon host is no easy thing. It will feel as though your soul is being flensed."

"You're insane," Annja said, unable to bite her tongue.

"No, Miss Creed, I am very, very sane. I have dedicated most of my adult life to the pursuit of this justice, and it will be mine. It ends here. And your friend Roux will help me by bringing the final item here to trade for your life. Alas, he does not understand that it is actually your mortal soul he is trading for, not the flesh."

Annja had no idea what the man was rambling on about; she focused on one thing he'd said: Roux was on his way.

She would bide her time.

There was no need to do anything to jeopardize her safety; as long as the madman didn't have his final gris-gris he couldn't carry out his ritual. And he wouldn't hurt her if he truly believed she was possessed of some all-powerful demon for fear of waking it.

She had time.

Under normal circumstances Roux's arrival would have meant Garin wasn't far behind, but after what had gone down at the chateau with Garin stealing from the old man, that meant these weren't normal circumstances. She had to assume they'd be on their own. If he turned up, passing for whatever version of white knight Garin Braden could muster, then that'd be a bonus.

"What do you want me to do with her?" Monique asked her brother.

"The basement, I think. Then turn the heat on down there so she won't freeze to death. Make sure she has food and drink, too. We aren't barbarians."

"How am I supposed to eat when I've got my hands tied behind my back?" Annja asked, doing her best to make it sound like a question, not a challenge. She didn't care about food. It was all about getting her hands free.

He looked at her, a slow smile spreading across his face. "Let me guess—we free your hands, your demon conjures that sword again and you attempt to cut us down where we stand? Is that the plan?"

Annja shrugged.

"Why not?" he said. "Once you're down there you can play with your sword to your heart's content. Your hands have been tied for hours. It'll be a miracle if you can manage to lift a teacup. I don't think we need to worry about your sword for a while."

"Are you sure?" Monique asked. "We don't know what the bitch is capable of."

"Unless you want to nursemaid her for the next two days, I don't see that we have any choice."

"We could just sedate her again," Monique said.

"That's always an option," he agreed. "I'll leave it to you. Just try not to break her."

Monique turned to Annja. "It looks like it's just the two

of us for a while." Before Annja could say anything Monique propelled her toward the door with a vicious shove.

As far as Annja was concerned, Roux couldn't get there soon enough.

38

Roux set the GPS on Garin's rented 4x4 even though he could have found his way without it.

It had been a long time since he had last made the journey—and from Roux's perspective a long time meant centuries, not months or years. The last time it had been on horseback.

There had been times—plenty of them—when he'd been glad that he had hidden the piece of history somewhere that Garin would never find it. As much as their relationship was one of love and hate, the one thing fundamentally lacking was trust between the two, and that had been damaged for centuries with Garin doing everything in his power to stop the old man from tracking down the scattered shards of Joan's blade. Go up against someone often enough and that feeling of distrust would never go away. Now, Roux contented himself with trusting Garin Braden about as far as he could throw him.

It had been years since he had last read Guillaume Manchon's ledger. The court scribe had been right there at the end, or for Garin and Roux, the beginning. There was enough in there to betray the both of them, but more, he feared, there was a clue that might lead the right reader to the one thing that Garin had so desperately craved: the chance to make sure the sword of Saint Joan was never whole again. Garin Braden would always do what was best for Garin Braden. It wasn't about them now, though. It was about Annja's life and what those documents—so filled with ancient superstition and religious dogma— might mean for her.

He could not allow the sword to be shattered again.

The light was dying as the weak winter sun sank low in the sky despite the fact it was only late afternoon. He had no thoughts of stopping for a break, not even for a second.

It would be fully dark before the jagged outline of the Pyrenees rose in the distance. All he could do was concentrate on the road ahead and hope that the time would pass as quickly as the distance. He tried to keep to a steady speed, but the narrow roads weren't plowed with the same regularity as the city streets he'd left behind. More than once he found himself closing in on a truck a little too quickly, risking a slide as he touched the brakes, or had to pull out into the path of another vehicle in an aggressive passing maneuver only to be greeted by the blaring horns and flashing lights of the oncoming traffic.

As he drove, the words of Bernard Gui played themselves over and over in his mind.

He had read them often enough over the years, understanding the notes he had made and believing them without an ounce of doubt.

There were plenty of others who followed after him who colored their writings with their beliefs, with the edicts of the church and the declarations that the world wanted to hear, not the independent thinking that challenged the world around them. Gui had been different.

He had written only the truth as he saw it. And that was why Guillaume Manchon's papers were of such importance. Coupled with Gui's writings they spoke of secrets never to be told.

Like it or not, he was in a race, the finish line: getting to the people who still carried the knowledge before Cauchon did.

Roux had trusted them in the past and had no reason to suspect that they would let him down now, but if his enemy was prepared to go to the extremes of murder to get what he wanted, then they were at risk. He didn't like putting innocent people at risk. It went against every vow he'd ever made and still held dear.

The journey might have taken only three hours on a good clear day, but when the latest snowfall began to transform into a proper storm he knew it was going to take a lot longer than that on these roads.

Trucks that had been racing down the road slowed alarmingly as the conditions deteriorated rapidly. Big wheels lost their grip, sliding in the compacted surface as the road began to climb. Roux slowed, but not as much as the others, fishtailing on the ice to save a few precious seconds with each corner.

The traffic began to thin over the course of the next twenty minutes, the driving conditions growing harsher until he could barely see a couple of feet beyond the hood for a mass of snow falling faster than the wipers could sluice it away.

He hadn't risked the fastest route, deliberately. He wasn't a risk taker in general, and the fastest route involved running hard around high peaks where there were no barriers on the side of the treacherous roads to stop him from plunging hundreds of feet down into any of the many snow-filled ravines. This way involved fewer deathly drops and border controls. The border police, such as they were in this region, were primarily interested in the heavily loaded trucks passing though in a steady stream, some bringing contraband over the border.

The main difference between him and them, though, was that he wasn't heading into Spain. He was aiming for the tiny principality of Andorra in the knowledge that it would have changed beyond all recognition in the intervening years since his last visit.

The country had a population of less than a hundred thousand, but attracted more than ten million tourists every year because, while time hadn't exactly stood still, life had moved at a very different pace to the rest of Europe and the skiing was good. As was always the case, many of the locals had embraced the opportunities tourism presented while others resented the presence of so many visitors. But then, plenty of people clung to the past as if they were afraid that it would be taken away from them and lost forever.

He crested the final hill and began the descent into Andorra, passing the yellow sign that marked the city limits for the parish of Canillo.

Even through the churning snow Roux could see so many changes, most notably the arrival of electricity, and streetlights that lit the place like Bastille Day.

Eventually the car crawled into the parish proper.

He pulled over to the side of the road, realizing just how tightly he'd been gripping the wheel. A car like that was built for rough travel, winding coastal roads, cross-country trips and inclement weather. Even so, the goat tracks he'd taken it down were pushing it to the extreme and his white knuckles were living proof of that.

Roux flexed his fingers to relieve the cramp, glad that his joints didn't feel quite as ancient as they really were.

He opened the door and clambered out of the 4x4. His boots crunched as he stepped onto the fresh snow.

The boots, along with the coat that he grabbed from the passenger seat, would help deal with the elements at least, but he was going to need more than that if he was going to come out of the next twenty-four hours alive.

It was only a short walk to the meeting place, but as the snow began to thicken it made walking difficult, the wind driving it into his face, into his mouth. He walked with his head down, knowing that the last thing he wanted to do was to be stranded in this place, and every hour the snow fell the greater the likelihood of that happening became.

He forced himself to walk faster, leaning into the wind.

After a couple of minutes he couldn't feel the cold on his face; he'd lost all feeling in his extremities. He didn't slow down. For almost fifteen minutes he trudged down the hillside, stopping every now and then to try to see if he could make anything out ahead of him beyond the vague glow of lights, but all he could see was white.

He turned back the way he had come to check on the car, but after a couple of hundred yards it disappeared from view, as did everything else.

He felt so incredibly isolated, like the last man alive in a savage frontier.

The wind picked up as he descended, making walking wet and uncomfortable and chilling him to the bone just as the snow getting into his lungs made it difficult to breathe. It didn't just sting his lungs; it felt as if Mother Nature had reached down his throat with her icy fingers and ripped them out with each breath.

He lifted his head, scanning the horizon, then continued down.

Up ahead, he saw the dark shape of a man.

For a moment he was sure that he was looking at a ghost.

39

"The car has stopped," Cauchon said, looking up from his laptop.

"The benefits of modern technology," Monique said. They had watched the blip of the GPS signal as it had moved across the map, moving closer and closer toward them.

"Indeed, but alas, we still don't know which one is in the car," Cauchon cautioned. "Braden somehow avoided arrest, despite our best efforts, though I must admit I enjoyed the fact that he switched the stolen Ferrari for a rental car. It's just unfortunate for him that our man at the airport was able to switch the tracker before he took delivery of the new vehicle. But then, anything he can think of, we've already considered it, haven't we, my dear?"

"We've had years to," she agreed. "They are working on instinct."

"And we've gathered enough evidence to know just how dangerous their instincts are," Cauchon agreed.

"Like taking candy from a particularly old and ugly baby," Monique said.

"Let's not get ahead of ourselves, Monique. Yes, Mr. Braden might have succumbed to your more obvious charms, but I wouldn't expect him to fall a second time."

"Perhaps not, but let's not give the old man too much respect, either. That's just as dangerous a mistake to make."

Cauchon raised an eyebrow.

He hadn't shared quite everything about Roux's lineage and longevity with his sister, and now wasn't the right time to start. She'd only think it was fairy tales, anyway. It would be better in the long run if she continued to believe this was all about money.

Money and revenge.

They were motivations she could understand.

She'd seen the footage of Annja going to town on those idiots Dugarry and Rameaux when they tried to bring her in, but even seeing Creed conjure her sword from out of thin air hadn't made her a believer. She had studied the footage, trying to disprove the illusion, looking for the trick in it. The only aspect of the attack that excited Monique was the proof that, despite all appearances, Annja Creed was dangerous. The thrill she took from that was undeniably disturbing, but as long as she harnessed that deep-seated need to give and receive pain she was a tool he could use in this game. She was wrong to underestimate the old man, but how could he tell her that?

"Roux is more dangerous than he looks, believe me."

"Once upon a time, maybe. But that was twenty years ago. It has been a long time since he was anything but an old man. And yes, I know this—" she pointed at his wheelchair "—is all his fault. And I know that he's the one that this—" this time she gestured all around them "—is all about. But let's not turn him into some sort of bogeyman."

"He wanted me dead, Monique. I will never forget that."

"And neither should you. But he's twenty years older now… He isn't the man he once was."

"Neither am I. Tell me, would it surprise you if I said that looking at him now, it's impossible to tell that he has aged a single day?"

There was no change in her expression.

He knew she heard him, but didn't—couldn't—believe him.

Why should she? It was impossible in the world she lived in. A world where demons didn't live hidden away beneath the skin suits of immortal men.

"He's still an old man. Just because he uses product for young-looking skin doesn't change anything," she said dismissively. "Once he takes possession of this relic you're so keen to get your hands on, I can take it from him. There is no need for us to bring him here. Why take the risk? Just kill him. An accident on one of those old Pyrenees roads in these conditions would hardly raise an eyebrow of suspicion. Why make things more difficult than they need to be?"

"I understand what you are saying, Monique, I do. But I want him here. I want him to see who has brought this all down on him. I want him to know that this is all his fault. Everything that is happening to the people he holds dear is because of him and his actions. I want to see him suffer. It is as simple as that. I haven't planned this for nearly half of my life just to be denied the opportunity to savor it."

"I get that," she said. "I do. So if you want to bring him here, then that's what we'll do. But I'll be honest. I'd feel a lot happier if I went out to get him, like I did with the girl. Roux wouldn't trust the man who has already stolen from him once this week to collect something so precious, would he? So Roux is in that car. The only question is whether he is alone or not."

"Go. But do not engage if he isn't alone. Understood? If Braden is there, you keep your distance. You may be a unique woman, my dear sweet sister, but I am not sure even you could take this pair side-by-side." He waved off her objections. "We wait until they have the treasure and then we make sure that only one of them comes up the track. That is how it is going to be."

He wasn't a fool; he'd made the mistake of trusting Roux once—and underestimating him. That wouldn't happen again. He'd surrounded the property with dozens of surveillance cameras. There wasn't a single angle of approach he couldn't monitor from his wheelchair.

He would be ready for whoever came up the mountainside.

In the meantime, Cauchon intended to savor every moment of the old man's struggle; this would be his test. His inquisition.

The small flashing light on the screen of the laptop had remained stationary for the past few minutes, confirming that the car was no longer moving.

His fingers moved deliberately across the keyboard, calling up information about the car's location. It had crossed the border into Andorra. He would never admit to the flutter of panic that had risen in his chest when he'd thought the old man had somehow found his location and was driving to his door. As much as he longed for the final confrontation, he just wasn't ready for it. Not face-to-face. He wasn't some blind idealist who couldn't see reality; he knew that he couldn't stop the man in a physical fight. He needed Monique for that. More importantly, he needed to complete his preparations. There was nothing that said the fight had to be fair.

The papers he needed were spread out on the table, the incantations prepared for when the armor and the woman were brought together again.

Did Roux have any concept of the power contained in those writings of Gui and Manchon?

A small pop-up opened on the screen.

The car had stopped in the parish of Canillo. As far as he could recall, there was nothing there to interest the old man unless he planned on taking the gondola to the ski resort of Grandvalira.

But those mountains were remote enough to provide a good hiding place.

Of course, there was nothing to say he was going to pick up the armor; that was just wishful thinking on his part. The old man had two days to do that. If not the armor, then what? Could he be meeting someone?

40

Annja's shoulders screamed with pain.

She stretched out her arm in the dim light of the basement, trying to keep the blood circulating. She clenched her teeth as she rolled her shoulders, working the muscles. The pain was deep-rooted, but not so desperate she needed to do something stupid. Not yet. She did a series of squats to work life back into her legs, and make sure she had good movement in them.

Her legs were going to be important in the coming fight, and she was in no doubt that it was coming.

At least she wasn't bound anymore. Monique had shoved her down the ramp into the basement no more than a second after she'd sliced through the plastic ties. As she lost her footing, Annja had thrown her hands out in front of her face, expecting stone steps where there were none and taking the brunt of the fall as she went down into the darkness. Monique hadn't turned on the light until she was sure Annja was lying at the bottom of the ramp, and for all her heightened reflexes and martial arts, a fall into darkness was indefensible.

The muscles and ligaments in her shoulders took the worst of the impact because she twisted as she fell, landing on her side rather than flat on her face. It wasn't a graceful maneuver, but it saved her a few broken bones.

The door slammed closed.

She heard the sound of a key turning in the lock, and that was it. She was alone.

Annja didn't move for a full minute, and even then it was just to bring herself into a sitting position, propped up against the whitewashed wall. She reached into the air before her face, seeing the raw wounds around her wrists and the slick blood on her skin even as she felt the blade in her hands. Despite its incredible heft, the blade felt weightless in her grip. Even so, it would take time to get a full range of movement back into her shoulders. And the only way she was going to do that was by forcing her body into action. Annja ran through an agonizing series of katas, keeping the blade low because of the confines the ceiling imposed.

When that door opened, she was going to use that one chance it presented.

Each kata felt like a thousand needles being pressed into her bones.

Annja embraced the pain.

The woman wouldn't know what hit her when she opened the door.

Her blood ran down her palms, staining the sword's hilt. She pushed herself harder, working her body as she moved around the room in a solo dance.

The basement was sparsely furnished, giving her plenty of room to maneuver. There was a desk with a gooseneck lamp illuminating papers that lay on its surface. The papers were weighted down by a piece of rock. A bookcase was crammed with books in a variety of languages, all of them seemingly obsessed with the occult and witchcraft.

After twenty minutes, breathing hard, sweat sheathing her skin, Annja stowed the sword in the otherwhere, willing it away, safe in the knowledge it was never out of reach.

At the far end of the basement there was a single bed covered with a plain blue comforter, which she took to mean she was going to spend a lot of time down here. Or at least that was their plan. Not that Annja was a stickler for plans, especially when they belonged to other people and involved her. She was more for improvising.

A door beside the bed led to a cramped bathroom that had clearly been specially equipped for wheelchair access.

Annja glanced back at the desk, realizing what was missing. A chair.

So this was Cauchon's working space.

Did it double as his bedroom?

Was he so devoted to his obsession that he spent his life down here, immersed in it, hiding away from the light? Annja couldn't imagine spending most of her life cooped up in a cell, hidden away from the light. There was nothing like being outside, breathing in that invigorating fresh air. Nothing came close to making her feel so alive.

She checked the small cabinet in the bathroom, aware that it was much lower on the wall to facilitate easy access from the wheelchair. There was a first-aid kit inside. She took it back to the bed, perched on its edge and checked the kit's contents.

There wasn't much to treat the abrasions and torn skin, but she found disinfectant and dressings to bandage the raw wounds. The bite of the antiseptic went way beyond a sting, but it had to be done.

She dressed and bound the wounds, then flexed her

fingers over and over until she could feel the life returning to them. After the workout she was in a much better
state both mentally and physically. She knew that she was
special. Her body reacted differently than other people's.
She should have been broken. Instead, she was in better
shape now than she had been two hours ago, despite the
blood. She brought her hands together, bracing the muscles in her shoulders, then pushed them apart. Standing,
she slowly worked her way through a dozen slow-motion
katas without the sword, testing the feel of her muscles
as the burn slowly subsided.

She closed her eyes, concentrating on the image of the
sword in her mind until her fingers closed around the hilt
again, and this time when she drew it out of the otherwhere the move was almost painless.

She still didn't fully understand the changes her body
had undergone over the past few years, that it was capable of superhuman strength, speed and agility. That was
something she took for granted now, but the recuperation
period? The recovery period? The fact that, like a broken
bone, it came back *stronger*? That was still new to her.

Annja looked at the door, knowing that if it had opened
outward rather than inward she could have broken through
it. But there was no point hurling herself at it, because the
frame would take a battering before it surrendered. Better
to just prepare herself for Monique's return. She found a
pair of nail scissors in the first-aid kit that would transform a punch into a lethal blow. They would do nicely.

She riffled through the desk drawers but failed to turn
up anything particularly interesting. Certainly not as interesting as the papers on the desk.

The pages were covered with a tight scrawl, barely
decipherable, and all of it seemed to relate to theories of
medieval witchcraft and the casting out of demons. She

turned over a couple of the papers, reading both the Latin and English notations. Lots of them referencing back to other material, documents held within the Holy See or lost forever, and to specific cases of demon possession and the symbiotic relationship between host and demon that granted the host immortality in exchange for the use of the body.

She was only just beginning to grasp the level of delusion Cauchon was living under.

How could he possibly think there were things like demons in this day and age of enlightenment?

Six hundred years ago this kind of thinking was dangerous.

Now it was so much worse.

She gathered the papers and retreated to the bed to read them properly, adjusting the lamp on the nightstand to better see them. They weren't the originals. Each of these pages were copies of ancient pages. Some of them, she realized quickly, had to have been the missing chapter of Bernard Gui's book, the pages stolen from the museum in Carcassonne. That helped another piece of the puzzle drop into place. Obviously Cauchon hadn't signed out the papers. Someone would have remembered the man in the wheelchair. So he'd used someone else to do it in his stead.

She struggled to decipher a lot of the notes, but the same three letters kept appearing.

JdA.

They sent a shiver up her spine.

Surely she was wrong in her thinking.

She had to be.

But no matter how much she tried to convince herself she was jumping to conclusions, Annja knew instinctively that those three letters could only represent one thing. Or, more accurately, one person: Joan of Arc.

Dread came with that realization—dread that this was so much more screwed up than any of them had ever considered and went beyond the insanity of demons into a very real and very chilling place right at the heart of their lives.

How much did Cauchon know?

Really?

Had he somehow stumbled on the truth?

How was that even possible? It wasn't like any of them ever broadcasted the nature of their relationship or the ties that bound them.

And yet...how could it be anything else?

Roux was right. There was no such thing as coincidence, meaningful or otherwise, and not when it came to something like this.

Looking at the pages again, she realized what the madman upstairs believed, as incredible and ridiculous as it was: that she was possessed by a demon, and that demon was the same entity that had possessed the Maid of Orleans all those centuries ago.

That changed everything.

She couldn't just wait for this to play out anymore.

41

"Roux?" The man's voice left his mouth as a shout, arriving as a whisper. Roux stared down the hill at him. The wind and snow whirled around his blurred outline, transforming him into something almost ethereal.

"That's my name," Roux replied, taking another stumbling step in the snow. He was cold to the bone, despite being dressed for the elements.

The man held a hand out to help him take the next few steps. Roux took it with gratitude, glad of the firm grip that both supported and stabilized him until they were looking at each other eye to eye.

"This way," the man said.

The shape of a building emerged through the snow with each stride.

The church of Sant Joan de Caselles.

The church was dedicated to a different Joan, predating the Maid's time, but Roux had *always* felt like it was the right place to hide the breastplate. He could never have explained why, what link it was he felt with the place, but he had always known he needed to hide her armor, and where. Now, though, for the first time in centuries, he was beginning to think he had made a mistake and that it should have been smelted down all those years ago.

They turned the helping hand into a handshake.

"Is it still safe?" he asked.

"But of course, my friend," the man said. "Still safe."

Roux did not know the guardian's name; that was part of the arrangement. He could never give up what he didn't know. The man, like his father and his father before him down the generations, had been entrusted with the safe-keeping of the armor.

He had spoken to this man only once before today, or maybe it had been his father. Sometimes it was difficult to be sure with normal lifespans feeling like mayfly-years to him. There had been a time when he had received a letter once a year, posted from anywhere in the world, that always said the same thing, one word: *safe*. Nothing more.

Roux followed him to the church.

A lamp burned on the altar, casting a dull glow at one of the windows. It looked bleak in this weather and yet it still remained a haven, a place of tranquility.

The door opened under the lightest pushes, swinging open. He'd been wrong, it wasn't a lantern. At least twenty votive candles burned on the altar table.

The man shook the snow from his long coat and hung it on a hook near the door.

Roux didn't remove his.

The man wore the vestments of a priest, as had been the case with the first keeper to whom Roux had first entrusted the armor.

"Are you sure it's safe?" Roux asked.

"I am in here every day. If it was ever to be disturbed, I would know about it, believe me."

Roux nodded. He knew that the man was right. He

had chosen the hiding place carefully. He struggled to remember the name of the first priest who had colluded with him and was now old bones somewhere in the ground outside the church.

"I never expected to meet you," the man said. "I never thought anyone would actually come. I know that my predecessor was never visited."

"Did he tell you what you are guarding?"

The man shook his head. "I don't think he knew, even at the end. He had his suspicions, as have we all, but all I know for sure is that the box is well preserved, and has not been opened for a hundred years or more."

"You've never wanted to know what was inside?"

The man shrugged. "At first, maybe, idle curiosity, but then it just became part of the many rites and rituals that are part of the job. You carry them out without question knowing that there has to be a meaning or a purpose to everything that you do. Beyond that, it doesn't really matter, only that you preserve the rite."

Roux wasn't sure he believed the man.

"Have you been told what's inside?" the man asked.

It took Roux a moment to realize that, of course, the man couldn't possibly know that he had been the one who had first placed the box in its hiding place. Obviously he assumed that Roux was a descendent of that man, just as the priest was a successor of the first caretaker.

"I know what's inside," he said, neither lying nor completely telling the truth.

The priest nodded, but didn't press further. The man understood the meaning of the word *discretion* and wouldn't push for more just because of curiosity. He walked the length of the church, a small chapel never meant to service more than the spiritual needs of a small mountainside community. Now, under the snow, the landscape bore the scars of the leisure industry.

The priest stopped at the lectern and placed a tight grip on it before he took a deep breath. Wood grated on stone as the structure began to move, slowly, inch by inch, until it was freed from whatever held it in place and then slid smoothly until the floor beneath it was completely exposed.

Roux watched as the younger man knelt and used a key to scrape away the accumulated grime from the joins in the stone; again, not rushing, carrying out the act with a significant amount of reverence. Like those before him, he had never considered the possibility that the box might leave his care.

Eventually a catch was revealed.

The man looked up at Roux.

"Would you like me to open it?"

Roux nodded.

He had waited a long time for this moment, and had thought to wait a lot longer, so he could wait a few seconds more.

A sudden fear rose in his chest: all it took was for one of the priests down the long line to have failed him and everything he was trying to do here was undone. What if someone opened the box only to find it empty? What then? What could he do to help Annja? How could he buy her life? Or would he be forced to walk away and leave her to her own fate? He'd told himself a thousand times over the past twenty-four hours she was big enough to take care of herself. But...

Stone ground against stone as a piece of the newly exposed floor began to shift from its resting place. Considering how many years it had set in place, it was a miracle of fishes and bread proportions that the ancient mechanism still worked, Roux thought irreverently.

The priest managed to get a grip under the exposed edge of stone and slowly a slab began to rise, even if just a couple of inches.

Dust trickled and fell into the space below, landing on the dark hidden shape.

And then it was free.

The priest lifted the slab and moved it to rest against the lectern.

He stood back, allowing Roux the opportunity to retrieve the box himself.

He had always remembered it being a little larger than it was. Funny how the memory played tricks on you, he thought. The box was less than two feet wide, only a little longer than that and less than a foot deep.

Roux peeled away the cloth that protected it while it was in its resting place, a piece of sacking that had at some point replaced the material he had carefully wrapped it in the first time it had been hidden away.

The box itself barely looked older than the day he had buried it. He had seen chests that had been buried for far less time and suffered far more from the effects of damp, mold and insect attack, but not this one. If there had been an escutcheon protecting the simple keyhole, that would have pitted and decayed, regardless, but the chest lacked protection or ornamentation.

Roux reached into his pocket and pulled out a bunch of keys he always carried with him.

Sometimes he thought that keeping things hidden would not be a bad thing. Too many of those items could prove dangerous in the wrong hands.

The breastplate itself wasn't something that was a danger to the world at large, a rallying point for fundamentalists looking to start another Holy Crusade, but in this case it could prove fatal for Annja if Cauchon didn't keep his word. Or if he did, and tried the rituals Manchon and Gui extolled. The box, like Pandora's, could never be closed once he'd let its secrets out. Was he really prepared to do that? Even for Annja?

"Do you want me to leave you?" the priest asked. "If you need some privacy…"

"It's fine," Roux said. "It's only fair that you should see what you have spent your life protecting, even if I can't tell you what it truly represents. With luck, it may yet be returned for your safekeeping."

The man nodded, but showed no sign of moving any closer.

Roux felt for the right key, knowing its shape within the bunch without needing to see it; some things were burned onto his soul.

He paused as he slipped the key into place in the ancient lock, and felt the tension as it engaged, hoping that the mechanism itself hadn't corroded or fused together. It wasn't a sophisticated lock; the lock had never been meant to protect it. That was why he had gone to such lengths to hide it.

The key moved smoothly, needing only the slightest amount of force to turn.

Roux held his breath as he lifted the lid, his heart skipping a beat as he saw the piece of red silk he had used to cover the armor, still undamaged, as pristine as if it had been placed there yesterday.

He folded back the edge of cloth, so fine in texture compared to the sacking that had provided the first layer of protection, to reveal the breastplate.

The metal beneath possessed a strange glow in the candlelight, as if there was a sheen to it that might not be seen in normal light, making it seem almost magical. It still bore the scars of battle, and the leather straps that had once held it to the young woman's body were all but dust. They were of no consequence. Beneath it lay the other smaller object, essential if he were to make his trap work. He closed his hand on it and palmed it away into his pocket without drawing any attention to it.

"It looks very precious," the priest said, his voice reverent.

A sudden breeze entered the church, threatening to extinguish the candles.

Roux had been concentrating so much on the box and its contents that he'd almost forgotten that he wasn't alone, taken aback by the simplicity of the statement.

"It is," said a voice from the doorway.

42

Annja felt the life returning to her muscles.

She closed her hand around the nail scissors, prepared to use them. Something so sharp, punched in hard, could do serious damage, even if she didn't take the woman unawares. She didn't need her sword to take care of a threat like Monique. Annja had dedicated a lot of her life to physical training, sparring, learning the fighting techniques of martial artists, hand-to-hand as well as with weapons. She was more than a match for anything the woman could throw at her. And on top of that she had the sword.

She worked her joints again, keeping the muscles supple.

In the distance, she heard the sound of a car engine starting.

She couldn't tell if it was the truck she'd arrived in or the car she'd seen in the open garage. It didn't matter. It had tilted the odds very much in her favor.

Everything in those notes and papers, a mixture of ancient ideas and a twisted imagination, had obviously convinced Cauchon to believe he could separate her from the spirit of Saint Joan that somehow possessed her. Yes, there was a bond between them. Roux had explained his belief after she'd grasped the shattered sword and made it whole again, but even then she had never quite swallowed all of the more mystical aspects of Roux's beliefs. Some things she knew were undeniably true. The sword for instance was proof of that. But there were still gaps that she constantly tried to bridge with concrete understanding without seeing the big picture because she was in the thick of things.

In Cauchon's mind, she was sure, there was no happy ending for her.

Annja rubbed her shoulder one last time before reaching out for the familiar grip. She drew it gently and smoothly from the otherwhere, the blade crystalizing into existence before her eyes. One moment there was nothing, a ghost of a sword, and then the weight solidified, taking on substance and form, its molecular structure attuned to hers, the vibrating in time with her flesh on a quantum level. She was the sword. The sword was Annja. Smiling, she let it return to its resting place.

She climbed the ramp to examine the door.

It was considerably sturdier than she had hoped; this was no re-formed fiber door that one good kick could break down. This was a solid, thick century-old cured timber that was intended to keep fire at bay. It was fitted with a heavy mortise lock. It was old—if not as old as the door itself, still not something that had been fitted purely because they intended on holding her hostage down here. Cauchon valued his privacy. It was as simple as that. Even in a place as remote as the farmhouse, he did not want to risk being disturbed by anyone while he devoted himself to his obsession. But then, who in their right mind would try to break into a house out here in the middle of nowhere?

How had her captor made the connection between Roux and Joan of Arc? How had he made the further connection to her and the sword? She had a lot of questions and very few answers. The only thing she knew for sure was that he had made the connections and he'd brought Garin into this, too. He was pulling their strings, all three of them, manipulating them. And that sounded like a very dangerous situation.

She had nothing with which to pick the lock, and nothing to get at the screws that held the hinges in place. It was as secure a prison as any that could be improvised.

She imagined being trapped down here with a raging fire. It wasn't something she really wanted to contemplate, but there was a smoke alarm and the sprinkler system set into the ceiling. Could she use them to her advantage? Even if she could scavenge everything she needed to start a fire, would anyone come if the alarm went off, or would she be left to burn?

There was no sign of matches or a cigarette lighter, nothing she could easily start a fire with, but there was plenty of material that would work as tinder, including the wadding of the comforter and mattress on the bed, which she could cut open with the nail scissors. There was nothing that would make a spark.

Frustrated, she stared at the paperweight on the desk and an idea began to take shape in her mind.

Annja made a nest out of a bundle of towels scavenged from the bathroom along with a mixture of fibers and paper gathered from around the basement. Her thought process was simple. Lots of different materials, all dry, all flammable. All she needed was one of them to hold the flame if she got something to ignite. Logically, the comforter stuffing and the mattress fibers were probably flame retardant, but she wasn't going to discount them because of logic. If there was a chance, even a slim one, that they might burn, she was happy to risk it.

It was all going to come down to the spark.

The exercise had done her good.

Her shoulders were moving with something approaching freedom, even if she could still feel a lingering tightness. She reached out, the sword singing in her hand as she brought it back again. She rested the point in the nest of tinder and held the blade upright before striking it with the paperweight.

Nothing.

She tried again.

This time a spark flew when the two materials collided.

It wasn't enough to start anything smoldering.

She hit harder and the blade vibrated with the impact, sending something akin to an electric shock surging up the length of her arm. She felt it sear the already strained and tender shoulder joint.

Again.

This time a shower of sparks ran down the blade into the wadding, paper and feathers and the first wisp of smoke began to rise.

Annja removed the sword from the bed where the embryonic fire was just beginning to take hold. She leaned it against the ramp before going down on her knees and lowering her face to the wisps of black smoke curling up from the towels.

She blew softly across the surface, drawing the fire to life as it finally caught hold.

All she could do now was pray that she set the alarm off without the whole place being engulfed in flame.

Because if there was one thing in her life that gave her nightmares, it was fire.

43

"Garin."

"Disappointed?"

Garin closed the heavy church door behind him.

The air had been enveloped in a draft that felt so much colder than when Roux had come inside only a short while before.

"What are you doing here?"

"Helping."

"When did you become so altruistic? Or," Roux said, drawing out the insult, "did you come here to steal this artifact for yourself? Maybe you have a buyer lined up?"

"Don't be absurd."

"Absurd? You can just walk away from all of this. What does it matter to you what happens to Annja?"

"Now you're just being insulting, Roux, but I'll forgive you this once because you are upset."

The priest gave Roux the briefest of glances, obviously made uncomfortable by the exchange. Roux placed a hand on his shoulder.

"There is nothing to be concerned about. This is

Garin," and a second later, deliberately insulting, he added, "My apprentice."

"Once upon a time, maybe. Look, Roux, we both know just how stubborn you can be," Garin said, walking toward the front of the church.

Roux replaced the silk over the breastplate and closed the lid of the box before Garin could catch a glimpse of what was inside. He would recognize it, and that would just lead to questions Roux had no intention of answering. Instead, he asked one of his own. "How did you know where I was?"

"I didn't know. I just tracked your phone. You should be used to the modern world by now, *sir*. It isn't the way it was even a couple of years ago. And I know, old dog, new tricks, but you really ought to embrace the future instead of burying your head in the past. For a while I thought you were on a suicide mission actually, heading straight to Cauchon to fulfill some romantic idea of a showdown. I figured he'd told you where to come and you thought you were being all noble. This is a nice surprise."

"Disappointed?" Roux asked, throwing Garin's word back at him.

"Well, let's just say I didn't like the idea of not getting to put things right between us and leave it at that."

"So you just hopped in a car and came after me."

"So I just hopped in a car and came after you. Seemed like a smart idea, and now it looks like I got here just in time. Believe me, there's no way we're getting back down the mountains in this weather." He shook his head. "Not tonight."

Roux didn't need to check outside to know he was right; the snowfall had been intensifying during the journey here, and the roads were barely passable before he'd pulled over to walk the remainder of the distance. Even the 4x4 would struggle, and in the dark, it'd be flirting with the reaper if not outright suicide.

"But lucky for you, I came prepared. Snow chains for the wheels."

"Sounds like you've thought of everything."

"Not everything," Garin said. "But hopefully you've got the rest of that covered, boss."

Roux saw that his gaze was resting on the box that he had been in the process of wrapping.

"The longer we stay in here, the less chance we've got of getting out of the village, with or without snow chains," Roux said. He thanked the priest and told him that he would return, but knew in his heart of hearts this was no longer a safe hiding place, not now that Garin knew about it. He wouldn't be coming back here in this lifetime, no matter how many years remained in it.

"Give me your keys," he said, holding out his hand to Garin.

He turned to the priest and passed the keys to him. "We'll pick this up when we return. Feel free to use it in the meantime."

"Roux! It's a Porsche! You can't just go giving away a luxury car!"

"I'm not, you are. Now be gracious."

"But I was just getting to like her."

"You'll like another one tomorrow," Roux assured him. "Something bigger, flashier and more expensive."

Garin nodded. "And with more under the hood." He grinned, and for a moment it would have been easy to think he was talking about a woman, not a lump of metal.

The priest was lost for words.

It was unlikely the poorly paid priest would be able to afford to run a car like that in a place like this. He told the man, "Feel free to sell it. I won't be offended. Use the money for something good."

"I will," the man promised. "I will. Absolutely. Yes."

His thanks were still ringing in Roux's ears when they stepped outside, leaving him to clear up.

"Where are we heading?" Garin asked.

"No idea," Roux said. "But I assume you are about to tell me. After all, you didn't follow me here only to drive all the way back to Carcassonne. That means you've worked it out. So, where is he hiding?"

"You're getting better at this, old man," Garin said.

"So?"

"Cauchon made his first mistake. He tried to call his thugs in Carcassonne just after you left. The phone wasn't connected to the network for long, obviously, with them being tied up with the local law. He didn't leave a message. The good news is that it was long enough to narrow his position down to within a five-mile radius."

"Is he still here in the Pyrenees?"

"He sure is. We get ourselves into that circle and wait for him to contact us. With a little luck he'll still think that we are miles away, up at the chateau even. That should give us time to hit him where it hurts."

It sounded like the closest thing they'd had to a plan in a while.

Roux wanted to get to Annja without handing over the box. Nothing good could come of losing possession of Joan's breastplate to the man, even if Roux didn't believe in hoodoo or witchcraft or any other nonsense. Playing his game, going along with his delusion, was dangerous.

The wind dropped.

The snow still fell in an impenetrable sheet. There was no visibility. Roux walked on memory, edging a few steps at a time, looking down at his feet, clutching the box and its sackcloth to his chest like a shield. Garin's footsteps were still visible in the thick blanket of snow, but they were fading fast, being filled in like those left by Roux and the priest only half an hour earlier, long gone now.

Somehow he managed to lead them to the 4x4, opening the backseat for the box, while Garin brushed away the fresh accumulation of snow on the windshield before he climbed in.

"Well, are you going to tell me what's in the box?" Garin asked when they were both inside.

"You *still* don't need to know," Roux said, staring straight ahead as the wipers struggled to keep pace with the snowflakes settling on the windshield.

"Are you sure about that?" Garin asked.

"For now, yes."

44

The towels smoldered rather than burned.

That was good. Better than burning herself alive. It didn't take long for Annja to get the smoke to rise, as if she was sending good old-fashioned smoke signals to the ceiling detector. It didn't need flames to go off. She offered another steady encouraging breath to try to muster flame from the smoldering cloth, feeling the heat starting to grow. She caught a lungful of acrid smoke and had to turn away for a moment, choking as it burned her lungs. She covered her mouth with her hand before she turned back in time to see a single tongue of flame reach a few inches into the air, surrounded by a belch of smoke.

It was a start.

She got to her feet and took a couple of steps back, still coughing.

The room filled quickly with thick tendrils of smoke, but then the near-silence was replaced not by the sound of an alarm or the spray of sprinklers bursting into life, but by the incessant hum of an extractor fan venting the smoke out of the small room.

"Oh, no you don't," Annja rumbled. Some cheap piece of household gadgetry wasn't going to stop her getting out of there.

She wafted the flames, willing the fire to really take hold as the room started to fill with smoke despite the extractor's best efforts. And then the smoke alarm sounded, bursting into shrill life.

Annja covered her ears just as the sprinklers came on.

She moved toward the bathroom door, realizing the one major flaw with her brilliant plan—she wasn't going to survive too long out in the blizzard if she was dripping wet. Hyperthermia would take her out in a matter of hours. It was too late for second thoughts with constant water raining down on her head.

She needed to be quick about it. The door could open at any moment.

She grabbed the sword and slid the weapon back into the otherwhere.

Her thoughts were focused on escape, not killing. Primary objective: get outside. Secondary objective: find someplace to hide out until she was ready, or Roux arrived, whichever came first. As she gave up her grip on the sword, she heard the sound of a key in the lock.

Annja shouldn't have been surprised to see Monique standing in the doorway, hypodermic syringe in her right hand. She'd assumed the car meant the woman had gone, but of course it must have been customized for Cauchon.

It changed things, but only slightly. It just meant it would be harder not to kill the woman because she wouldn't back down.

Annja snatched up the remnants of the comforter from the bed, some of its stuffing spilling out as she started to sprint up the ramp. Annja intended to use it as a shield, much like a gladiator might have used a net. That needle wasn't going in her arm again.

She didn't give Monique the chance to back out of the room; instead, she was on her in a second, knowing this was her one and only chance to escape—hopefully bloodlessly. She wasn't about to waste it. Monique hadn't been prepared for the ferocity of the attack. Too late, she tried to backtrack up the ramp and simultaneously block Annja's path. Caught between the two maneuvers, the woman was trapped in an instant of indecision that cost her.

Badly.

The shredded comforter was too bulky to allow Monique to jab the needle through it and into Annja's skin. There was nowhere for it to go as Annja's momentum knocked the woman off her feet.

Annja didn't give Monique any time to fight back; she landed on her hard, driving her knee into the woman's gut in a solid blow she couldn't fend off. Annja drove her elbow into the woman's face, feeling the crunch of bone and blood as she rolled away. She was up on her feet in a heartbeat and running, not looking back. She had to keep moving. Annja guessed only Monique and Cauchon lived in the farmhouse. Others, however, could be there. But for now she focused on the fact that the wheelchair-bound Cauchon was gone.

She knew that in her place Garin would have acted differently. Leave no enemy behind was a mantra he seemed to live by. It would have made sense to go back and finish the woman, or even just stick her with her own damned needle and take her out of the fight for a few hours, but that wasn't Annja's style.

She pulled the door closed behind her, turning the key that was still in the lock.

Sometimes old-fashioned mechanics were every bit as effective as fancy drugs and cruel violence.

The fire alarm was still shrieking in the basement, and the sprinklers would have the fire under control in a few moments. Monique wasn't going to drown down there, even if the fire department couldn't make it up the mountain tonight. The same almost certainly went for any calls for the police. With the storm of the century building, the emergency services would be more concerned about accidents and keeping the roads open than a little petty crime in some remote farmhouse.

Annja was on her own.

She didn't even contemplate Roux's white knight act.

One look outside the window killed that particular fairy tale stone dead.

She scoured the place for keys. She could hear the woman in the basement pounding against the door, venting her frustration. All of the factors that had made it difficult for Annja to break through that ancient door still held for Monique. She was going nowhere. But without keys, neither was Annja.

There was a box beside the door, but there were no car keys on the bunch that hung inside it; that would have been too easy.

She headed straight for the front door, hit by the incredible cold against her soaked skin as she stepped out. The truck was still parked by the house, but fresh tracks alongside it showed where the other vehicle—Cauchon's car—had set off down the mountainside. The back of the truck was still open. She closed it.

The keys were in the ignition.

It was a trusting neighborhood, but then again it was very isolated.

She didn't waste any time clearing the windshield, despite the thick layer of snow that had built up there. She simply pushed aside a huge armful and relied on the wipers to do the rest.

Even so, the wipers labored under the strain, but not the engine. That fired first time. Annja threw the truck into gear. The wheels turned slowly through the snow, crunching over the fresh fall as she pulled away gently. She picked a path carefully, not wanting to risk getting caught in a deep drift. She checked the side mirrors, but the reflection was filled with snow. She'd just have to drive blind and trust that no one was crazy enough to follow her down the mountain road.

The tracks from Cauchon's car were still clear ahead of her, giving Annja something to follow. She still needed to control her speed, easing the brake whenever she needed to, but mainly trying to slow by inertia rather than risk sliding on the sheet of ice buried below the snow. She did her best to keep to the center of the road.

To her right, the mountainside fell away steeply, though a person would not have been able to tell without actually focusing on the landscape to notice where one started and the other began, which made a mockery of perspective. The drop, she guessed, was both steep and long. On a clear day no doubt she'd have been able to see for miles. Tonight, Annja was focusing purely on the few feet in front of the truck's hood and no farther.

She drove on into the blizzard, visibility down to mere inches, and even then all she saw was a blanket of snow.

THE ENGINE COMPLAINED as she shifted through the gears, using the engine to try to slow the vehicle as the descent began in earnest. It had little effect. She could feel the truck's weight and gravity's helping hand as the vehicle picked up speed as the gradient increased, caught up in its spell.

She saw the bend too late and had to fight with the wheel to try to get it around while the truck sought to take flight.

The wheels caught in the snow. The truck slid sideways, hitting a bank of snow and beginning to tip, as if trying to stand on two wheels. Annja leaned against the door, as if her weight alone could bring it back onto four wheels.

It was a pointless move.

Her action didn't affect anything apart from make it more difficult for her to steer into the slide. The truck continued to slide in the opposite direction. The back end slewing toward the precipice as one wheel caught on the edge, tantalizingly churning snow and the dirt beneath it for a heart-stopping second until the tread caught and pulled the truck back onto the road. Annja fought every instinct to yank the wheel hard, willing the huge vehicle to stay under her tenuous control, but the momentum was too strong to fight.

She wasn't an idiot. It was only going to be a matter of time before she hit a turn the truck couldn't handle and it went over the edge.

She had to make sure that she got out of it before that happened.

Annja clutched the wheel, knuckles white, willing the wheels to get some real traction on the road beneath her. The snow swirled and churned and spun, turning the air absolutely white, blinding, as she released the seat belt.

The next bend could be her last chance.

With one hand she gripped the wheel, with the other she groped for the door handle, throwing it open. As ice cold air flooded the cab, she launched herself out of the truck. She had no means to prepare for her landing. She could have hit an outcrop or a dry stone wall just as easily as she could have slammed into a tree or any other part of the landscape that wasn't a snowdrift to cushion her fall.

Suddenly, she was in the air and then she hit the road, hard, rolling away. The truck hit a rock, the back end lifting off the ground before it tipped back onto two wheels again, and slewed, twisting well beyond the balancing point, wheels spinning freely in midair.

Annja was on her hands and knees, looking up in time to see the truck slide over the edge in slow motion, and then it was gone.

She heard rather than saw it roll, each horrible impact echoing through the mountain range, before the explosion tore through the eerie stillness and sent a tongue of flame into the sky.

The sound of the falling truck almost masked the oncoming vehicle that was climbing back up the track.

She pressed herself low in the snow, trying to take cover, sure that it wasn't the cavalry riding up the hill to rescue the damsel in distress.

She was right.

In the dull glow of the dashboard as the vehicle crawled past, Annja caught a glimpse of the gaunt reflection of Cauchon, hunched over the wheel seemingly oblivious to the accident that had taken place only minutes before.

He was not alone.

She counted three other men in the vehicle with him.

He couldn't have *not* seen it. There was no way he could have missed the shaft of flame. He just didn't care. That said something about his psychopathy right there.

Who were the men who were with him?

She didn't have time to waste thinking about that.

Not with the extreme cold, the lack of protection from

it and the wet clothes already beginning to freeze to her skin.

She needed to move, to keep up her body heat. But even then there was a limit to what she could withstand before the elements won. Being lost, alone in the heights of who only knew where, she didn't exactly have the luxury of making any mistakes. The problem was, there was nothing, no sign of civilization, no promise of warmth or salvation, as far as the eye could see. Although that didn't mean much, given the storm, as she could barely see beyond her outstretched hand.

Think, Annja urged herself. *Use your brain. You are not helpless. You're not a victim. Don't act like one.*

She could run, but where?

She could stand on the roadside and trust that Roux was coming, even if he knew he was heading into a trap, but when would he arrive?

She could go in search of a phone, get a message to Garin. That was an option, too.

Whichever one she decided on, she needed to start walking if she was going to get off the mountain before the cold killed her. That much she knew. She could already feel death creeping into her bones.

45

Even driving through conditions as bad as this gave Cauchon a sense of freedom.

The car offered him a level of control he never would have imagined possible even a few years ago, and *almost* allowed him to forget about his lifeless legs. It was miraculous to think that while he couldn't use them to hold his own weight he could still drive. Maybe one day in the future they'd perfect some sort of stem cell surgery that could rebuild his legs, like those of a bionic man. Until then he'd settle for little miracles like this and focus on revenge, which was far more effective for pushing him on than hope ever had been.

Truthfully, he didn't care if he ever walked again; that had been a hard realization to come to, but once he'd made his peace with it, it made living in the chair so much easier.

Monique had insisted that he be the one to make the trip down the mountainside to pick up the men who were going to keep the house secure. It made sense. Should Roux arrive at the farmhouse when he was alone, he wouldn't have been able to fight him off. This close to the endgame, Cauchon was taking no chances. He knew just how dangerous Roux and his friend Garin were, hence bringing in extra muscle. His original plan had been for the two men he'd hired to bring Annja Creed in from Carcassonne to serve as guards, but he hadn't been able to make contact in the past twenty-four hours. He had to assume that they had been arrested by the police. They couldn't reveal who he was, but it meant that he needed to burn that number, too. He couldn't risk that they'd somehow lead back to him.

It was all about planning for the worst now. The extra muscle shouldn't be necessary, but better to have it, and have the grunts sitting around wondering why they were there, than not have them and need them.

The price was having to pick them up from the village during a major storm.

Cauchon didn't care about the snow or the storm or anything that fell outside of the sphere of his single-minded purpose. His entire universe funneled down to one thing: Roux. Nothing else mattered.

Even with satellite navigation, the muscle would never have found the farmhouse in this weather.

Monique was more than capable of handling Annja Creed; he was absolutely sure of that. There was nothing his sister couldn't do if she put her mind to it, and nothing another shot of tranquilizers couldn't handle if worse came to worst.

Even so, it frustrated him that he had to rely on his sister so much. She, conversely, relished it. Monique would rather have kept Annja sedated for the entire time they held her. There was sense to that, of course. A passive hostage wasn't likely to cause trouble. But he couldn't help thinking that Monique was more interested in tormenting the woman than keeping her pliable. Annja Creed was the innocent in all this, only the vessel that something else had taken possession of.

The tracker on Roux's 4x4 had remained stationary for a long time before Cauchon left the farmhouse, leading him to believe that Roux was in place, retrieving the armor. Not that he was naive enough to think that he could trust the old man to keep his word. He would be scheming hard, planning a scheme to renege on his promise. That was his nature. Even if he was in place, the weather almost certainly meant he wouldn't be able to move out even if he could retrieve the armor before morning. That didn't matter to Cauchon. He knew where the man was. That was the important thing.

Once he was below the line of the heaviest snow, he joined a wider road where a snowplow had cleared away enough of the fresh fall to allow two cars to pass side by side in comfort. He pulled over.

It was time to make the call.

He'd been looking forward to this for a while. He wanted to enjoy it, not be worried about concentrating on the road and icy conditions.

"Do you have it?" he asked when the other man answered.

"Not yet."

Cauchon thought about calling him a liar, just to rattle Roux, strip him of a little more arrogance. Cauchon could have told the old man precisely where he was. That would have really thrown the old man, but he thought better of showing his hand. Right now he had an advantage, as slight as it was, and he did not want to relinquish it too easily.

"When, then?"

"First light," Roux said.

That sounded reasonable enough. Almost like it could be the truth.

And it wouldn't hurt if Roux was forced to spend an uncomfortable night in the car instead of some plush hotel.

The connection wasn't good. The line kept cracking and dropping out as the poor weather interfered with the signal.

Cauchon looked at his watch. How long should he give the man to retrieve the armor? Less than he'd initially offered obviously, to keep the man on his toes, keep him thinking that he was on shifting sands.

"You've got until 6:00 p.m. tomorrow to get to Pau. The conditions should be good enough for you to be able to take that plane of yours, but if they deteriorate any further you'll just have to put your foot down and pray that 4x4 of yours doesn't get you killed."

"But…" Roux started to interrupt him.

Cauchon silenced him. He was not going to let him get a word in. "I will call you with instructions." He ended the call and slipped the phone back into his pocket. It was imperative that he stayed in charge of the situation. He was so close to getting what he wanted.

It was going to be on his terms from now on.

He put the car back into gear and set off.

Roux was going to pay the price for what he had done.

46

"Pau," Roux said as he slipped the phone back into his pocket. "He'll give us directions once we get there."

"So the mountain goes to Muhammad," Garin said.

"Or the spider draws us into its web."

"The difference being we've got an advantage. We pretty much know where the spider is. It doesn't know we know. Now it's just about playing his game. Part of me wants to head straight to the airport at Pau. He's probably planning on sending that woman out to meet you. I wouldn't mind meeting her again. We've got some unfinished business."

"Don't worry, I'm sure you'll get your chance soon enough. He trusts her to do his dirty work. If you trust someone that much, you want to keep them close. With Cauchon's two thugs sitting in cells in Carcassonne, out of contact, we know he'll fall back on her soon enough. If he hasn't already."

"Good. I'm going to enjoy our second date far more than she does," Garin promised. "So, come on, you've obviously got an idea of what's going on here, certainly more than you're letting on. Time to 'fess up, old man. What has he got against Annja? Or me for that matter."

"You? Nothing. Annja, I'm not so sure about. But I think his problem is with me, and you are the collateral damage. He's just using people to get what he wants."

"Just like I do, you mean?"

"I didn't say that," Roux protested, though in truth he couldn't deny the similarity. It had been the first thought that had crossed his mind.

"You didn't have to," Garin replied.

His phone rang almost as soon as he had finished speaking. He checked the caller ID before answering.

"What have you got for me?" he asked, then listened with the phone pressed to his ear, nodding.

He started the engine but made no effort to pull away.

Whatever the voice on the other end had to say was worth listening to.

"I think we just hit pay dirt," Garin said. "I told you my guy was monitoring that phone number? It seems Cauchon just made his second mistake. He used the same number to call you that he used for his heavies in Carcassonne. We've got a fix on the point where the call was made."

"Then we've got him." Roux smiled. He could barely believe their luck. "Time to make a surprise visit."

"Oh yes, and you're going to appreciate this. He hasn't turned the phone off. We're still picking up a signal. He's on the move at the moment, but at least we should be able to keep track of him. Assuming he heads home, we should be able to turn up on his doorstep before daylight."

47

It was daylight when Annja woke with a start.

She looked around, disorientated, lost. For a moment she couldn't get a fix on her surroundings. They didn't fit with what she remembered. She was lying on a real bed with a comforter thrown over her, still dressed. What she remembered was stumbling down the mountainside, struggling to stay on her feet in the ice and snow, stumbling every few feet, each step sapping another ounce of strength from her body. Even with her superhuman reserves of strength, she couldn't go on forever. Close. But when it came right down to it, not close enough when that kind of frozen death was on the line.

All she could remember was the absolute bone-chilling cold. And then all she had wanted was to sleep. It didn't matter how hard she drove herself, how determined she was to keep going. As her knees buckled and her thoughts became jumbled and confused, all that remained was the promise of warmth if she just lay down. And that was when she'd drawn the sword, wanting it there with her, needing it.

But now?

Nothing made sense.

The air was warm.

She tried to move, noticing the great sword was on the bed beside her, and she still had one hand gripping it tightly.

"Ah, so you're back in the land of the living," a man's voice said. "I must admit, I was rather worried for a while that you wouldn't make it."

Annja tried to say something as she rolled over, but her lips were numb, her throat raw. Every muscle in her body ached. She saw an elderly man edging closer to the bed, a mug of something hot in hand. He offered it to her as she sat up.

The steam warmed her skin as she held it close to her face.

"When I saw your truck go over the side I headed out, hoping there'd be someone left to help. It was a mess. And, I'm delighted to say, I got lucky," he said, settling back into his chair. "But nowhere near as lucky as you were. You wouldn't have made it through the night out there. Even if the cold didn't get you, I've known people to suffocate, getting caught in snowfalls on this mountain. It's not a safe place to venture out on foot, especially when you're not properly equipped. I couldn't get you to a doctor. Not tonight. So I made a judgment call to bring you here and try to warm you up."

"I don't know how to thank you," she said quietly, knowing that simple words would always feel inadequate.

"No need to. I only did what any decent person would have done. However, I must admit I'm rather impressed with your makeshift walking stick. That couldn't have been easy to carry. Even when you were dead on your feet you simply wouldn't let go of it."

Annja smiled ruefully.

"I can only imagine how precious it must be for you to have risked your life to salvage it from the wreckage," he said, peering over his own mug.

Annja nodded. "It's an old family heirloom," she lied. The best lies were always close to the truth. This was as honest as she could be and still be believable. The man nodded as if that made perfect sense, then took a sip of his drink. Maybe he believed her, maybe he didn't.

"Not that it's my business what you were doing on the mountain, but there's only one house that track leads up to," he said.

"You know them?"

"Not really. I've seen them drive up and down but they don't get many visitors, and they keep to themselves. The wife has waved a couple of times when she's driven past, but that's about it."

"Sister," she corrected him, but it only caused more confusion on his face. "They are brother and sister."

"Ah, I had no idea. Like I said, they keep to themselves. Anyway, I can give you a lift the rest of the way down into the village when you feel up to it, as long as the road isn't too bad."

"Do you have a phone I could borrow? I need to let someone know I'm okay."

"Sorry."

"No phone?"

"No phone, no television, no electricity," he said.

She glanced around the room and realized that it was an oil lamp at the side of the bed, the glass chimney stained with smoke.

"Do you live here alone?" She was asking questions just to save any uncomfortable silence. It was hard to understand why anyone would choose to live like this. But

part of the rationale behind the questions was that maybe
if she understood why he did, she could better understand
Cauchon's motivations behind choosing such an isolated
place to make his home.

"I only live here for a few months of the year. I come
here to get away from the world."

"You don't think it's a little…bleak?"

"Bleak?" He laughed. His smile was kind. "My dear,
this is one of the most beautiful places in the world. This
is the kind of place you don't want to spoil by having to
share it."

She wanted to ask how he filled up his time here, but
the edge of sadness in his voice stopped her. Perhaps not
so long ago there had been a Mrs. Good Samaritan and
now he was hiding from the world that no longer had
her in it?

She needed to get in touch with Roux, at the very least
to warn him he was walking into a trap.

But even warned, she wasn't sure that would stop him.

She finished the coffee and put the mug on the nightstand, then rose unsteadily to her feet. She left the sword
on the bed.

"How are you feeling?" the man asked, though he made
no attempt to get up to support her. Annja stretched her
joints, feeling her muscles complain from the exertions of
the previous night. He made no comment about the makeshift bandages around her wrists. She realized how it had
to have looked to him. Did he think she'd escaped from
some distant asylum by brandishing an ancient broadsword?

"I'm fine," she assured him. "Don't worry. I'm pretty
resilient."

"I'm sure you are, but believe me, the cold can take a
lot out of you."

"I've been in worse," she said. He raised an eyebrow, but didn't ask where she might have been that could have been colder than midnight in the midst of a blizzard on a lonely mountaintop.

"I'm sure you have," he offered instead. "I'll venture outside to see how bad it is."

And with that, she realized the elderly man had probably been in that chair all night, watching over her.

Annja saw her boots resting beside a fireplace where the remnants of burned-down coal remained in the hearth, still casting its heat into the room.

She'd definitely had a lucky escape.

"How far is the village?"

"A couple of miles. Too far to walk in this weather, if that was what you were thinking. Especially if you're trying to carry that thing."

"Oh, the sword? That's no burden at all. There's a trick to it."

"Well, then, at least let me pretend to be a good host and offer you some breakfast before we argue about you going outside again."

She smiled, and didn't object. To borrow a favorite line of one of the nuns at the orphanage, her stomach felt as if her throat had been cut. She couldn't remember the last time she'd eaten. It felt like forever since Philippe had been moaning about food. Toast and another mug of coffee sounded too good to be true.

"You really don't have to, but I'm starving so I won't say no," she said, reaching down for her boots. They'd dried out in front of the fire.

"When we're in the village we can call mountain rescue about your car, but whatever was in there is gone now. Those things burn pretty hot." The way he said it made Annja realize it wasn't the first time he'd seen a car go over the edge. Again, she didn't want to ask. "You are a very lucky young lady."

"I know," she said, not for the first time feeling that she was living a charmed life.

48

Roux and Garin drove through the night, taking turns at the wheel to allow the other man the chance to take a break from the hypnotic rhythm of the windshield wipers and the glare of oncoming headlights.

The roads were fairly clear once they had dropped below the permanent snow line, even the fresh snow turning to slush when it met the gritted asphalt.

Roux was able to rest his eyes when Garin was at the wheel, but managed no more than that.

Garin on the other hand seemed to slip into a deep sleep without any difficulty. Obviously he didn't have a care in the world.

Roux saw several cars abandoned at the side of the road while they drove through areas in the clutches of heavier snow, high-performance cars that simply couldn't perform in the stormy conditions.

Garin was convinced they'd have no trouble tracking Cauchon to his lair. That the technology he was using was like a noose he'd put around his neck and was drawing tighter and tighter by the hour. During the drive, Garin took two updates from his contact, one detailing Cauchon's simple journey down into the village, and included a pause of no more than a couple of minutes, before returning back the way he had come. Messages had then started to come through while Garin slept. Roux hadn't woken him. When he was sleeping Roux felt that he could almost pretend that he wasn't there.

Beside him, Garin stretched, working the kinks out of his muscles. "My turn?" he asked.

Roux had kept the radio on low so that any road traffic warnings would be heard. The drone of a late-night radio host was the same in whatever language it was spoken, the soft understated tones that were barely enough to keep the listener awake, but smooth enough to wash the world away.

"Next service station," Roux said. "No point pulling over when the roads are like this."

Garin looked at his phone. "You should have woken me," he said without glancing up from the screen. The backlight haunted his face. "These might have been important."

"I'm not your social secretary," Roux said. "Are they?"

"Important, yes. Urgent, no."

"Then there's no harm done."

"My guy has not only managed to pinpoint the signal, he's even nailed it down to the house in question, which means we know where he's holding Annja."

"Directions?"

"Better than that. Pictures."

"How did he manage that?"

"Technology, my friend. Technology. Everything is out there. You just need to know where to look, and be determined to look pretty hard. The aerials will be from satellite feeds, easy enough to track down. It's not like the old days when you needed to hack into a military satellite to get at the good stuff. The floor plans, however, took a little ingenuity. The place was on the market five years ago. The real estate agents put up stylized layouts, not strictly accurate to the inch, but more than good enough for us to know exactly what we're walking into. You should think about going back to college, do a course, before the world leaves you behind."

"I've got you for that."

"I'm sure you'd find another use for me."

"True. I could set you up into the property recovery game."

Garin fell silent.

Roux concentrated on the road ahead.

The glow of lights appeared a short distance ahead. He signaled to pull over. The car was running on fumes. He'd been counting down the miles to the next rest stop hoping they'd make it all the way. He checked the clock on the dash. It was a little after six in the morning. If he hadn't known, he'd have been able to guess reasonably close to the hour because the traffic was already starting to pick up, the early birds off to work to make sure that they still managed to get into the office despite the conditions.

"How much farther?"

"An hour or so. I'll drive the rest of the way," Garin said.

He released his seat belt, but made no effort to get out.

Roux knew Garin was happy to sit back and let Roux fill the tank. After all, the world waited on him, hanging on his every word, so why should the old man be any different?

Right now Roux was focused on making sure Annja was safe. After that he'd reassess his relationship with Garin.

The forecourt was strewed with sand and grit. Snow stood in heaps around the perimeter where it had been shoveled clear of the pumps.

Roux walked around the car. His boots crunched with every step.

The counter ticked over quickly as the gas pumped, filling the seemingly bottomless tank.

A full tank should mean they wouldn't need to stop if things went wrong at the farmhouse just outside Pau. Not that he intended to run away. This was going to end here, today. He wasn't going to let a threat hang over his head and live out the remainder of his days looking over his shoulder for Cauchon. He had no idea what, in reality, they'd find waiting for them in Pau. A small army? It didn't seem reasonable, but very little of what Cauchon was doing was reasonable. Not so very long ago it had felt as if the future stretched out forever before him, but that had changed the moment Annja had pieced the shards of Joan's sword together. It was as though a clock had started ticking inside him at that precise moment, counting down the seconds, measuring out the rest of his days in precise ticks and tocks like everyone else in the world. And now he simply felt old. Garin could behave like a teenager, chasing women, drugs, money and whatever hedonistic pleasure crossed his mind.

There was nothing fair about the world.

A car pulled up at the next pump.

Roux's heart leaped. In the briefest of glimpses he imagined he'd seen Annja at the wheel only to be brought crashing back to earth as a pretty young woman climbed out. She gave Roux a smile; she wasn't Annja.

The cashier at the checkout offered Roux the kind of look that was part sympathy, part disbelief, but then, they were out at an ungodly hour, in poor driving conditions.

Who in their right mind would do that willingly? Roux ignored him, paid quickly, and headed back to the car.

Garin had moved over to the driver's seat.

When Roux opened the passenger door, he saw that the box on the backseat was open.

"Couldn't resist," Garin said, offering a *what-are-you-gonna-do?* shrug as he ran his fingers over the breastplate.

Roux said nothing.

He raged inwardly, but he refused to let his emotions show.

Instead, he leaned into the back and replaced the silk covering before closing the box. It was no one's fault but his own. He should have known that Garin wouldn't be able to resist temptation.

"So, is that what I think it is?" Garin asked, breaking the silence as he pulled out into the road again.

"I'd say that rather depends on what you think it is, wouldn't you? I mean, if you think it has anything to do with you, you're sadly mistaken. Likewise, if you were laboring under the misapprehension that it was a bacon sandwich, you'd have clearly lost your mind."

"Funny guy. The only person's armor I can imagine *you* having stashed anywhere would be a certain martyred maiden."

"Then why ask a stupid question?"

"Don't play games with me, Roux. This is serious. *Why* do you think Cauchon wants a piece of Joan's armor? Something that's been close to her skin?"

"He's a collector…" Roux began.

"There's more to it. And you know it. You're lying to me. If you believe that story, you're only lying to yourself, old man. Normal people don't go to the extremes of kidnap just to add something to their collection."

"Normal people?"

"People who aren't psycho crazy."

"Then I guess you have your answer, don't you? We're dealing with someone who's unstable."

"I'm not buying it."

"What more do you need? We are dealing with a crazy man who has got it into his head that he wants to possess everything that still exists that is connected with Joan in some way."

"Don't try to con me, Roux. I know a con when I hear it. That doesn't explain why he wanted the Gui papers, does it? Hell, it doesn't even explain how he knows that the armor still exists. I didn't even know you had it, so how could he?"

"I don't tell you everything, Garin. I never have."

"Clearly. But you share with a madman? Or let's put it another way. If you've been so careless that Cauchon could find out about that—" he hooked a thumb over his shoulder, indicating the box on the backseat "—what else could he have found out? I mean, exactly how careless have you been with our secrets? These are our lives we're talking about."

Roux hesitated. He'd been thinking about this for a while now, not so much the fact that it had happened as the guilt that came with the accident that followed. "It's not the first time that someone has tried to put together the pieces of a puzzle even if they didn't know what the big picture was like."

"What do you mean, not the first time?"

"There was someone else, a long time ago."

"How long ago? A few years? A hundred? Two hundred? Right now you need to be a hell of a lot more precise."

"Twenty," Roux said, the memory flooding back again. He'd done so well to bury it away in the recesses of his mind where it would no longer haunt him. Now he was willingly letting the genie out of the bottle.

"Twenty years? That's nothing. That's like *yesterday*. What it is not is a long time ago and you damned well know that. Talk to me, Roux."

Roux shrugged, not really sure how much to tell him. Should he confess how close that French journalist had come to exposing them? He had thought about it many times over the years, usually in moments like this when the urge to break off contact with Garin was strong. There was logic to it. The more they were seen together, the more likely it was for people to connect the two of them. Side by side it was impossible not to notice the one single unique trait they both shared, and now, with the proliferation of cameras and living lives out on social networks photographing absolutely everything in the minutia of life, it wouldn't take much to bring trouble knocking on their door.

"Someone—a journalist—found a few pictures of me that were quite a few years apart…"

"…and you didn't look a day older," Garin completed for him. "That's it, isn't it. That's what's happened here. You got careless and someone found out about us."

"There's nothing to worry about," Roux said.

"How can you possibly know that? Certainly there's something to worry about." Roux raised a hand to cut him off before he could launch into a tirade about how he'd compromised them, but he stopped midbreath. "He's dead, isn't he? That's how you know. You killed him. Jesus, Roux. How many secrets are you hiding in that head of yours?"

"Plenty," Roux said. They were not strangers to death, but like it or not, the journalist hadn't deserved what happened to him.

In the light of the headlights coming toward them, Roux could see that other man was smiling, that he thought that this was in some way something to be proud of.

"It was never my intention to kill him."

"Of course you didn't." Garin laughed. "It just sort of happened. You keep telling yourself that if it helps you sleep, old man. Just remind me not to piss you off for a while, eh?"

"Leave it," Roux said.

"Okay, you say it's over, but what if this journo of yours told someone else? What if he left notes?"

"It's irrelevant. The two events aren't connected."

"How can you possibly know that?"

"Because they hired you to steal from me."

"No. That was happenstance. A collision of good fortune. They didn't know where the documents were," Garin said.

"And you are stupid enough to believe that? You are quite possibly the only person in the world who could conceivably know that I had Guillaume Manchon's papers in my vault. I mean, who in the world was he? Some hanger-on from the court at Rouen? Do you even remember him? I do. He was a nobody. A vile creature always fawning over more powerful men, a sniveling wretch with a perpetual cold who was obsessed with demons and devils and couldn't set foot outside the church without invoking every damned holy rite known to man. That was Guillaume Manchon. And our tormentor just happens to be looking for the ramblings of this demon-obsessed scribbler? A man who stood there when they burned Joan and watched, relishing every second of it, rubbing his hands with glee over the flames as they bit into her flesh. A man who believed there was a demonic entity inside her that needed to be exorcised? And he wants you to get them for him? You, one of the only two people in the world who were at that execution. Sometimes, Garin, you are a true idiot."

It was Garin's turn to fall silent.

Roux settled back into the seat and listened to the beat of the windshield wipers and the *swoosh* of wet snow as the wheels churned it up for mile after mile.

He needed to think.

If he pretended to sleep, Garin might just shut up for once.

49

In the end Annja talked her host out of giving her a ride into the village.

She was feeling much better than she had for a couple of days; the second cup of coffee and a plate of eggs and toast made the world of difference.

She had told him that instead of heading down the mountain to the village she'd just double back and head up to the house she'd been visiting, explaining that they had a phone there and right now the most important thing was getting in touch with her friends who'd be worrying about her. He nodded, understanding, and no doubt relieved he didn't have to get his car out given the treacherous conditions.

Even so, she could feel his eyes watching her as she made her way from his house to the road that led back up the mountain.

She desperately wanted to slip the sword back into the otherwise, but wouldn't risk it until she was sure he could no longer see her, even if that meant balancing the huge blade on her shoulder as she slipped and slid up the road.

She felt much stronger, strong enough to take on whoever was in that house.

She wasn't running away.

It wasn't her style.

Besides, if Roux was coming to save her, this was where he'd come, and he was going to need someone to save his ass when he sprung Cauchon's trap.

Going back into the lion's den was the only option.

Even if Cauchon had returned and freed his sister, even if he had a small army hidden up there, she was *ready*.

And they were about to find out just how ready.

Before she reached the road, she heard a car coming up the mountain.

She held back, scrambling over a low wall at the side of the road and ducking out of sight.

She didn't get more than a glance at the car as it passed, but the old man had said there was only one place this road led to.

As she reached the track she turned to see that the man who had saved her was still standing in his doorway, watching her. What had he thought about her scrambling over the wall? It couldn't be helped, but so much for not doing anything to rouse his suspicion. She gave him a wave. He returned it and went back inside, closing the door on his little mountainside sanctuary.

Confident that she was away from any prying eyes, Annja swung her sword, feeling its weight as her muscles worked through a routine, easy, graceful, filling her body with warmth. With each swing she felt stronger, as if the sword was giving her more energy. Energy that surged through her like an electric charge, invigorating her, restoring her.

She didn't need to walk up the mountainside; she felt strong enough to run, knowing she'd be strong enough to do whatever she needed to do when she reached the top.

She was alive.

Vital.

Invincible.

Annja's heart rate accelerated, the blood pumping through her veins to the rhythm of the sword's raw power, surging through her system, firing her synapses. She slipped the sword into the otherwhere, not needing its revitalizing thrill, and she strode on, determined to reach the house in the mountains as quickly as she could.

The storm had subsided into a crisp calm morning of clear blue skies as far as the eye could see, dazzling against the blanket of white that lay over the mountaintops.

It didn't take long to reach the bend where she'd lost control of the truck and then the subsequent one where she'd bailed out. The night's snowfall had obliterated the worst of the scarring the accident had done to the landscape. All that remained were a couple of faint marks in the surface from where the vehicle had overbalanced in the final seconds before going over the edge. Considering the wind, in a few hours even they could be gone.

She walked to the edge and stood there, the wind battering her as she gazed down to where the tangled wreckage of the truck had burned out. It had fallen a long way. Snow had accumulated on the wreck as winter claimed it.

There was no sign of any other dwellings nearby.

There was still plenty of ground to cover.

She wanted to deal with these people before Roux arrived, or at least be in a position to stop him from doing something stupid. She knew how he was about her. He didn't think rationally. It was some misplaced father instinct. It meant he made bad decisions, but they all came from the right place. The old man had a big heart. He cared. Sometimes caring, though, was a problem, especially if it meant dealing with kidnappers on their terms.

Annja turned her back on the incredible vista, and noticed the snow at her feet, or rather the fact that it had been compacted by another vehicle during the night. She ran on, using those tracks for the grip she needed to break her stride into a run and attack the incline. It felt good to push on, to feel her heart pumping blood into her muscles, the icy cold air in her lungs. She wanted to scream at the top of her lungs and hear her voice echo from peak to peak before rebounding and filling her ears with its raucous chorus.

She drove herself on, arms and legs pumping hard, teeth gritted against the elements, savoring every single step on the road.

This was it, woman against mountain. She would win. She always did.

No matter what it cost her physically or emotionally. She always won.

50

"Someone's coming," one of the men said, looking up from the video-feed he'd been monitoring on a laptop.

Cauchon wheeled across the room and pushed him aside, getting a clear look at the screen. Despite the angle and its reduced clarity, he was sure he was going to see Annja Creed staggering back up the mountain toward the house, defeated, coming to beg for mercy and warmth because the mountain had beaten her. He would see her on her knees. He would listen to her teeth chatter and watch as she was reduced to a pitiful wretch, and then he would drive her demon out.

He breathed in deeply, savoring the thought.

He was just.

He was on the side of the angels.

He was doing God's work.

He was finishing what had begun six centuries ago.

When he'd returned to the isolated farmhouse with his hired muscle, he'd found his sister locked in the basement, with no sign of the Creed woman. She was treacherous. Devious. The demon in her skin was cunning. Underestimate the devil's minions at your peril—that was the message her escape had reinforced. He didn't know how she had done it, and certainly didn't doubt she had used her powers. How else could she have tricked Monique?

What he didn't know was if the woman's demon granted her the same sort of immortality that Roux and his sidekick seemed to have, in which case would driving it out leave her in danger of dying? How many lives had she already lived? It didn't matter, he thought, staring at the screen. This was the last one. That was all that mattered. And dead or alive, Roux would still come to the farmhouse trying to save her. And he would still bring the armor with him.

Some things were just too perfect.

The more he read from those ancient pages, the more he realized that he would be able to achieve so much more than just ridding the woman of the spirit that possessed her.

A 4x4 passed the security camera, traveling slowly enough for him to see the vehicle's sole occupant.

He had stared at the man's face, seen in so many pictures, taken from so many years, some almost a century apart that he would even have been able to pick him out in the dark.

Roux.

How the *hell* did he find us? he wondered. Why didn't he know that the devil was coming?

He tapped a couple of keys to bring up the map with the tracker signal. The signal hadn't moved. It was still sitting where it had been since early morning, moving north on a highway seemingly heading to Paris. The old man had realized that there was a tracker on the car and switched it to another vehicle heading north. Cauchon's frustration threatened to boil over.

"Get your weapons!" Cauchon demanded, pushing his chair back from the screen. It didn't matter *how* Roux had managed to find him. That was irrelevant. He was here now. It saved having to give him directions from Pau. The only thing that mattered was he'd come alone, and that was the last mistake the old man was ever going to make.

The house was full of sound and movement; it was hard to believe that there were only three men and one woman readying themselves for war, but that's what it was—war.

"Watch the old man's approach," Cauchon ordered one of his goons. All he could do now was to put his faith in others; it wasn't a position he enjoyed.

But he wasn't completely helpless, even if most of it was illusion.

He retrieved a Browning Hi-Power pistol from its place in the cupboard.

He had tried to fire the gun once and the recoil had almost tipped over his chair, but that didn't mean that the weapon didn't offer the same feeling of power that it did to able-bodied men. It was time he came face-to-face with Roux.

He checked the screen again.

Roux's car was coming into sight of the second camera. He watched the 4x4 travel up the road.

The contractor who'd installed the system had tried to convince him that he was going over the top with the number of cameras he wanted, but the man hadn't understood that Cauchon was planning for war. This wasn't about home invasion. He followed the progress from image to image as Roux neared, until the old man reached the last checkpoint.

He called out distances to his men, Monique beside him, urging them to be ready for Roux's approach. He watched as Roux brought the 4x4 toward the farmhouse, then stopped watching and wheeled himself toward the door.

Cauchon wanted to be there to greet him.

He wanted to see the look on the old man's face when he realized that they were ready for him, that whatever trickery he'd used to find his way here hadn't been enough.

Monique stood at his shoulder, an Uzi at the ready.

"I can hear him," she said needlessly. The vehicle's engine was the only sound in the mountains.

Cauchon wheeled himself out onto the stone slab area outside the front door. The snow had been cleared that morning, and with the heat of the sun had melted little that remained on the steps. He sucked in the cold morning air.

The winter sun glinted off the mountain peaks in the distance.

Today was going to be a good day.

Today was going to be the day when wrongs were righted and revenge exacted.

Today was going to be the day when Roux finally met his Maker.

The car crawled around the last tight curve that led to the farmhouse. Two of the guards took a step forward to intercept the driver, not waiting for instructions. They had looked capable of feasting on lions when Cauchon had picked them up, but now, dressed in black, fully armed, they looked like cold-blooded killers, standing out in stark contrast to the whiteness that surrounded them.

The car stopped.

Roux paused before he opened the door to get out.

Cauchon watched him. Did the old man remember him? He had changed, of course. A lot. Life had happened to him. Whereas he would have recognized Roux anywhere. The man was unchanged. It was as if he'd been carved out of the landscape.

"Welcome," he said as Roux climbed out of the vehicle.

The old man made no show of acknowledging the guns aimed at his chest.

"I trust you haven't come all this way empty-handed?"

"Of course not," Roux replied. "I've got what you want, but before I take another step, where's the girl?"

"Ah, not so hasty. All in good time. I want to savor our reunion. We have much to talk about, so why don't you come inside out of the cold? It's been a while."

51

Garin approached the farmhouse, keeping low, moving as quickly as he could across the uneven ground, listening to the sounds of the mountain.

He'd abandoned the warmth and comfort of the car farther from their destination than he would have liked. Hell, in an ideal world he'd have curled up on the backseat with a blanket over him and pretended he wasn't there, but even a bunch of incompetents would have seen him. He had no choice but to go in by foot.

He scrambled forward, hands pawing at the high snow as his feet sank into the drifts. Each stumbling step ended with the snow up around his knees. The two hundred feet to the crest of the hill was a colossal undertaking. He stumbled and nearly fell three times, dragging himself forward, eyes on the prize.

He crested the next hill, keeping low, and saw the farmhouse up ahead. He made out six people, several of them with odd silhouettes that seemed to have distended and disjointed arms: submachine guns. That was an unexpected and unwelcome development. Garin wasn't unarmed. Only a fool went into the lion's den naked. But he didn't like the idea of pitting his Colt Mustang against an Uzi. The XSP was good for concealed carry, weighing less than a pound even when loaded with six shots of .380 ACP. But heavy ordnance it was not.

He dropped to his stomach and lay still as Roux made his way around to the passenger's side of the car. He regretted it immediately. The snow was bitingly cold against his skin. He wasn't twelve anymore. This wasn't fun.

The old man retrieved the box from the backseat.

The guards watched him closely.

From this distance, with the wind whipping across the mountaintops, it was impossible to hear what words passed between them no matter how hard he strained to hear. The mountains carried words away on the wind and wrapped them up in snow. He watched Roux and the others enter the house before he made his move.

He had no way of knowing if any of them would continue to monitor the feeds from the security cameras, but had to hope not.

There was a track that ran around the outbuildings, which offered some cover from the windows of the farmhouse. Garin scrambled forward, bolting for cover. He fell before he made it thirty feet, and slid twice as far down the slope, and then was up on his feet again and running hard for the stone wall, dreading one single sound: the crack of bullets from an Uzi echoing around the mountains.

He couldn't hear anything over the crunch of snow and his own ragged breathing.

Garin kept on running, knowing that he'd feel the killer bullet before he heard it, anyway.

That was no comfort.

He forced himself to go on, driving his legs through the deep snow, staggering and stumbling but not stopping.

He hit the wall, hands out to brace him against the impact, then waited, listening.

Nothing.

Not a sound.

He crept to the edge of the stone barn.

There was no sign of the guard, but that didn't mean they weren't scouting the area.

He watched, waiting, but nothing changed.

Silence.

Not even birdsong to break it.

The quiet rang in his ears.

Lights were on in a couple of the rooms. The curtains were open in the largest of the downstairs windows, but in others they were closed. He saw dark shapes move across his eye line inside. No lookout was posted at the window. Garin scanned the farmhouse and parking area, picking out a route to the door that would get him as close as possible with minimum risk of anyone seeing his approach. It was harder than it looked, because he noted that half a dozen cameras had been fixed on the corners of the various outbuildings, seemingly covering most angles of approach. Cauchon really valued his privacy.

Crouching, he rushed from cover to the trunk of the 4x4, keeping low as he hid at the back of the vehicle, making sure to keep it between him and the house. The distance to the other vehicle was about a dozen yards—twelve long strides, a few more if taken in a crouch, but it was all it would take. The problem was that he was going straight through the middle of an area monitored by a security camera, but there was no other means of getting to the front door—assuming the front door was the only entrance.

He took a breath and closed the distance before he released it.

Cauchon might not be expecting reinforcements, but surely he wasn't so arrogant as to leave the front door unguarded.

Garin edged a little farther around the vehicle, keeping low, inching forward, coiled, ready to sprint for his life, twelve steps to the corner of the house. It wasn't a lot. Twelve steps.

Now or never, Garin thought, pushing himself to his feet in the exact same second that one of the guards stepped out of the house. Garin froze—half up, half down—and didn't dare move so much as an inch. The guard didn't look particularly interested in securing the area. He scanned from left to right and back again, then reached into his pocket and pulled out a pack of cigarettes. He adjusted the gun that was slung on his shoulder and leaned against the wall, but even so, that made lighting up his smoke awkward, so he slipped the gun off his shoulder and balanced it against the wall.

Garin had just gotten lucky.

Someone should have told this bozo that smoking would kill him eventually.

He wasn't about to let the man enjoy the cigarette.

Garin ran the numbers in his head, calculating the time it would take him to cover the distance between them. He knew it was impossible for him to sneak up on the guy, and he needed to be close enough to overpower the guard before he realized what was going on and grabbed for the Uzi. The answer was: too long.

The man took two satisfying puffs on his cigarette.

Garin watched the smoke corkscrew with the vapor of his breath. He pushed himself all the way up, ready to burst into movement, but stopped suddenly as a hand clamped over his mouth.

52

"It's been a long time, Roux," the man in the wheelchair said.

"You've changed your name."

"I'm a different person now." Cauchon waved one hand as if to highlight the state of his legs and the wheelchair that he relied on to get around. "I'm the man you made me."

"I thought you were dead."

"Patrice Moerlen is dead. If you searched the internet, you would find plenty of reports of his tragic death."

"And yet you're still here, living and breathing."

"You shouldn't have left me the way that you did."

"I didn't mean for it to happen, not like that. I only wanted to scare you off," Roux said. It was as though it had happened only days ago, not decades. The image of it was so vivid in his memory. "I'm sorry."

"Sorry?" Cauchon sputtered. "No. Don't be sorry. I want to thank you." Roux looked at him, not understanding. "My sister—" he reached up a hand to rest on the woman's hand, which in turn rested on his shoulder

"—managed to get me to the nearest hospital, get me the best treatment. She even identified another body as mine, allowing her to claim the not insubstantial insurance policy on my life, which paid for everything I could possibly need. So, no, don't be sorry, Roux. I'm not sorry. I'm not even bitter. I was angry for a few years, but even that passed. The truth is, without you, without what happened at the Eiffel Tower that day, I would never have made the discovery that will soon make me so much more than I am now, so much more than I was before."

It would be easy to dismiss him as deranged, a dangerous lunatic, damaged forever by that accident, but Roux knew that would be a mistake. The woman stood behind her brother, not breaking contact with him. It was the woman who had waved so flirtatiously at him, the same woman who had drugged Garin and tried to frame him for murder. The old man had absolutely no doubt that she was capable of identifying another man's body as her own brother, or that she would have put on a good act doing it: handkerchief at the ready, leaning on the supportive policeman's shoulder for comfort when they peeled back the sheet to reveal the wrong dead man to her, the choking sob, the nod. He had met people like that before. He recognized the type, knew the body double had been living and breathing when she found him.

"I hate to admit it, but you have me at a disadvantage here," Roux said. "I've brought what you want, but I still don't know what I'm doing here, why you are so interested in getting me here." Almost as an afterthought he added, "Where is Annja?"

The man nodded and the two guards who had been standing behind Roux took the box from him. They pulled his hands behind his back. His instinct was to fight against the restraints, but there was no point. Until Annja was free he had no choice but to go along with whatever they had in mind, no matter how much damage it did to him physically.

When she was safe, then things would be different. Then he could rain holy hell down on these people.

The two men pulled the plastic cuffs tight and pushed him into a chair, putting him on a level with Cauchon. Face-to-face. Eye-to-eye. The woman took the box from the guard and placed it in her brother's lap. Her smile was vile. His eyes lit up like a child's on Christmas morning.

"Not to put a damper on things, but this is meant to be an exchange, but right now I feel more like Santa Claus. Where's Annja?"

Cauchon didn't look up from the ancient box until he had pulled the sacking away, revealing the lid. The expression on his face was cruel and twisted.

"Gone," the man said.

"What do you mean gone?" Roux felt rage surge up inside, from the depths of his being. They were lying. They had to be. He said as much.

"Now why would I lie to you? Your little friend is *very* resourceful. You should be proud. She managed to escape from my little prison, and bested Monique."

Roux tried to keep the smile from his lips.

He hadn't noticed the dark bruise beneath the blonde's eye. The makeup concealed the worst of it, but the swelling was hard to disguise. This changed things. If Annja was safe, then he'd handed over the breastplate for nothing. They could have come in here guns blazing.

"If she's truly gone and you have what you want, then we are done here," Roux said.

"Done? Oh no. No, no, no. We're not done. We haven't even started."

Cauchon opened the box.

He carefully pulled back the silk wrapping that protected the metal from contact with the wood, and breathed in deeply as he gazed upon the object of his obsession.

"Joan of Arc's breastplate. Part of the armor she wore on the days of her final stand against the enemy."

"That's what I was told," Roux said.

"You lie!" Cauchon yelled suddenly, all trace of restraint blown. "Stop lying to me! I still don't know quite *what* you are, but I know that you are not a mortal man. I am not stupid. I do not believe in fairy stories."

"People say that I have a very familiar face."

"Shut up, shut up, shut up."

"There are a lot of people who look like me. It's always been like that."

"Stop lying, old man. I *know* you were there when she wore this armor. I *know*. I have seen enough pictures and paintings dating back centuries to know you were there at some of the most important incidents in history."

"You don't know what you are talking about. I told you before. You are mistaken."

"And then you tried to silence me, if I recall. That is not the act of an innocent man, Roux. You know it and I know it. The fact you were able to lay your hands on her armor without difficulty is damning in itself." He patted a palm against the dented metal.

"You're making logical leaps that have no grounding in reality. This is what I do. I've dealt in all kinds of things over the years. Not all of them with any kind of provenance."

"Really? Then how do you explain Miss Creed?"

"Annja? What about her?"

Cauchon sighed heavily. "I've seen the trick she does, drawing that sword of hers out of nowhere."

Roux waved the notion away. "I don't know what you're talking about."

"Yes, you do. But let's pretend you don't. Let me explain it to you."

"Please do," Roux said, purposely stalling. He needed to give Garin time to infiltrate the farmhouse and even the odds. Cauchon didn't seem to mind. He was enjoying himself. He'd imagined this meeting for a long time and had no intention of rushing it, even if his ultimate endgame was Roux's death, which was a possibility that grew all the more probable the longer they spent together. For Cauchon this was about revenge; for Roux, suddenly, it was about atonement. This didn't have to end in death. Not this time.

"You see, I am a scholar. I have devoted my life to research."

"An honorable pursuit," Roux said.

"And an enlightening one. The more you look, the more you see."

"I would imagine so," Roux agreed.

"I have seen a lot. Almost as much as you, I suspect."

"More, probably," Roux offered. "I'm not particularly observant."

"No need for self-deprecation, Roux. You are with some of the only people in the world who truly understand all of the marvelous things you must have seen during your life."

"No so many marvels."

"You are too modest. Perhaps we should share. Let me begin with one of the incredible things I've witnessed, shall we?"

"Please do."

"I've seen her sword before."

"Sometimes a sword is just a sword," Roux said.

"I've seen it in several paintings. You see, it's the Maid's sword, isn't it? Jeanne d'Arc. Saint Joan. *La Pucelle d'Orléans.* Joan of Arc. That's quite a coincidence, don't you think?"

Roux shrugged, the ties tugging at his wrists as he did so.

He was starting to think that there was no point in trying to deny anything.

The man had clearly made his mind up and nothing he could say was likely to change it, especially as it would be a lie.

Cauchon lifted the breastplate from the box and turned it over, examining every inch of the metal on both sides.

"Do you know what this is capable of? No, silly of me. Obviously you do. The clues were all in the notes that your friend retrieved from your own home. A better question would be, did you follow the clues that were in there? Did you find the proof that I found?" Cauchon waited for a moment, clearly wanting Roux to respond.

The old man knew that silence would be the way to beat him.

"Guillaume Manchon only scratched the surface when he suggested that there was a secret magic being practiced, but you know that, don't you? Even Bernard Gui had suspected it was more than the mere hedge magic of charms and curses, of love potions and medicines. But neither of them could have known quite how demonic this magic was, could they? Because at heart they were good men who didn't understand how corrupt their world really was. Unlike you."

Roux refused to speak.

He wasn't about to risk a word until he knew what Cauchon knew, what he believed and just how far from the truth his obsession had taken him. He already understood that Cauchon had picked at the thread of something that had more than an element of truth, but how far did that thread go? A link between Annja and the young woman who had once wielded the sword? A further link to his own incredible longevity? Both seemed likely. Both were too close to home. And, in truth, both contained answers he didn't want to hear in case Cauchon had stumbled across something that could end it, something that could give him the power to draw a line under this life if ever decided that he had had enough of it. And there were days when all he longed to do was die.

"Nothing to say? Come on, Roux, I'm sure that you must have given the matter some thought. After all, you had plenty of time, even just over the past twenty years since I went to visit you. Since then, I have dedicated my life to studying this. I had one intention—to find your Achilles' heel and make you suffer. But things changed. I changed. I realized that more than just pain, I wanted to give you the opportunity to show true penitence."

"I've already told you that I'm sorry," Roux said, breaking his silence. "I thought that you had died."

"No. That's what you *wanted* to believe, you mean," the man snapped, revealing again the anger he barely kept in check beneath his veneer of calm. "Because it was convenient. Because it was better for you. Safer."

He took a deep breath and looked Roux in the eye, holding his gaze unblinking for longer than Roux found comfortable. "Even though you seem awfully reluctant to confirm what I already know to be true, we'll just take it as a given that you comprehend what I'm talking about. We both are aware that Annja Creed is connected in some fashion to Joan of Arc. She has her sword, and somehow reaches across time to draw it. How could this be possible? I wondered. How indeed, unless she is possessed by the martyr's spirit? That set me to thinking. And eventually I found what I was looking for, ancient documents that show the rites and incantations that could have been used to keep her spirit in this world. Papers that detail rites that bind a spirit to this world by offering it a safe haven, a vessel that it can remain in until the mortal flesh is no longer able to sustain it. Imagine that. And while it survives in this vessel, the possessing spirit gives the body a strength that it would not otherwise have, cures it of wounds and sickness that should end its life and sustains it."

"I'm sorry, but that's rubbish. Superstitious nonsense. You do understand that, don't you? There's no such thing as magic. There is no 'supernatural.' What you are holding in your hands is a rusted piece of armor. A treasure? Yes. Undoubtedly. It was worn into battle by one of the greatest women this world has ever known. But that doesn't make it magical, just precious," Roux said.

"Far from it. Something sufficiently advanced may indeed seem to be magical, but that does not necessarily make it so. It only underlines the fact that we do not see all there is to see about this space we live in or how it works."

"Now you're mixing science and superstition to suit your need."

"And you are willfully trying to goad me. That makes a lot of sense. You must be frightened. All these years living in the shadows, your secret safe, only to have the spotlight turned on you."

"I'm not what you think I am," Roux said.

"There are a number of rites and incantations that need to be completed to recall the spirit from the body."

The woman laughed. He'd almost forgotten she was there, standing at her brother's shoulder.

Had she been allowed inside the insanity that existed inside his head? Was she party to his madness?

The two thugs remained silent, seemingly unfazed by this talk of immortals and spirit possession. It was above their pay grade.

"It sounds like your sister agrees with me," Roux said, weighing his words carefully. "Maybe she knows that this is all some madman's obsession with no basis in reality."

The woman crossed the room in less than half a dozen strides, then swung one hand, slapping him hard across the face without warning.

The noise rang out loudly. His lower lip split under the impact of the blow and his mouth was suddenly filled with the coppery tang of blood. There was no anger behind the slap, more a satisfaction that he had given her the opportunity and excuse to do it. She enjoyed inflicting even this little pain.

She returned to her place behind her brother.

"You must forgive my sister," Cauchon said. "She is very protective of me and sometimes does the things she thinks I would like to be able to do but, because of the constraints of this chair, am unable to. She is very loyal."

"I get the picture, even if I don't really like what it looks like."

"That's good," Cauchon said. "Very good. Now perhaps we can get on with this. I'm a changed man. I would hate for you to suffer for any longer than absolutely necessary."

"That's very decent of you."

53

Annja held her hand over Garin's mouth.

"Move back behind the car, keep down. I'll draw him closer," she whispered. "Not a sound."

Once he nodded his understanding she released her grip and allowed him to move.

She had been surprised to see Garin crouching beside the vehicle. There would be time for questions later. Right now she was just glad the band was back together. She grinned at him.

"It's good to see you."

He put his finger to his lips.

Annja had caught a glimpse of Roux inside. He wasn't having tea and biscuits with the madman and his homicidal sister. She resisted the temptation to make some ironic dig about how her white knights had come to rescue the damsel in distress only to wind up needing to be rescued themselves. There'd be time for that later. She gave Garin just long enough to hide himself before she rose.

The guard showed no sign of realizing she was there,

even as she stepped away from the car. He was clearly savoring his nicotine-fueled meditation.

She made a show of stumbling to her knees.

This time he looked up.

"Help," she said in a voice that was barely above a whisper, weak but just loud enough for the man to hear.

She slumped forward and waited as the man grabbed the Uzi and flicked his cigarette to the ground.

He was faster than she'd expected. She lay still, her eyes closed, listening to the sound of boots running across the snow toward her.

She felt the man's breath on her cheek as he bent down to be closer.

"Are you all right?" he asked.

It was a stupid question, but was exactly what she would have asked. It was a human response to someone who was hurt.

She resisted the urge to open her eyes until she heard the sound of him being hit—*hard*—and falling. He landed on top of her, driving the air from her lungs.

A moment later the weight was lifted.

Annja scrambled free.

"Well, that was easy," Garin said.

He relieved the man of his Uzi.

The guard appeared to be dead.

"They're interrogating Roux," Annja said, nodding toward the closed door. "What exactly are they chatting about in there?"

"I wish I knew," Garin replied. "The old man's not exactly forthcoming at the moment. I think he's got some noble plan to save your life, but beyond that?" He shrugged.

"So have you boys kissed and made up?"

Garin winced. "Not yet. But at least he isn't trying to kill me."

"Would you blame him if he was?"

"Probably not, but I'm not too stubborn to admit we can all make mistakes."

"Big of you."

Garin grinned. "I'm just here to try to put things right. You can't hold that against me, surely?"

"Putting things right by letting Roux sacrifice himself?"

"It's not about me. It's not about you. It's all about Roux. Roux's the one that this Cauchon has been after all the time. It was about a bigger prize than those papers I stole from the old man's vault."

"Talk to me, Garin. I want to know what we're going up against. I really hate surprises. You should know that by now."

"He was very secretive about it, but he's brought a piece of armor here. A breastplate. Joan of Arc's," he added meaningfully.

Annja shook her head. It wasn't a denial; she was trying to understand, to put the pieces together. "But why would he think Roux would have that?" She didn't like the only answer she could come up with.

"He knows about us."

"What do you mean, about us?" She frowned.

"The guy must know that there's a connection between the three of us, and with Joan. That's what has the old man rattled. All of our secrets are beginning to unravel."

"How? How is that even possible?" How could Cauchon have discovered this about them?

All Garin could do was shrug.

They weren't going to learn anything more outside.

Every minute they delayed meant another minute that Roux was alone in there.

"Time for the cavalry," Garin whispered, holding the Uzi at the ready. He checked that the safety was off and the selector was set to 3-round bursts. "Aren't you forgetting something?"

She didn't understand until he made a swishing gesture with the muzzle of the Uzi.

Annja reached out and drew the sword into the here and now.

She smiled as she felt the surge of energy flood into her body, pulsing through her skin and bone, bringing her alive.

Garin nodded.

They rushed side by side to the doorway.

"Here goes nothing," Annja said as she placed her fingers on the door handle. "Let's hope we get the drop on them."

"Rock and roll," Garin said wryly.

54

Cauchon pressed the breastplate close to his chest.

It was a tight fit, even if the man's emaciated torso was skin and bones.

Roux could only imagine how severe his injuries had been, and what he had gone through during his recovery, but years in the chair had destroyed his musculature. He'd wasted away, lost in the search for knowledge.

"Not a good look," Roux said, deliberately trying to goad Cauchon into lashing out.

"You still don't understand, do you?"

"Educate me. Make me understand."

"This—" he rapped his knuckles off the breastplate over his chest "—is going to get me out of this wheelchair." He let that sink in for a second. "I am going to walk again. I will be whole. Better than whole. I will invite the demon into *me*."

Roux rejected the notion at once. So that was it. The confused fool had pinned his hopes of salvation on a piece of metal, wishing somehow it would conduct whatever he believed was inside Annja—Joan's demon—into him.

He didn't understand that sometimes a piece of metal, no matter its history, was just a piece of metal.

"That's not going to happen," Roux said, sympathetically this time, no gibes, no goading.

Cauchon ignored him. He didn't want to hear anything that conflicted with what he needed to happen.

"Those papers, the ledgers and lost chapters, the secrets that the Inquisition never wanted released to the public, I have read them. I've studied them. I understand them like no one before me. I can see the whole picture, putting together the suppositions and revelations of all of these other, better men, and I *know*. I know. All I need are things that were touched by people close to her. Things that she came into contact with."

"It doesn't work like that."

"No? You would say that because you are frightened. You would say that because this is your doing, and it will be your undoing. I know. I know," he repeated. "I will rise. I will. And that scares you, doesn't it? That scares you down to your core."

"No," Roux said, "nothing would make me happier. I never wanted this."

"You say that, but words are cheap. Anyone can say that. They only have to move their lips and it all comes flooding out, all of the lies. But I have spent years gathering the truth, a quest for understanding. All of those papers, including Gui's, even Cauchon himself, the real one, the man who signed her death warrant, I have items of his. I have held in my hand a piece of paper that so many other men put their hand to at the time. Holy men frightened of the demon spirit inside the girl. But the thing I needed most, the prize that would make the rites work, was something she had touched herself, something she had held tightly that would have absorbed some of her very essence. And now, thanks to you, I have it. All that remains is to speak the words—words as old as the entity inside her, words that bind them even now, the mirror of the words that saved her soul when the flames burned away her skin."

Roux looked at him sadly. This wasn't at all what he'd wanted or expected. He didn't fear the man or hate him. He pitied him. "And what then? Do you suddenly rise up? Does the demon get sucked out of Annja and drawn here, into you? Is the devil going to materialize and claim us all?" He glanced at the others in the room. "Will we all be drawn into some hellish vortex, stripped of flesh, shredded and scattered to the four winds? How is this supposed to work?"

He gestured at Cauchon's sister. She made no obvious sign of making a move.

"Nothing so dramatic," Cauchon said. "But the essence of Joan will abandon Miss Creed. She will be free of the curse. What happens to the vessel after that? I do not know."

Roux closed his eyes, trying to gather the strength he needed to face this madness head-on. "It won't work. There's no such thing as magic, Patrice. There is no miracle cure for your injuries. I'm sorry. I truly am, but this is madness. She's not even here. How can you perform any sort of ritual without her?" He knew he was feeding the man's delusion, but it was another way to buy a few more seconds. Where the hell was Garin?

Cauchon laughed. It was a deep, throaty, totally genuine laugh. "Oh, she is. She's here somewhere. Did you look out of the window on your drive here? She couldn't possibly have gotten down off the mountain last night. And my men tell me there is a burned-out wreck where her car went off the road. She's here. She knew that you were coming for her. She knew that you wouldn't abandon her here. She won't leave you to your fate any more than you would leave her to hers. As for the ritual, it is about connecting with that singular moment in time, that one instant when all these things collided. It's not about where the spirit is now."

Roux said nothing, still struggling to digest it all.

He fixed on one thing the man had said: there had been an accident. A crash.

Roux had no way of knowing if she was out there still, battered, bleeding, freezing to death, or if she'd been in the car while it had burned. Fire frightened Annja. That was something she'd gotten from Joan. A relic. Like the sword. He'd seen her tossing and turning in her bed, having nightmares, fever sweats, the word *fire* on her lips.

He couldn't even begin to contemplate the possibility that his enemy might be right, that the bond she shared with the sword could be severed and leave her helpless, bereft of the protection it conferred. It wouldn't be the end of the world for her, but it would change the very nature of who she was now and everything she had become. She was as much a part of the blade as it was of her.

What if she was close? What would happen then, if the words truly had some kind of power to them?

Roux had seen too much in his long life to dismiss the otherworldly as impossible; he was walking, living proof that it wasn't, even if he couldn't explain *how*. If she were out there, beyond the farmhouse walls, close enough that if the madman stumbled upon the right words? What then? What would happen if the energy somehow flowed between the sword in her hand and the madman's tongue? Would she survive? Would any of them?

He wasn't the kind of man who jumped at shadows and

looked for angels and demons hidden in every corner. Not anymore. He'd spent centuries burying that man.

Even so, just the possibility that something, some relic from the old days, could undo what he'd spent centuries repairing, shattering the essence of the blade, ending all of this, sent a shiver to the core of his being. He clenched his fists.

Roux was prepared to pay the price, whatever the price, if it kept Annja far from this, if it kept her safe. He wanted to know that his sacrifice would give her the chance to live brilliantly, and grow old with kids and grandkids, and stories, oh, what stories…

What he didn't want was to live with the image of her being destroyed in front of his eyes.

But that couldn't possibly happen, could it?

Matters were out of his hands.

His fate, hers if the impossible were true, rested in Garin's hands.

And, oh, how he hated that.

He knew Garin well. He knew his strengths and his flaws. He was venal, self-centered, selfish, all of those things, but what he wasn't was a coward. And when it came right down to it, there was no one better he'd trust his life to. Not that he would have ever admitted that to Garin's face.

Cauchon held the armor close to his chest, hugging it tightly with one hand while he held one of the pages that Garin had stolen from Roux's vault.

Slowly, he began to read from the sheet, the tongue a form of medieval French that Roux hadn't heard spoken for longer than he dared try to remember. Manchon had recorded the rite in his papers, and they'd appeared in part in the missing chapter of Bernard Gui's *Practica inquisitionis heretice pravitatis—Conduct of the Inqui-*

sition into Heretical Wickedness—where the Inquisitor wrote about sorcerers, diviners and the invokers of demons. That's what these words were, the invocation of a demon. Manchon had written his own warning besides his tight scrawl that these words should never be spoken out loud for fear that they would conjure up a spirit capable of untold harm to the invoker.

Roux had traced his own finger along those lines more than once, never once daring to vocalize the words because superstitious or not, he wasn't about to tempt fate.

He grinned at that, and then realized how Cauchon would interpret the smile and stopped.

The two thugs fidgeted at either side of Roux.

They were out of their comfort zone, unsure what they'd signed on for, and no matter what denomination of currency they'd pocketed, neither really wanted to do anything beyond flex a few muscles and look menacing.

The blonde woman was different.

She looked like she was anticipating all hell would break loose.

And it was coming.

It was inevitable.

"You do realize what is going to happen when you finish reading that, don't you?" Roux asked, but Cauchon showed no hint of even taking a breath, let alone stopping his recitation. He was absolutely absorbed in the words. Lost. He'd obviously learned them by rote, the sounds of the words perfect but stilted, nothing natural about his delivery. "You're going to kill everyone in this room. Is that what you want?"

"Don't be ridiculous. Of course we're not going to die," the blonde woman said.

Roux looked up at her. "You're right. We're not. Do you know why? Because it isn't going to work. This magical passage of verse isn't going to tear the essence of Joan from Annja, because she's not possessed by Joan. Joan is long gone. At rest. There is no demonic entity. There's nothing to release, nothing to summon, nothing to bind. Your brother is sick. Ill."

"My brother is a great man," Monique contradicted.

"Are you sure about that? Really sure? Willing to stake your life on it? Because if he is great, if he's right and I'm wrong, he's the one in the chair with Joan's breastplate to protect him. What have you got? What's going to keep you safe?" She stared at him. "What about those two?" Roux deliberately turned it on the guards, the weakest links. "I mean, their friend's long gone. You noticed that, right? He slipped out when things went south. Ever think that maybe he knows something that you two don't?"

One of the men fidgeted uneasily, shifting his balance from foot to foot. Roux knew that he was starting to get under the tough guy's skin.

"Shut up," Monique spat.

Not once during that conversation did Cauchon's incantation falter.

If Garin came through the door soon, it was going to get messy.

It had nothing to do with magic; now that the incantation had started, everyone in the room was on edge, keyed up and ready to go off at a second's notice. Three of the five had an Uzi in their hands. Not a good combination.

"Still here?" he asked the uncomfortable guards. "You really don't have to stick around on my behalf. I'm not going to cause any trouble. Go."

The men didn't move.

But it was obvious they wanted to.

"Why don't you wait outside?" Monique suggested. "Nothing's going to happen here that I can't handle." She aimed her Uzi square at Roux's chest as though to emphasize the point that she had things covered. Roux was absolutely certain she'd pull the trigger. She was the real danger here, not her deranged brother with his head full of mystical nonsense.

The two men didn't need to be given the opportunity twice.

Without another word they both left the room.

Roux faced the black eye of the Uzi.

Cauchon continued his incantation, his voice rising and falling with the rhythms of insanity. The beat behind his words was relentless, on and on, fueled by his obsession.

There was no doubt he truly believed something as simple as this ancient rite could make him whole again.

It was tragic.

"This ends here," Roux said.

"Oh, I couldn't agree more," Monique replied.

55

Annja was caught off guard by the resistance of the door as it jammed in the frame, the wood swollen by the cold. A heartbeat later the door swung inward and she found herself face-to-face with two very surprised gunmen who'd been looking to make a sharp exit.

Beside her, Garin said, "I think we can safely say they're surprised."

Even so, they reacted smartly. Instead of taking a step back to raise their weapons in the confined space of the doorway, the first guard pushed his way through, barging past Annja as if she wasn't there. She wasn't about to let the second man through so easily. She brought up her blade and saw the sheer panic in the second man's eyes as he realized she was about to swing her sword.

The first man slammed the stock of his Uzi into Garin's ribs, sending him sprawling to the floor. He went down cursing. It was better than the alternative. The second man wasn't so quick.

Annja's blade flashed through the air, the tip no more than a whisker from the man's face before she pulled the blow. Almost too late, she noticed just how young he was. And just how frightened. All he wanted to do was to get out of there. That was the only reason he was fighting.

"Please," he begged, the word little more than a whisper. He released the grip on his Uzi and knelt, lowering it to the ground.

He looked up at her, on one knee, expecting the sword to drop and end it all.

It didn't.

Annja reversed her swing just in time, the blade whistling past him. The breeze in its wake tugged at his hair. "I can't let you leave here," she said.

He nodded, thinking she still meant to kill him.

She dragged back on the grip of the sword, just as he closed his eyes, unable to look death in the face. The pommel cracked against the side of his skull and he toppled over. His muscles relaxed in the same instant, like a marionette whose strings had been cut. Annja released the grip on her sword with one hand and half caught him to slow his fall.

"Sorry," she said, even though he couldn't hear her. She meant it.

The other gunman swung a boot at Garin, who scrambled at his feet for his own gun.

She felt his pain as the blow lifted him off the ground. He came back down on his knees, hard, gasping and shaking his head. Another forceful kick left him motionless on the floor.

The thug kicked Garin's gun out of reach, then turned to face Annja.

She was ready for him.

The man swung his Uzi in her direction, finger already on the trigger.

This man was not like the boy she'd dealt with. This was a man who lived for violence and knew nothing else.

Which was bad news for him.

"Drop it," he said. "Last chance."

"I think that should be the other way around," Annja said. "But don't worry. I won't hold the mistake against you."

Her sword was already moving as he unleashed the first stream of bullets, the shrieks of the hot lead breaking the silence of the mountains. Each one missed its target as Annja drove the steel of her sword into the joint where his arm met his shoulder. He ripped out another round, wildly, while he staggered backward, reacting to the serious wound she'd inflicted. Annja, a dancer on the edge of life, absolutely at one with the weapon in her hand, prepared herself again as the man screamed his rage and frustration into her face.

She closed in on him.

She had to end this and she had to end it quickly.

Everyone inside the farmhouse would know they were coming now. They'd be ready to face them, either as they came through the door, or they'd come out to meet them, armed to the teeth.

Wisps of smoke curled away from the blade as the sparks flew, each bullet that struck the sword turned back on the shooter.

Some became embedded in the wall of the house; others missed even that and struck the layers of ice and snow that clung to the side of the mountain.

The blade moved faster and faster, a silver barrier that stopped everything the man fired at her.

Annja faced him down, invincible. Mighty. Terrifying. Every bit the demon his master feared she was. But so much more than that, too.

Before she took the final three strides to close the distance between them, the firing stopped.

He stared down at the weapon, horrified.

He'd burned through his ammo, all seventy rounds from the Vector Arms high-capacity magazine. She didn't give him the chance to replace it.

Annja turned sideways, swinging the flat side of the blade toward him. He looked up from the traitorous gun in his hand to see the metal slam hard into his skull. He sank at the knees, dropping the gun.

Annja stepped in, driving the point of her elbow into the side of his head. He reeled, reaching out with his broken arm instinctively to stop himself from falling, only to scream as it buckled under him unable to take his weight. He fumbled for the gun as he fell.

Annja delivered a punishing blow, hammering her foot into his gut.

She backed away, content that he was done.

A single shot rang out.

The snow and ice around the thug began to turn red.

Garin stood beside her with a gun in his hand.

"Don't go all bleeding heart on me," he grunted. "He would have killed us both given half the chance. Let's just go in there and get this over with. I'm tired and I want to go home."

56

Not even the sound of the firefight on the doorstep was enough to distract Cauchon from the words.

The words were everything.

They spilled off his tongue. He was sure he could feel it. Sure he could feel the air as it began to crackle with energy. It was harder to breathe.

The two guards had left, abandoning him at his moment of triumph. He would hunt them down later, make them see the miracle they'd been too frightened to witness firsthand. The door that led to the main room remained closed.

"Should I go and see what's happening?" his sister asked. He wasn't about to break the incantation to answer her, not as it was so close to completion. She was smart enough to know what to do. He trusted her.

"We've got company," Roux said. Was the old man struggling to breathe? He seemed to be. There was a rasp to his words.

Cauchon peered down at the breastplate. This was it.

This was what he'd worked so incredibly hard for.

This moment.

The words came easily. He knew what each meant, even if the tongue was strange. He had studied them obsessively. He knew with absolute certainty which beats in the recitation would rip the essence from Annja Creed's flesh and instill it into his own.

He looked at Roux. Did the man know what would happen? Surely he did? Surely he had been the one who had first drawn the essence of the saint out of the burning girl back on the fields of Rouen? So then he had to know that he was doomed, that the saint's demon would restore him, that he would rise, a new man, capable of everything she was—the speed, the lethal grace, the agility and sheer athletic prowess. Would the sword answer his call? It didn't matter. He didn't care. All that mattered was that he would be able to walk again.

His sister ignored the old man's taunts and walked toward the door.

Cauchon wanted to warn her; they were trapped in here now, the room sealed until the ritual was complete. He willed her to understand. To snatch her hand away quickly before it burned her, the metal searing her skin.

She cried out.

He said nothing. Couldn't. He needed to focus on the words. A single misplaced vowel, a missed conjugation, a trip of the tongue, and maybe everything would be lost. Everything he'd worked so hard for. Their lives depended on him not making a mistake.

He closed his eyes.

The words were all.

Everything.

He heard something: a sharp crack. He knew what it was. It was the ritual. Every piece of metal in the place was responding to him, anything that would conduct power was resonating to the frequency of souls.

He heard the laptop, still open on the table close to him, begin to hum, the speakers inside the plastic unit vibrating in their casing. The hum twisted, a baleful counterpoint to Cauchon's chant in his own mind, then whip-cracked as the plastic shell could no longer hold the raw power surging through it. That sound, he knew without opening his eyes, was the rush of surging power. The sound was followed by a series of *pops*. Lightbulbs shattered. He felt the glass against his face as he threw his head back, still not opening his eyes. What was the point? There was nothing to see. He was absolutely focused on the words. The words were everything.

As Cauchon felt the changes happening in the room, every muscle tensed, taut, thrilling to the raw heat and strength of the universe, the words bringing him back to life. He bucked in his seat, back arching, and screamed out the penultimate syllables of the ritual.

ROUX SAW NOTHING, but a sick man becoming sicker.

As the man's wild ranting continued, Roux could no longer decipher the words. They were masked in screams as Cauchon's body bucked and writhed, contorting in paroxysms of agony.

"What is wrong with him?" Monique demanded. "You have to help him."

"It's too late," Roux said. "You should have listened to me sooner."

"Listen to you?"

"This can't work. This is in his head. All of it. There are no demons. Only the ones haunting him."

"You've got to help him," she repeated. "He's dying."

"A fit," Roux said coldly. "Let him ride it out. He thinks

he's summoning all the available power around him, I believe."

"You did this to him!" she screamed at Roux. "You did this!"

Roux refused the charge. "No. You did. You fed his sickness. He needs help."

"Then help him!"

CAUCHON OPENED HIS eyes to stare at his enemy. He liked what he saw. Roux's chest burned with the same electric blue flame as Joan's armor. The sparks danced across his chest. Yes, Cauchon thought, willing it to burn brighter, faster, more. Willing his skin to blister and brown and blacken as the flames quickened. Willing the old man to cry out for help.

He saw the metal crucifix the old man wore. The blue lines of elemental energy snaked toward the crucifix, which offered the magic a focal point. No. No. No! This couldn't be happening. The crucifix acted as a form of protection, like the breastplate, drawing the magical forces to it, absorbing them.

Cauchon was frightened then, realizing that the old man had come protected, prepared. Surely this was Joan's crucifix, Saint Joan's guardian, and then Cauchon's downfall?

They should have met in Pau as he'd wanted. Allowing him to come here was a mistake.

He couldn't take his eyes off the crucifix.

He almost lost it then, the complex run of syllables almost escaping him at the last.

The words were everything.

He couldn't allow panic to set in. Fear was the enemy. He would complete the ritual. He would draw the demonic spirit into his own flesh. He would walk again. He would rise. He would have his revenge on Roux, finally paying him back for the ruin of his life, and then he would turn on Garin Braden and end him. There was only room for one victor in Cauchon's world.

He thrashed in the chair, hands clawing into the armrests, head thrown back again as another wave of spiritual energy lanced into his soul, drawn to the breastplate. It worked like a magnet for the essence of the dead saint.

This was his moment.

It was always going to come down to this, the old man and him, and only one of them was going to walk away from the farmhouse.

The study door strained against its wooden frame, buckling inward.

Someone on the other side hammered against it.

"Roux!" the voice from the other side called.

Annja Creed.

The spell had worked; it had drawn her here.

Cauchon cried out the last few words gleefully, welcoming the devil woman to throw open the door and enter.

Everything was as it was meant to be.

He raised his arms wide above him, welcoming the ecstatic convulsions of possession, opening himself for the spirit.

"Come into me!" he cried. "Come, spirit! I am yours!"

The door flew open. Beside him, he felt his sister's hand on his shoulder, trying to restrain him, but he would not be restrained. He thrashed in the chair, trying to force his body to stand, willing himself up, even as he opened his mouth wide, knowing the essence would need a way into him.

Annja Creed stood backlit in the doorway.

Smoke swirled around her. He saw black tendrils spilling from between her lips. The demon spirit.

"Come in," he said softly, meaning Annja, meaning the long-dead Joan, meaning the spirit that would save his soul and give him back his life.

Annja stepped into the room.

Garin Braden was one step behind her, an Uzi was in his hand, aimed straight at him.

"Annja!" Roux shouted at the top of his lungs, the devil trying to warn his apprentice. An instant later his dear sister slammed the butt of her gun against the side of the old man's skull and the room came alive to the sound of gunfire.

57

She hadn't realized until that moment, standing in the doorway, just how afraid she was that he could die.

Roux wasn't impervious to bullets, and he wouldn't live on if his head was separated from his shoulders. Or at least she assumed he wouldn't. They'd never tested it.

She heard his cry almost too late to step out of the way.

Despite the bright day outside, the house was shrouded in stifling near-darkness.

Monique unleashed a rain of bullets, emptying the magazine into the doorway.

Annja threw herself to her right just as the first bullet splintered the door.

Splinters of wood filled the air as more shots tore into the wood, shredding it, and continued on, biting a line like a manic grin through the stone wall beside it.

On her knees, Annja knew she was vulnerable.

A long sliding silence filled the house after the final shell left the magazine.

She rose fast, her sword held out as a shield.

The automatic fire changed to single shots as Monique slammed a second magazine into the submachine gun.

The shots were enough to hold her back.

Then she saw him.

He was down.

Monique stood over him.

A bullet split the rough wood beside her, then another and another. Annja instinctively took in the madness of the room she'd stepped into. Cauchon was in his chair, dressed in an absurd piece of armor, head thrown back as if in the throes of a seizure as he moaned and shuddered and kept crying out, "Enter me! Come into me!" He looked utterly out of it. And that made him dangerous. Another burst of gunfire filled the air.

Monique backed away.

One step, then another, reluctantly putting distance between herself and her brother.

Annja closed the gap between them. "Put down the weapon," she urged. "It doesn't have to end this way. We can all walk away from this."

"No," Monique said.

"You'll only be able to get one of us, before we get you. This won't end well. Not for you or your brother. Be sensible." Annja held her sword at the ready, though she hoped her words would mean she wouldn't have to use it.

Monique made a last, desperate charge.

The magazine spent, she was no match for a real swordswoman. Annja stepped up to her, driving her elbow into the woman's face and, as her head snapped back, stepped in close and slammed her against the nearest wall. It was every bit as brutal as it was fast. She swept the legs out from under the woman, leaving her sprawling on the bare floorboards.

Annja stood over her as she tried to get up.

Annja kicked her, hard, driving her foot into Monique's gut, leaving her coughing and gagging as she gasped for air. She clutched at her stomach in pain.

"Roux," Annja said, running to his seemingly lifeless form.

He gave the slightest of groans as she knelt beside him. That was all she needed to hear. He was still in the land of the living. She helped him up and guided him to the sofa. His hands were bound with the same type of plastic ties that had bound her own wrists when she'd been held captive in the farmhouse. "Untie him," she told Garin.

Cauchon had stopped chanting, his dream seemingly over. The silence that replaced it seemed eerie.

Annja allowed herself a minute to examine the breastplate that covered Cauchon's chest. He was like a broken child playing dress-up soldiers. She felt an overwhelming sense of sorrow for the man.

58

"END IT," GARIN said bluntly.

Annja couldn't.

This was a broken man, mentally unstable. His rage was fueled by insanity, and had no point or purpose in reality. There was no magic here.

She held the sword firm in her grip, even as he tried to wrestle it from her.

Cauchon was stronger than he looked, but that strength was derived from madness, not from any natural reserve.

Garin stood beside her.

"End it," he repeated. "If you don't, I will."

Annja stared down at the man in the chair as he laid a hand on his stolen breastplate. What was he seeing when he looked around the room? What hallucination drove him on? He talked about holy fire, about light, magic, the devil in her body, the devil in his, but what kind of world was he *seeing*?

She shook her head.

"No."

"What do you mean, no?" Garin said in utter disbelief.

"These people have kidnapped you, tortured you, killed a man and tried to frame me for his murder. Rolls reversed, they wouldn't hesitate to kill you."

"I don't care," Annja said, unmoving. "Look at him. He's harmless. He's in some sort of fantasy world."

"He's not harmless," Garin objected. "Believe me, he's anything but. And like it or not, we can't leave him. He won't ever stop trying to kill you, or Roux, or, God forbid, me. You never leave an enemy at your back. Ever."

Garin put his hand on the sword. "We can do it together," he offered.

"No."

"You have to," Garin insisted. "If it helps, don't think of him as someone defeated. Think of him as someone who wants you dead."

She turned to Roux.

The old man looked at her, at Garin, at the sword in their hands and then at the madman in the wheelchair.

He didn't offer any answers.

"I can't do it," she said. "I just can't."

"Then I'll do it," Garin said. He raised the Uzi and pressed the muzzle against Cauchon's temple. "Stand back."

From somewhere outside Annja heard a deep rumbling sound. It built like thunder, increasing as the entire structure of the farmhouse began to tremble.

"What the hell is that?" Garin asked, finger on the trigger.

Roux was on his feet before he answered.

Annja didn't hear him as Monique was also standing.

The woman, desperate for any weapon now, had grabbed the fireplace poker and was slashing about wildly, trying to drive Garin away from her brother.

Annja wouldn't reach her in time. She acted on instinct, the sword an extension of her own arm.

The sword left her hand, turning end over end as it sailed toward its mark.

The woman dropped her makeshift weapon as the blade pierced her chest and sunk into the plaster of the wall behind her, pinning her in place, a look of absolute horror twisting her lips as she died.

Annja looked down at her hand and the sword was there, back in her grasp.

She heard rather than saw the woman slump to the floor, and looked up to see her blood smearing the wall with its sticky trail.

Outside the thunder gathered.

Only then did her brain register what that sound meant.

"Avalanche," she said.

59

Annja returned the sword to the otherwhere and wrapped an arm around Roux's shoulders. "Lean on me," she said. It was an order. "We're getting everyone out of here. Now."

"Go while you have a chance," the old man said.

"Stop trying to be a martyr," she told him.

The air was full of a gathering anger, close, overbearing.

They didn't have long. Minutes. Seconds.

She helped Roux to the door.

Garin hadn't moved. He stood over Cauchon, the muzzle of the Uzi pressed against his head while the madman cried out again, once more in the grip of some unseen image.

She looked back over her shoulder at him.

"Go," Garin urged. "I'll be right behind you."

"Don't do it, Garin," she said.

He didn't reply.

Annja half dragged, half carried Roux outside.

He stumbled twice, still disorientated from the blow he'd taken to the head.

Again she heard the not-so-distant rumble from the mountain. She didn't dare risk so much as a glance at the slopes. She didn't want to know how close that crushing death was until they were in the car and moving.

Outside, the young guard Annja had knocked unconscious was starting to stir. He pressed a hand to the side of his head.

She looked back at the doorway.

There was no sign of Garin.

He was taking too long.

She yelled for him to hurry.

She heard a crack—an unmistakable sound. It was like a gunshot echoing off the mountaintops. A moment later Garin emerged from the house. He was carrying something in his hands. It took her a second to realize it was the breastplate. He'd wrestled it away from Cauchon's shoulders. As he neared, she saw that the straps had been cut.

He looked at the young man struggling to get to his feet, and said, "One question, and be careful how you answer. Are you going to be foolish about this or can I buy out your contract?"

The young guard shook his head, not understanding.

"I'll give you a thousand euros for the day. You work for me now," Garin said. "Deal?"

The young man nodded slowly.

"Good. Help her get him inside the vehicle. We're getting out of here before the mountain comes down around us."

Garin opened the driver's side door and slid behind the wheel, tossing the relic into the backseat as if it were an item of no value whatsoever.

Everything was taking too long.

The ground beneath them trembled, the entire mountain shaking.

The young guard slipped Roux's arm around his neck and helped support him as Annja tugged at the rear passenger door. Together they helped Roux inside, slamming the door behind him.

It was as if the peak was falling apart.

Great slabs of snow and ice moved in slow motion, throwing up clouds of white powder each time they caught a ridge or created another crack in the surface.

Annja tried to judge the distance—half a mile, maybe, but the avalanche was picking up speed and heading in their direction.

Was it possible their gunfire had started the landslide?

It had to be.

The magic that Cauchon had been trying to summon couldn't be the cause…that was crazy, Annja thought. There was no such thing as sorcery.

They had to get out of there as quickly as they could.

Annja raced around to the other side of the vehicle, clambering in the back beside Roux.

"Get in!" she shouted at the young man who stood there, trapped in a moment's indecision even though he'd taken up Garin on his offer. Garin pulled away before the young guy was even in the seat, the door still open.

Annja reached over and helped Roux buckle up before fixing her own seat belt. She had a flashback to the last time she'd been in a vehicle on these slopes.

"Is someone going to tell me what just happened back there?" Garin asked.

For a while the question hung in the car, unanswered.

Garin drove hard, double declutching, hitting the corners faster than was safe but absolutely in control, years of defensive driving paying off. He negotiated each twist and turn at speed, racing the avalanche down the mountain.

Finally Roux broke the silence. "His real name was Patrice Moerlen. I killed him twenty years ago."

"That doesn't make sense," Annja said.

"Hush. If you want me to tell the story, I'm telling it my way. I watched him die. Or thought I did. He came to see me at the chateau with proof about me, having pieced the puzzle together. He was a bright young man, a journalist with a promising career. I only wanted to warn him off. I was prepared to buy his silence. We arranged a meeting. He didn't show. He was run down on the streets of Paris as I tried to reach him. It was a tragedy. An accident. I left, assuming he was dead. I shouldn't have done that.

"Somehow he survived. His sister, Monique, identified someone else as his corpse. She looked after him for twenty years. All the while he stewed, plotting his revenge, looking for something that could do what the doctors couldn't, make him walk again."

The vehicle bounced as it took a bend on the road and the mountain shook again.

Annja looked out of the back window.

"It's getting closer," she said, then looked ahead, seeing the point where the avalanche was going to swallow the road. "We're never going to make it."

"Of course we are," Garin said, ratcheting up through the gears. "Trust me."

She nearly laughed.

Nearly.

"So, what then?" she asked Roux. "He spent the rest of his life plotting some mad revenge and it drove him out of his mind?"

"Delusion. Obsession," the old man agreed. "But he wasn't a million miles away from the truth, I think. Or at least the truth as better men tried to describe it." He told her about the discoveries that Bernard Gui had made all those years ago, hunting witches and practitioners of the dark arts, chasing demons.

"Add that to Manchon's theory—Manchon was the court scribe whose notes Garin, ah, shall we say liberated, for now. He was a very deluded man who had witnessed the execution of Joan at Rouen, seen her sword shattered and swallowed the wild claims of the real Cauchon, who used devilry and demon possession as a way to explain why men, good men, normal men, would follow a woman into battle, which was about the most unnatural thing he could imagine."

"And the breastplate?"

"Joan's."

That said it all.

"This was hers?"

Roux nodded.

"So you gave him something that had been close to Joan's heart, feeding the delusion?"

He shook his head. "If I'd even thought that far ahead, I would have offered him this." His hand closed around the crucifix that circled his throat. "I took it from her body after they burned her. It was unharmed. Undamaged. But I wasn't thinking straight. I just wanted to give him what he wanted to get you out of there."

"Why did he want something of hers? What am I not understanding here?"

"He believed that there was a demon inside you that he could draw into himself, capturing whatever it is of Joan that exists in you."

"You didn't think…that he might be right? That there might be something of her in me…something that these incantations could release?"

Roux shrugged. "It was a calculated risk. I don't believe in magic."

Annja sat in silence as she tried to take it all in, but she couldn't get through the insanity of it.

"Hold on tight, folks, this is going to be uncomfortably close," Garin warned.

Annja looked through the window. The avalanche was carrying its massive weight of snow and ice down the ravine where the burned-out truck lay. In the moving mass she was sure that she caught sight of parts of Cauchon's house as the whole thing was swept away. Against the backdrop of raw elemental power on display, bricks and mortar stood no chance.

She redirected her attention away from the oncoming snow to Garin.

"Did you...?" She couldn't finish the question.

"It would have been mercy if I had," he said.

"Did you?"

He didn't answer her.

Instead, he yanked down hard on the wheel, the snow chains biting into the surface as the 4x4 slewed around a tight bend.

There was a man on the road up ahead, struggling with his unresponsive car.

Her Good Samaritan.

"Stop!" Annja yelled.

Garin slammed on the brakes. The 4x4 yawed, spitting ice and grit.

She threw the door open and called, "Get in!"

He looked up, fear etched in his face.

"Everything I have...everything...is here. I should stay."

"You'll die," Annja argued.

"I know," he called over the churning wind and snow chasing down the mountain. "Go with God," he said. "I've made my peace. I want to be with my love again."

"Listen to the man," Garin said.

He didn't wait for her to decide. He slammed the 4x4 into gear and put his foot down, the sudden movement nearly hurling Annja from the car.

She watched the old man face the mountain, amazed that someone could stand there so calmly, ready to embrace death.

She couldn't have done it.

The snow hit the road no more than twenty feet behind them.

Garin didn't slow for a second, not until they were safe on the outskirts of Pau.

* * * * *

COMING SOON FROM

GOLD EAGLE®

Available June 2, 2015

THE EXECUTIONER #439
BLOOD RITES -- *Don Pendleton*

When rival gangs terrorize Miami, Mack Bolan is called in to clean up the city, but the mess in Florida is just the beginning. The drug trafficking business is flourishing in Jamaica...along with the practice of voodoo and human sacrifice.

STONY MAN® #137
CITADEL OF FEAR – *Don Pendleton*

Able Team discovers that Liberty City, an economic free zone in Grenada, is a haven for building homemade missiles. Phoenix Force arrives just in time to provide backup, but the missiles have already been shipped to a rogue group with their sights set on the California coast...

SUPERBOLAN® #174
DESERT FALCONS – *Don Pendleton*

In the Kingdom of Saudi Arabia, a secret group is plotting to oust the royal family. Their next move: kidnapping the prince from a desert warfare training session outside Las Vegas. Mack Bolan must keep the prince safe—but someone in the heir's inner circle is a traitor.

COMING SOON FROM

GOLD EAGLE ®

Available July 7, 2015

THE EXECUTIONER® #440
KILLPATH – *Don Pendleton*
After a DEA agent is tortured and killed by a powerful Colombian cartel, Bolan teams up with a former cocaine queen in Cali to obliterate the entire operation.

SUPERBOLAN® #175
NINJA ASSAULT – *Don Pendleton*
Ninjas attack an American casino, and Bolan follows the gangsters behind the crime back to Japan—where he intends to take them out on their home turf.

DEATHLANDS® #123
IRON RAGE – *James Axler*
Ryan and the companions are caught in a battle for survival against crocs, snakes and makeshift ironclads on the great Sippi river.

ROGUE ANGEL™ #55
BENEATH STILL WATERS – *Alex Archer*
Annja uncovers Nazi secrets—and treasure—in the wreckage of a submerged German bomber shot down at the end of WWII.

SPECIAL EXCERPT FROM

Check out this sneak preview of
BENEATH STILL WATERS
by Alex Archer!

It was Doug on the screen. He was tied to a metal chair in a nondescript room.

Annja's anxiety propelled her closer to the hotel room's television as she turned up the volume on the DVD.

Not that Doug was speaking. His hands and forearms were tied to the arms of the chair, his legs to the legs of the chair, leaving his hands free and his bare feet resting on what looked to be a wet concrete floor. The camera was close enough that Annja could see that his face was bloody and swollen, as if he'd been subjected to a pretty thorough beating. A thin line of dried blood ran down the side of his face from his cracked and swollen lips. When he raised his head and looked at the camera, the one eye that he could actually see through was filled with fear.

"Help me, Annja," he said, and his voice was little better than a croak. It sounded as if he hadn't had any water for hours. "You have to help me. I don't care what he asks you to do or who he asks you to do it to—I'll die here if you don't do what he wants. Please, don't let that happen, Annja, please."

The camera zoomed in on his face and then slipped down to his body and stopped on his right hand. That close, Annja could see that his last two fingers were bent at odd angles.

She could hear Doug saying, "No, no, I didn't do anything! Don't!" She steeled herself for what was coming but she didn't turn away. Annja owed it to him to watch all the wrongs he was enduring, designed simply to coerce her into action.

A gloved hand reached into the camera frame. It was neither large nor small, so she couldn't really tell if it was a man's or a woman's, though she suspected the former. Not because a woman couldn't be that cruel—she knew from experience that that certainly wasn't the case—but because her mystery caller who'd sent the DVD had claimed to be the one who had kidnapped Doug, and she had yet to see anything that made her think this was anything more than a single nut-job at work.

The individual took hold of Doug's middle finger and without further ado snapped it in half. Doug let out a shriek of pain and the screen went blank.

That was everything on the disk; Annja used her laptop to search the disk's directory structure just to be sure.

Watching the kidnapper inflict pain on Doug for no other reason than to coerce her into action filled her with a righteous fury. She vowed then and there to make him pay for what he had done.

He'd picked the wrong woman to tangle with.

Don't miss
BENEATH STILL WATERS
by Alex Archer,
available July 2015 wherever
Gold Eagle® books and ebooks are sold.

"I'd say it's just about ready to get serious," J.B. said, sounding more interested than alarmed.

Krysty looked back. The people who had gone on board the barge to fight the fire in the fabric bales were scrambling back across the thick hawser that connected the hulls. She was relieved and pleased to see Doc trotting right across, as spry as a kid goat, holding his arms out to his sides with his black coattails flapping. Despite his aged appearance, he was chronologically a few years younger than Ryan. The bizarre abuse and rigors the evil whitecoats of Operation Chronos had subjected him to had aged him prematurely, and damaged his fine, highly educated mind. But he could still muster the agility and energy of a man much younger than he appeared to be.

Ricky came last, straddling the thick woven hemp cable and inch-worming along. But he did so at speed.

Avery had vanished. "You and Mildred best head for cover," Ryan said.

"They'll only hit us by accident," Mildred said, "shooting oversize muskets at us."

"They're going to have a dozen or two shots at us next round," J.B. said. "That's a lot of chances to get lucky."

"Looks like some smaller fry are heading this way," Ryan reported. "Krysty, Mildred—*git!*"

"Come on." Krysty grabbed the other woman's wrist and began running for the cabin. Though Mildred was about as heavy as she was, Krysty barely slowed, towing Mildred as if she were a river barge. She was strong, motivated and full of adrenaline.

Krysty heard Ryan open fire. Given the range, the bobbing of the approaching lesser war craft, and the complex movement of the *Queen*—pitching fore and aft as well as heeling over to her right from the centrifugal force of the fastest left turn the vessel could manage, she doubted he'd be lucky enough to hit anything significant.

The women had almost reached the cabin when the next salvo hit, roaring like an angry dragon. Krysty saw stout planks suddenly spreading into fragments almost in her face.

And then the world vanished in a soundless white flash.

Don't miss
IRON RAGE by James Axler,
available July 2015 wherever
Gold Eagle® books and ebooks are sold.